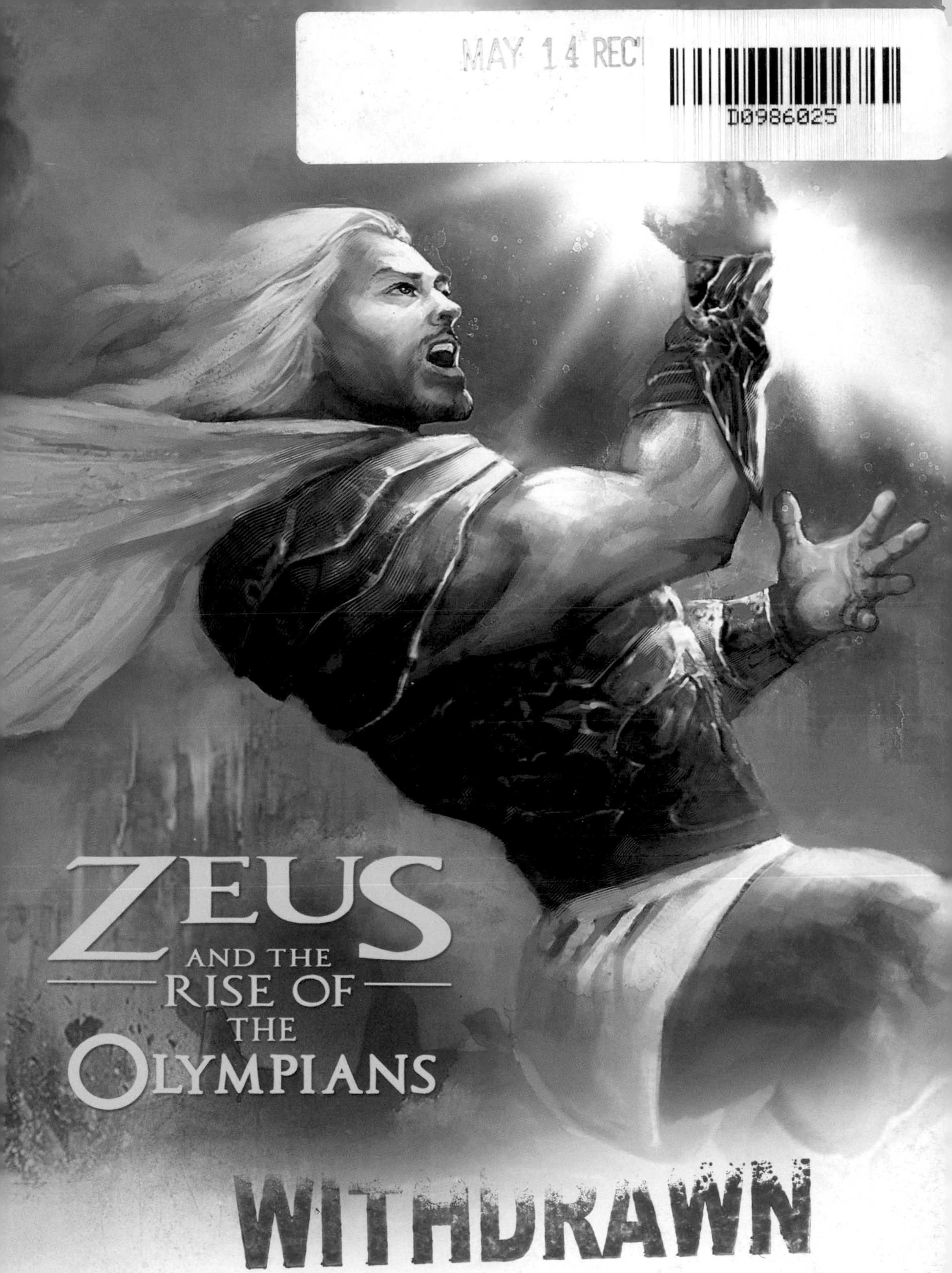

ZEUS AND THE RISE OF THE OLYMPIANS

CAMPFIRE™

KALYANI NAVYUG MEDIA PVT LTD
New Delhi

ZEUS AND THE RISE OF THE OLYMPIANS

Sitting around the Campfire, telling the story, were:

WORDSMITH **RYAN FOLEY**

ILLUSTRATOR **JAYAKRISHNAN K. P.**

COLORISTS **JAYAKRISHNAN K. P. & ANIL C. K.**

LETTERER **LAXMI CHAND GUPTA**

EDITOR **ASWATHY SENAN**

PRODUCTION CONTROLLER **VISHAL SHARMA**

COVER ART & DESIGN

JAYAKRISHNAN K. P.

CAMPFIRE™

www.campfire.co.in

Published by Kalyani Navyug Media Pvt. Ltd.
101 C, Shiv House, Hari Nagar Ashram, New Delhi 110014, India

ISBN: 978-93-80741-15-4

Copyright © 2012 Kalyani Navyug Media Pvt. Ltd.

Printed in India at Galaxy Offset

Ryan Foley

About the author

Born in 1974 in New Jersey, USA, Ryan Foley's obsession with comic books began during his childhood when his mother introduced him to characters like Spider-Man and Batman. He cites R. A. Salvatore's science fiction, *The Crystal Shard* (and its character, Drizzt Do'Urden) as having influenced him the most, for it drew him into a world of fantasy and inspired him to become a writer. He has worked with Image Comics and Arcana Studios on comic book series such as *Masters of the Universe*, *Dragon's Lair*, *Space Ace*, and *Tales of Penance: Trial of the Century*.

Ryan has adapted several Greek myths for Campfire, such as *Legend: The Labors of Heracles*, *Stolen Hearts: The Love of Eros and Psyche*, and *Perseus: Destiny's Call*.

Jayakrishnan

About the artist

A lively, enthusiastic digital illustrator, painter, and concept artist from Kerala, India, JK (as he is called by his friends) wishes to develop a career in the illustration and animation industry. He has worked as an assistant animator at Toonz Animation, Kerala, for three years and has collaborated on various animation series like *The Adventures of Tenali Raman*, *The Adventures of Hanuman,* and others.

JK has been with Campfire as a senior colorist for more than three years and has done the cover art and designing for many Campfire titles such as *Sita: Daughter of the Earth*, *In Defense of the Realm*, *Conquering Everest,* and many more.

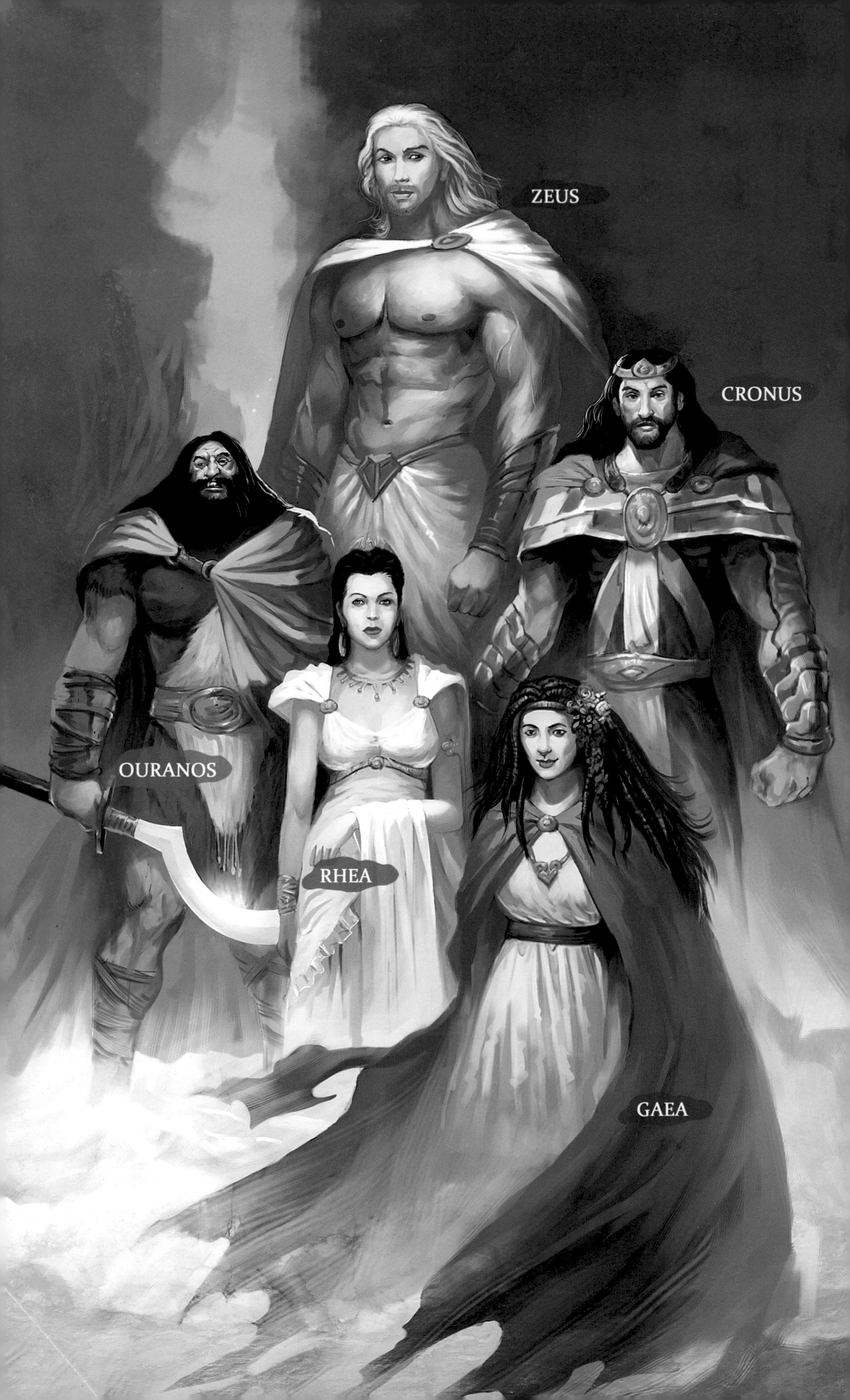
ZEUS
CRONUS
OURANOS
RHEA
GAEA

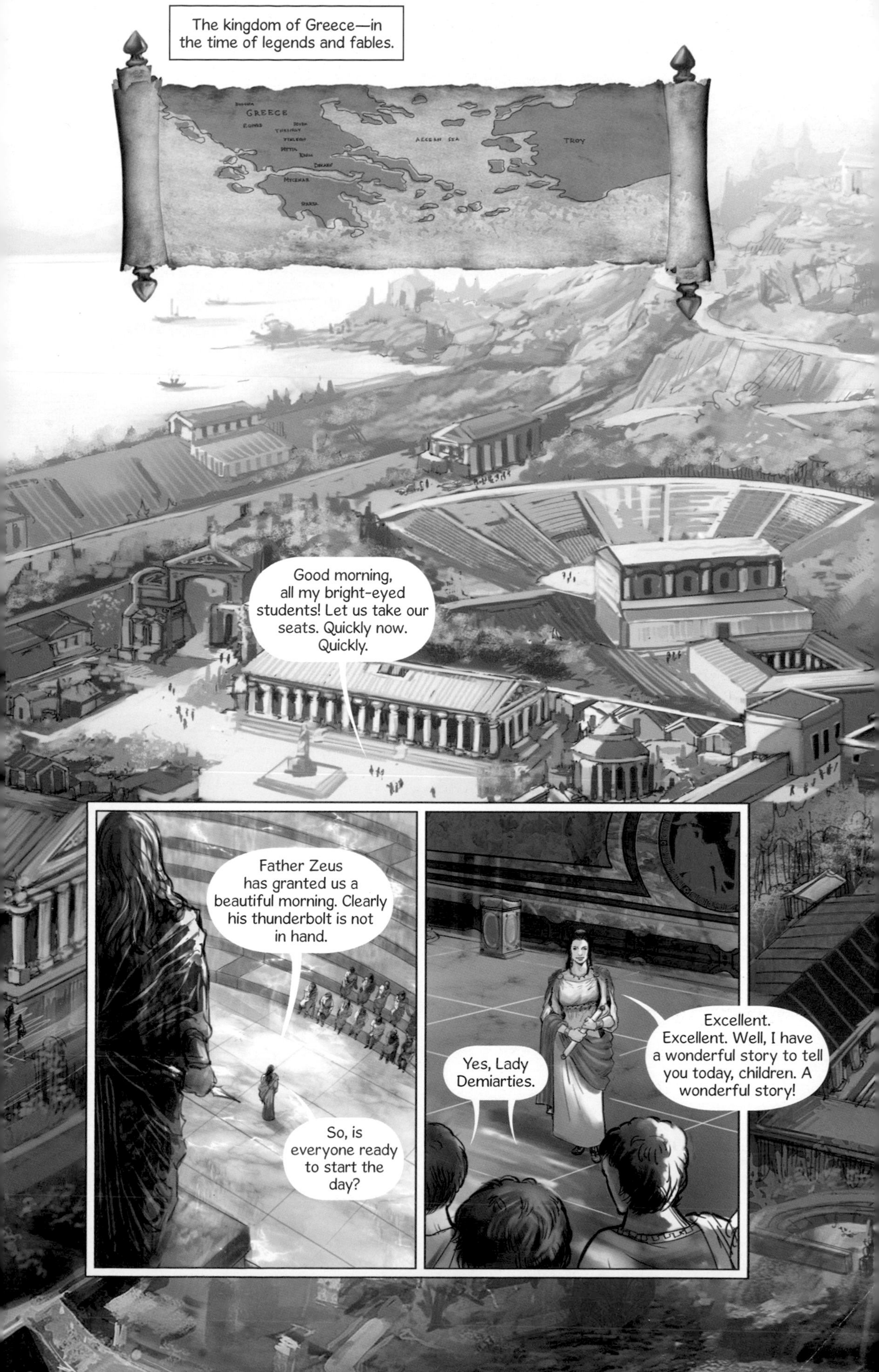

The kingdom of Greece—in the time of legends and fables.
GREECE
TROY
Good morning, all my bright-eyed students! Let us take our seats. Quickly now. Quickly.
Father Zeus has granted us a beautiful morning. Clearly his thunderbolt is not in hand.
So, is everyone ready to start the day?
Excellent. Excellent. Well, I have a wonderful story to tell you today, children. A wonderful story!
Yes, Lady Demiarties.

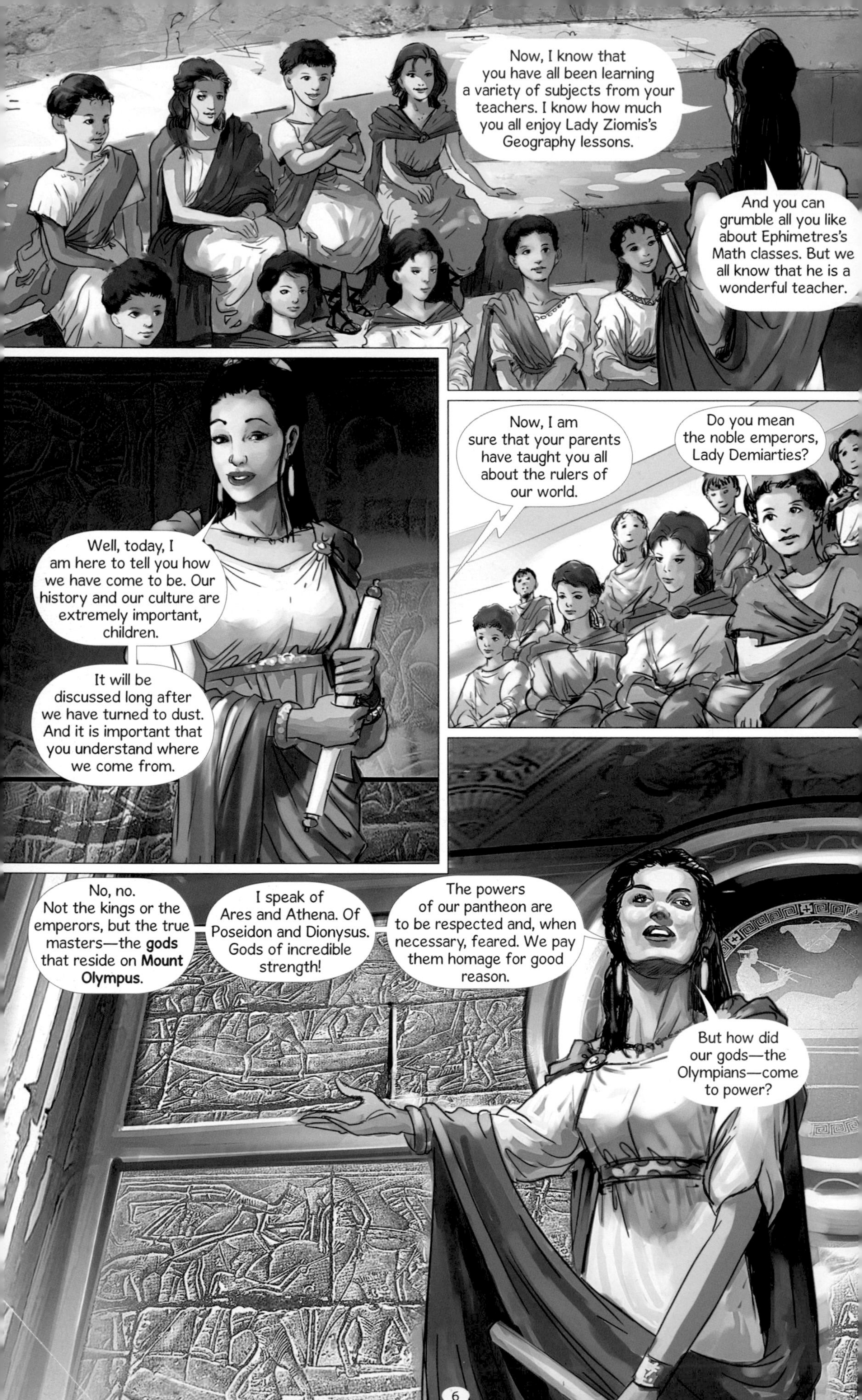
Now, I know that you have all been learning a variety of subjects from your teachers. I know how much you all enjoy Lady Ziomis's Geography lessons.
And you can grumble all you like about Ephimetres's Math classes. But we all know that he is a wonderful teacher.
Well, today, I am here to tell you how we have come to be. Our history and our culture are extremely important, children.
It will be discussed long after we have turned to dust. And it is important that you understand where we come from.
Now, I am sure that your parents have taught you all about the rulers of our world.
Do you mean the noble emperors, Lady Demiarties?
No, no. Not the kings or the emperors, but the true masters—the **gods** that reside on **Mount Olympus**.
I speak of Ares and Athena. Of Poseidon and Dionysus. Gods of incredible strength!
The powers of our pantheon are to be respected and, when necessary, feared. We pay them homage for good reason.
But how did our gods—the Olympians—come to power?

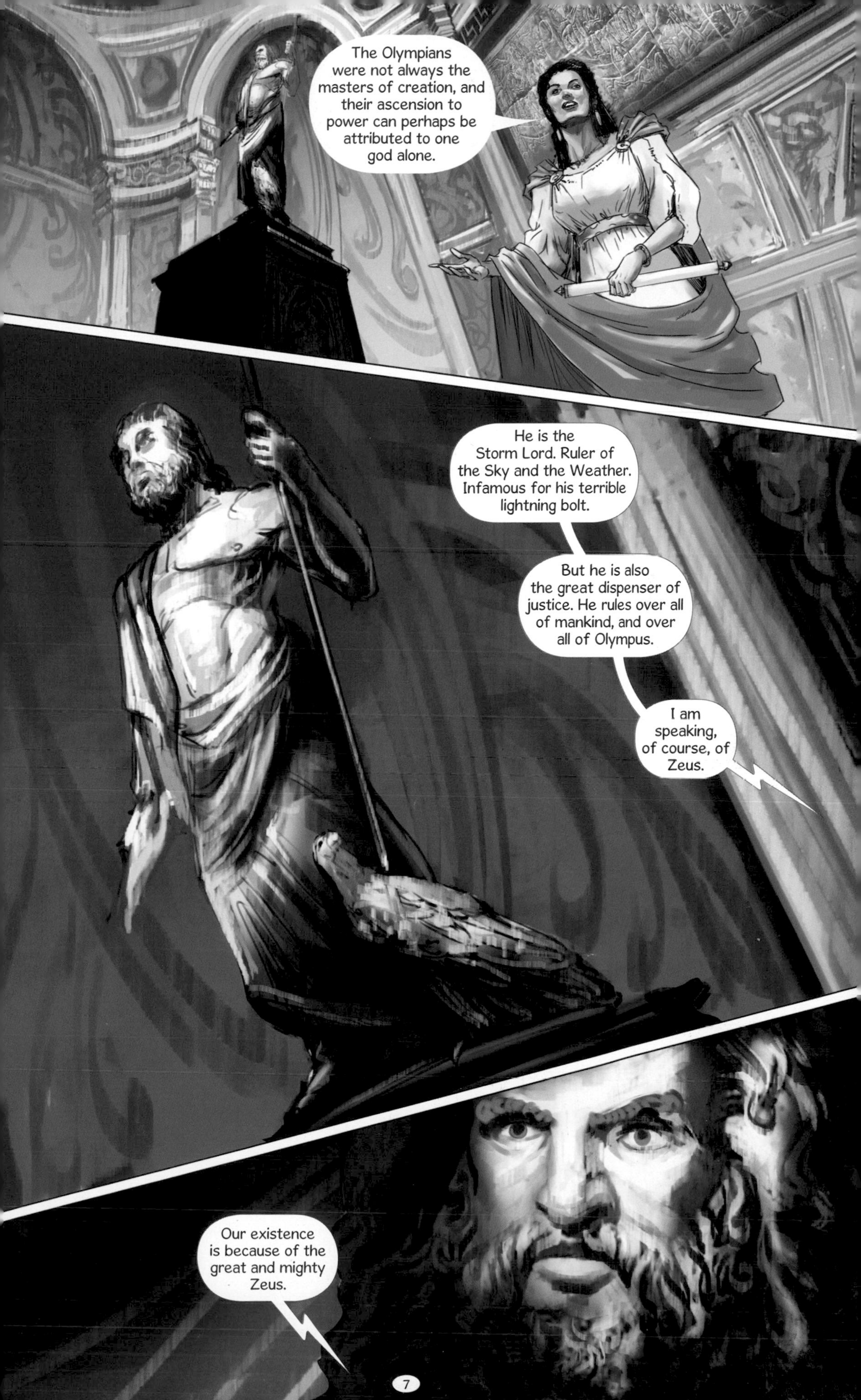
The Olympians were not always the masters of creation, and their ascension to power can perhaps be attributed to one god alone.
He is the Storm Lord. Ruler of the Sky and the Weather. Infamous for his terrible lightning bolt.
But he is also the great dispenser of justice. He rules over all of mankind, and over all of Olympus.
I am speaking, of course, of Zeus.
Our existence is because of the great and mighty Zeus.

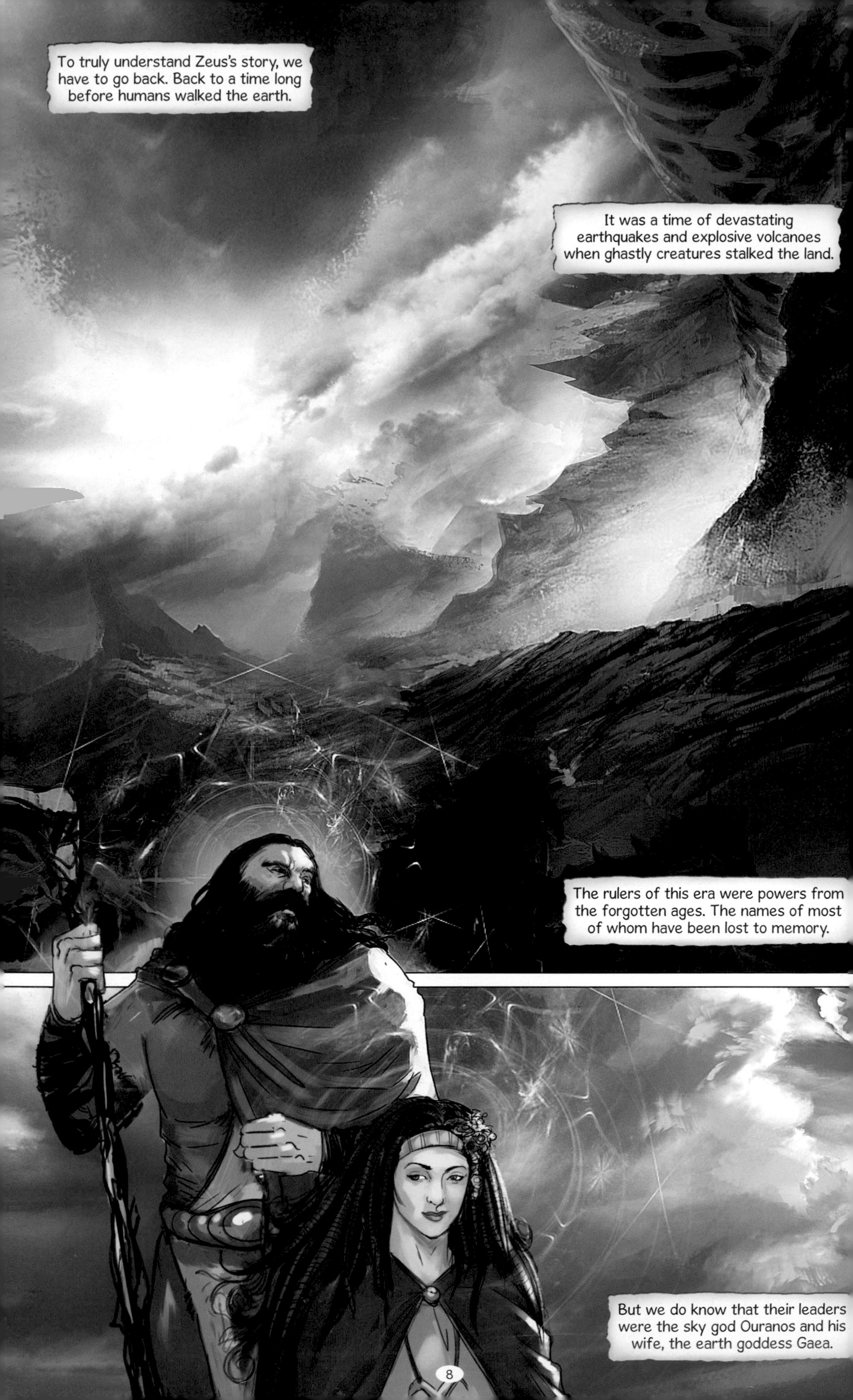
To truly understand Zeus's story, we have to go back. Back to a time long before humans walked the earth.
It was a time of devastating earthquakes and explosive volcanoes when ghastly creatures stalked the land.
The rulers of this era were powers from the forgotten ages. The names of most of whom have been lost to memory.
But we do know that their leaders were the sky god Ouranos and his wife, the earth goddess Gaea.

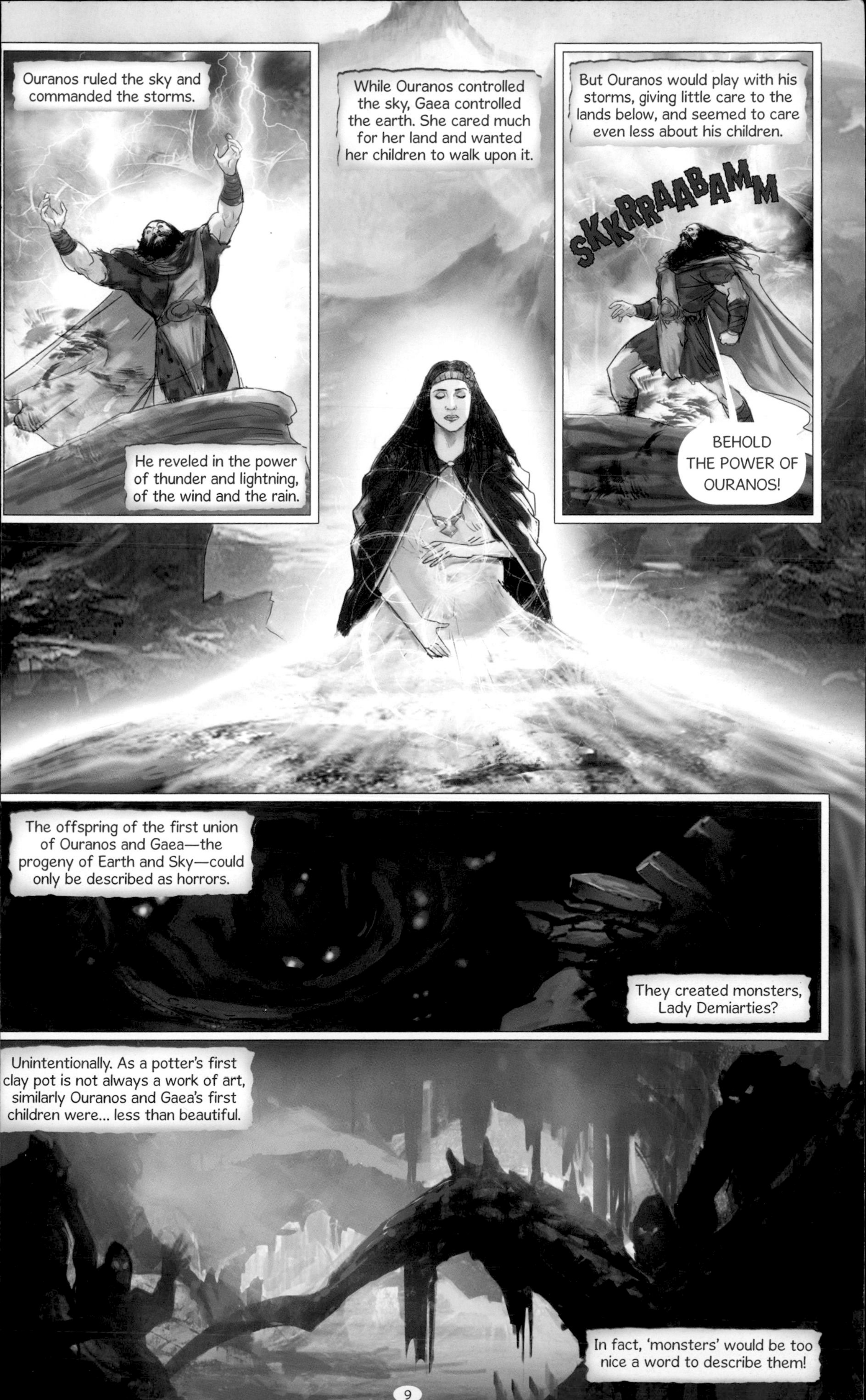

Ouranos ruled the sky and commanded the storms.
He reveled in the power of thunder and lightning, of the wind and the rain.
While Ouranos controlled the sky, Gaea controlled the earth. She cared much for her land and wanted her children to walk upon it.
But Ouranos would play with his storms, giving little care to the lands below, and seemed to care even less about his children.
SKKRRAABAMMM
BEHOLD THE POWER OF OURANOS!
The offspring of the first union of Ouranos and Gaea—the progeny of Earth and Sky—could only be described as horrors.
They created monsters, Lady Demiarties?
Unintentionally. As a potter's first clay pot is not always a work of art, similarly Ouranos and Gaea's first children were... less than beautiful.
In fact, 'monsters' would be too nice a word to describe them!

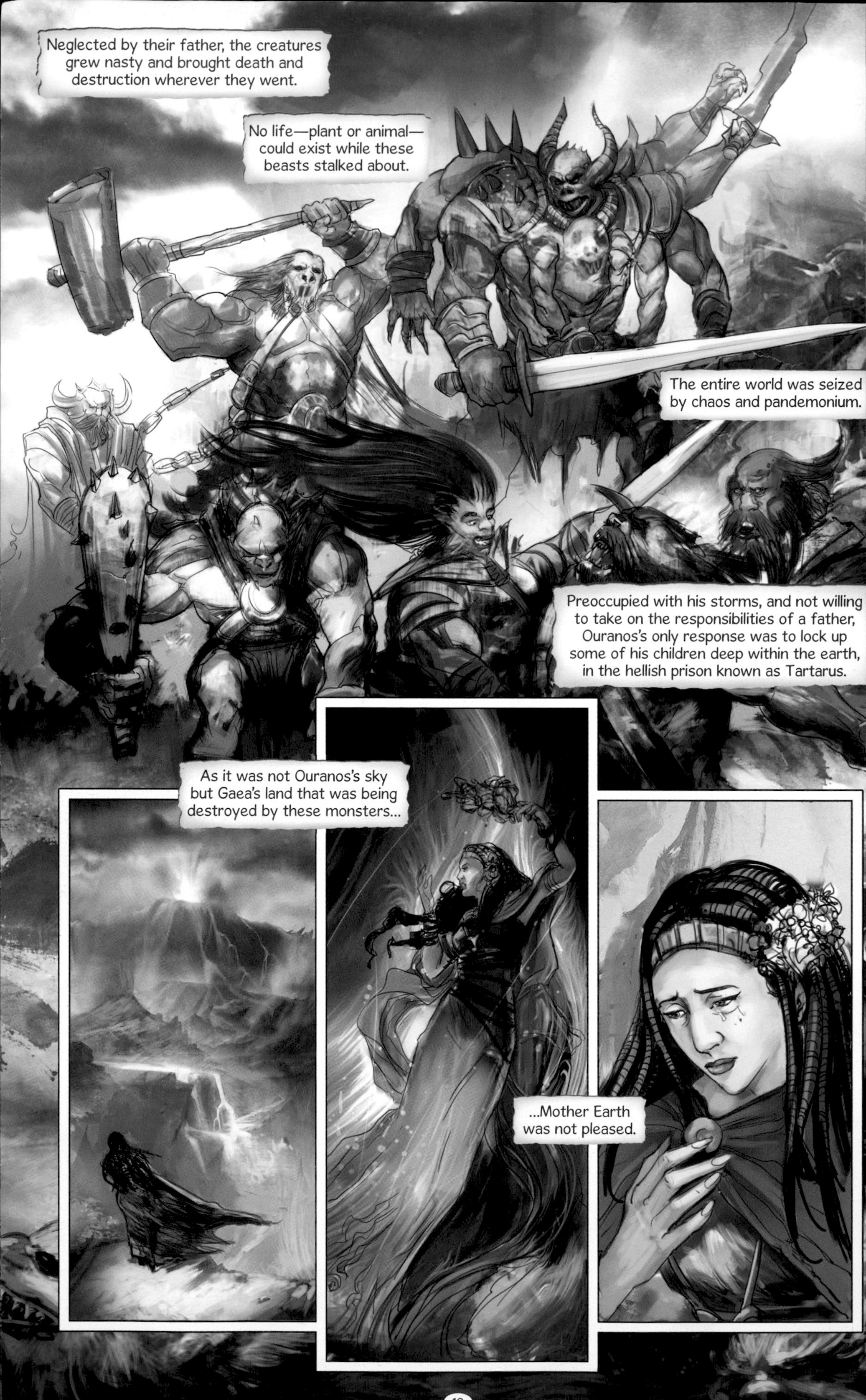
Neglected by their father, the creatures grew nasty and brought death and destruction wherever they went.
No life—plant or animal—could exist while these beasts stalked about.
The entire world was seized by chaos and pandemonium.
Preoccupied with his storms, and not willing to take on the responsibilities of a father, Ouranos's only response was to lock up some of his children deep within the earth, in the hellish prison known as Tartarus.
As it was not Ouranos's sky but Gaea's land that was being destroyed by these monsters...
...Mother Earth was not pleased.

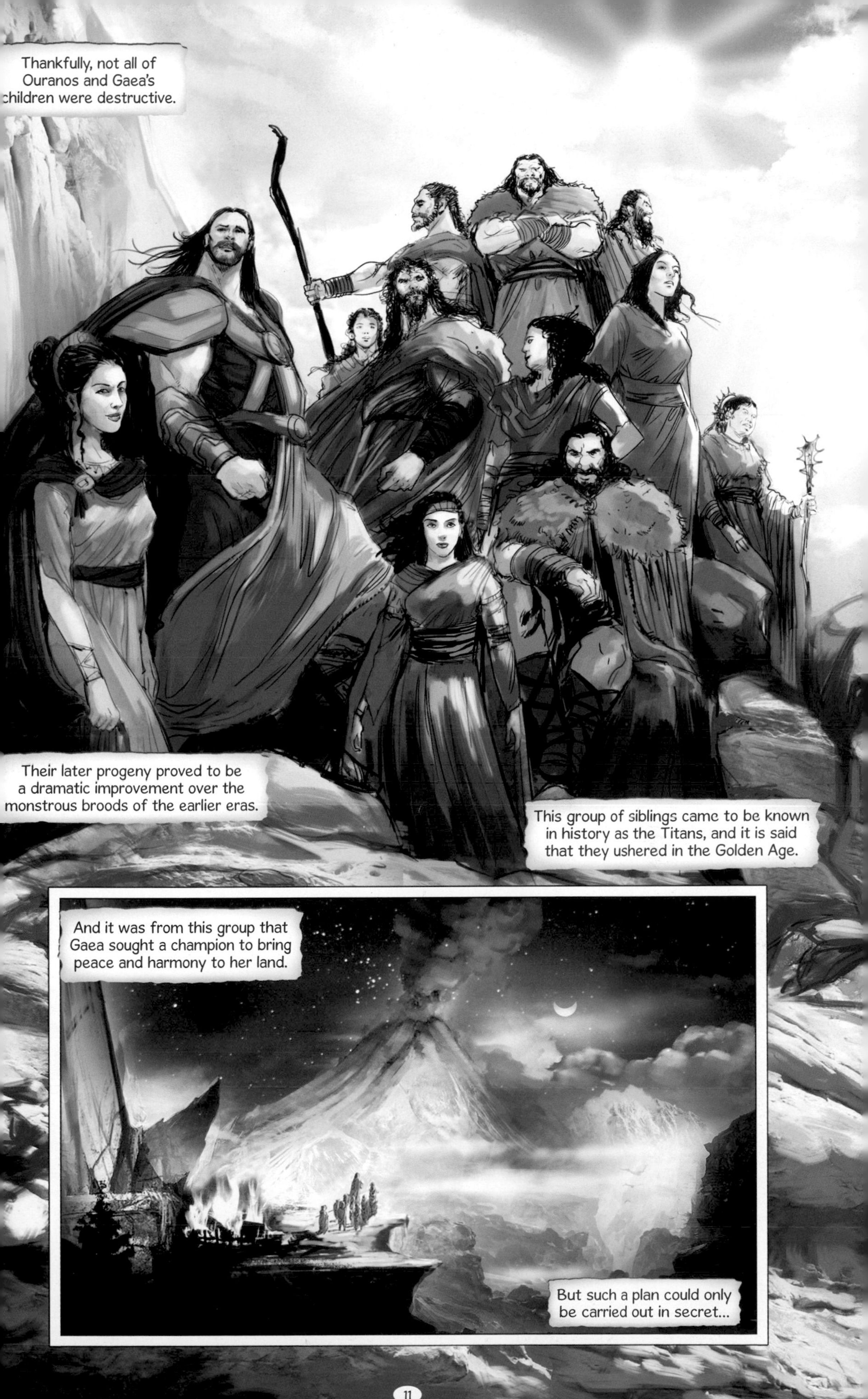
Thankfully, not all of Ouranos and Gaea's children were destructive.
Their later progeny proved to be a dramatic improvement over the monstrous broods of the earlier eras.
This group of siblings came to be known in history as the Titans, and it is said that they ushered in the Golden Age.
And it was from this group that Gaea sought a champion to bring peace and harmony to her land.
But such a plan could only be carried out in secret...

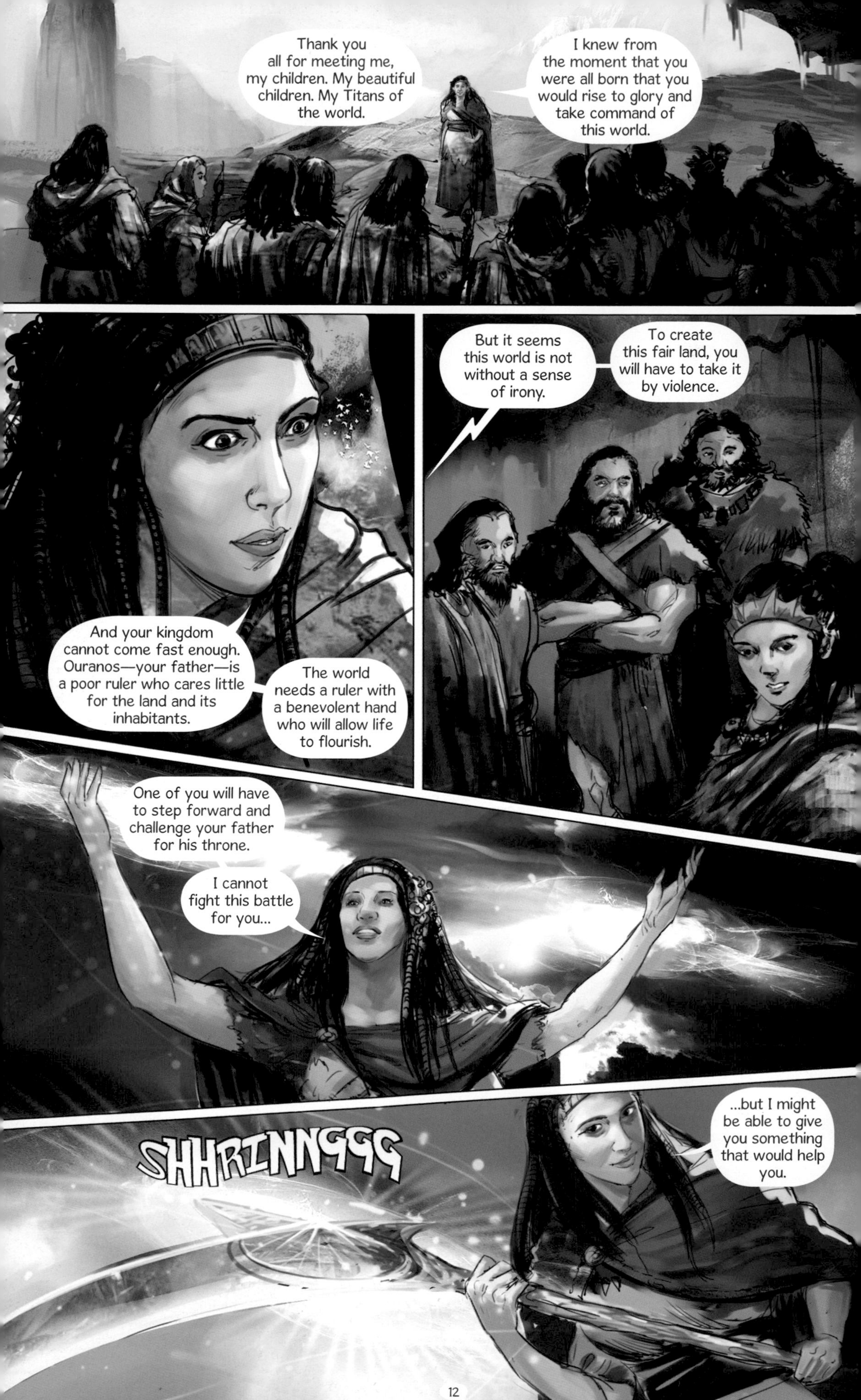

Thank you all for meeting me, my children. My beautiful children. My Titans of the world.
I knew from the moment that you were all born that you would rise to glory and take command of this world.
And your kingdom cannot come fast enough. Ouranos—your father—is a poor ruler who cares little for the land and its inhabitants.
The world needs a ruler with a benevolent hand who will allow life to flourish.
But it seems this world is not without a sense of irony.
To create this fair land, you will have to take it by violence.
One of you will have to step forward and challenge your father for his throne.
I cannot fight this battle for you...
SHHRINNGGG
...but I might be able to give you something that would help you.

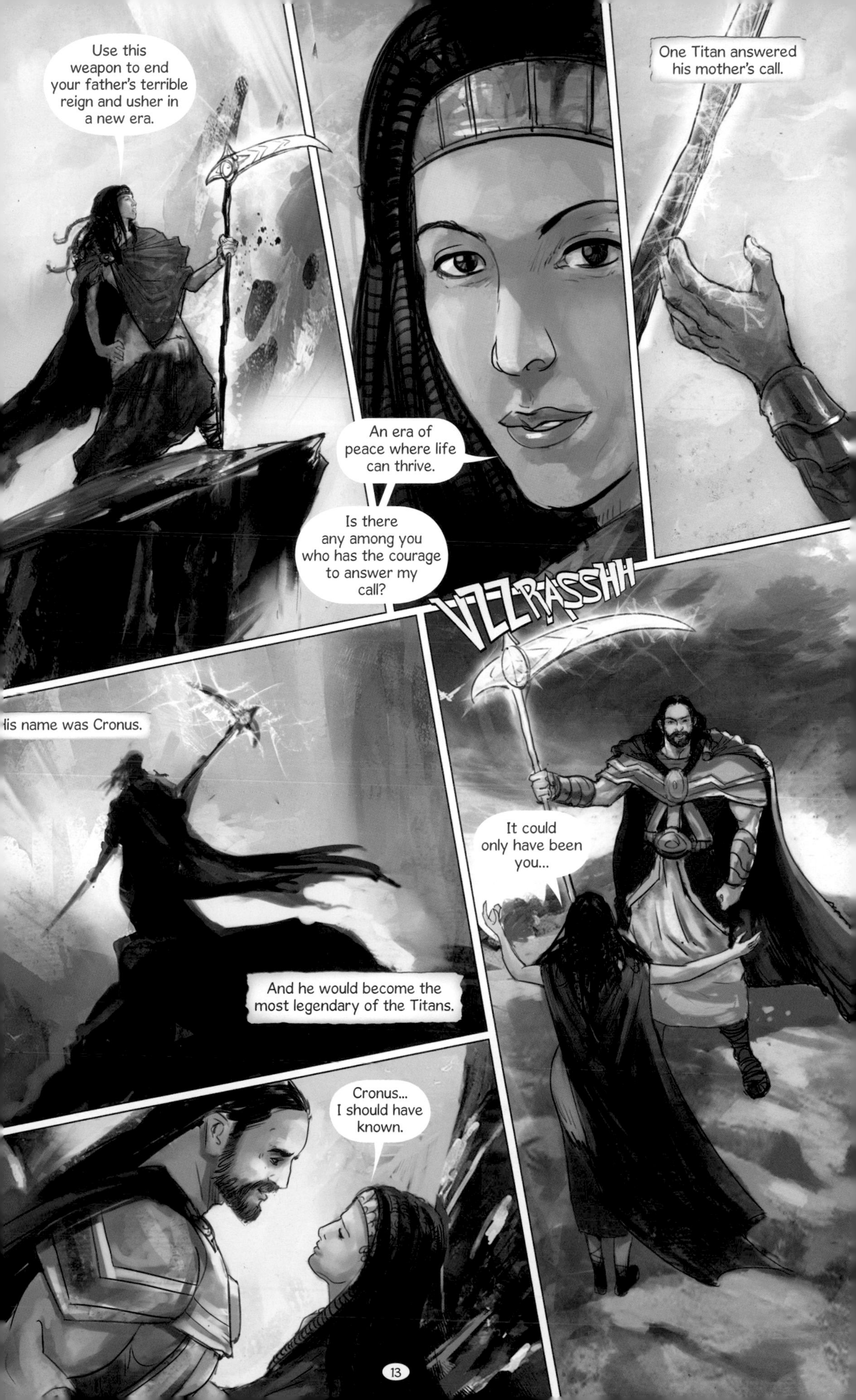
Use this weapon to end your father's terrible reign and usher in a new era.
An era of peace where life can thrive.
Is there any among you who has the courage to answer my call?
One Titan answered his mother's call.
VZZRASSHH
His name was Cronus.
And he would become the most legendary of the Titans.
It could only have been you...
Cronus... I should have known.

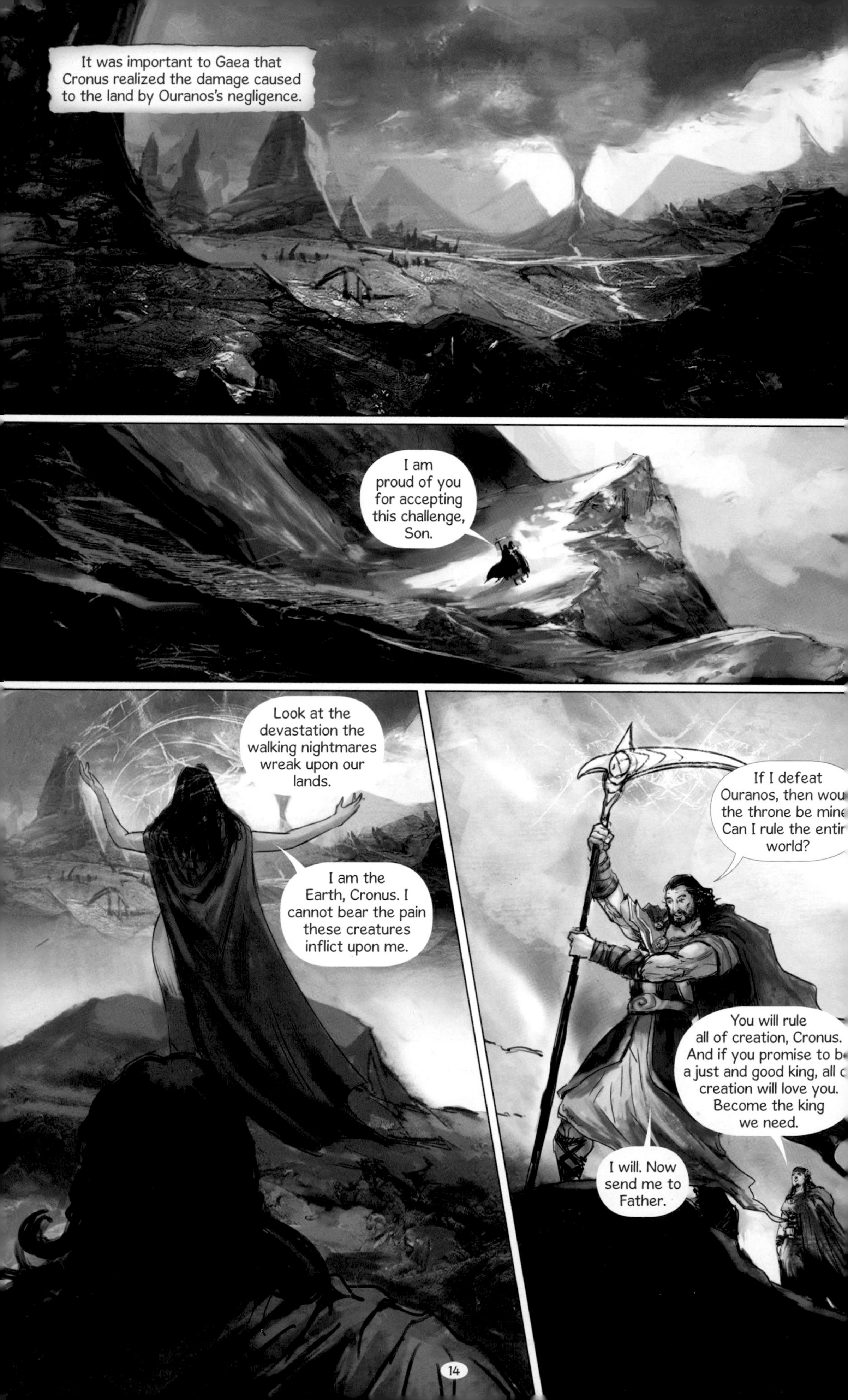
It was important to Gaea that Cronus realized the damage caused to the land by Ouranos's negligence.
I am proud of you for accepting this challenge, Son.
Look at the devastation the walking nightmares wreak upon our lands.
I am the Earth, Cronus. I cannot bear the pain these creatures inflict upon me.
If I defeat Ouranos, then wou the throne be mine Can I rule the entir world?
You will rule all of creation, Cronus. And if you promise to b a just and good king, all c creation will love you. Become the king we need.
I will. Now send me to Father.

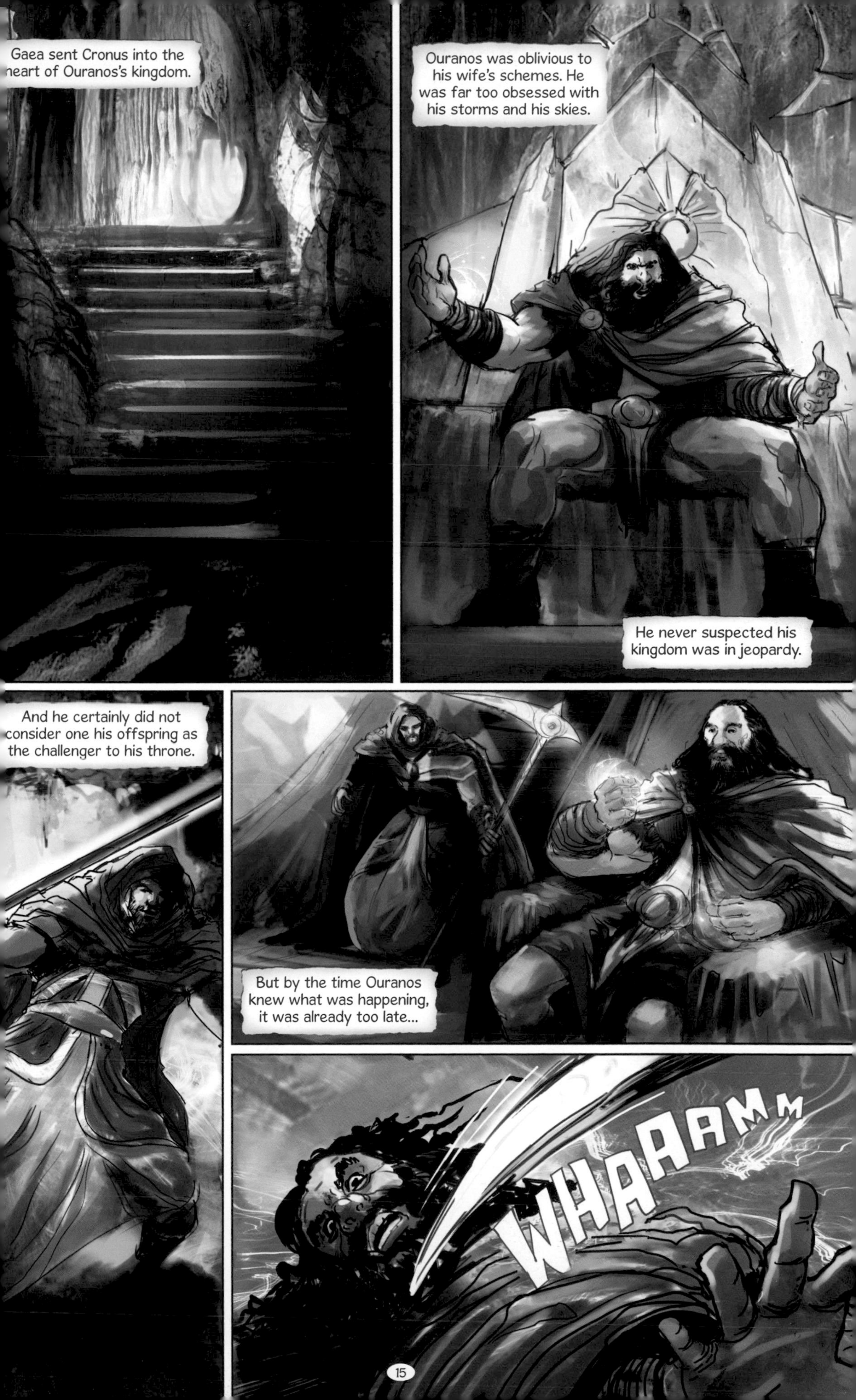
Gaea sent Cronus into the heart of Ouranos's kingdom.
Ouranos was oblivious to his wife's schemes. He was far too obsessed with his storms and his skies.
He never suspected his kingdom was in jeopardy.
And he certainly did not consider one his offspring as the challenger to his throne.
But by the time Ouranos knew what was happening, it was already too late...
WHAAAMM

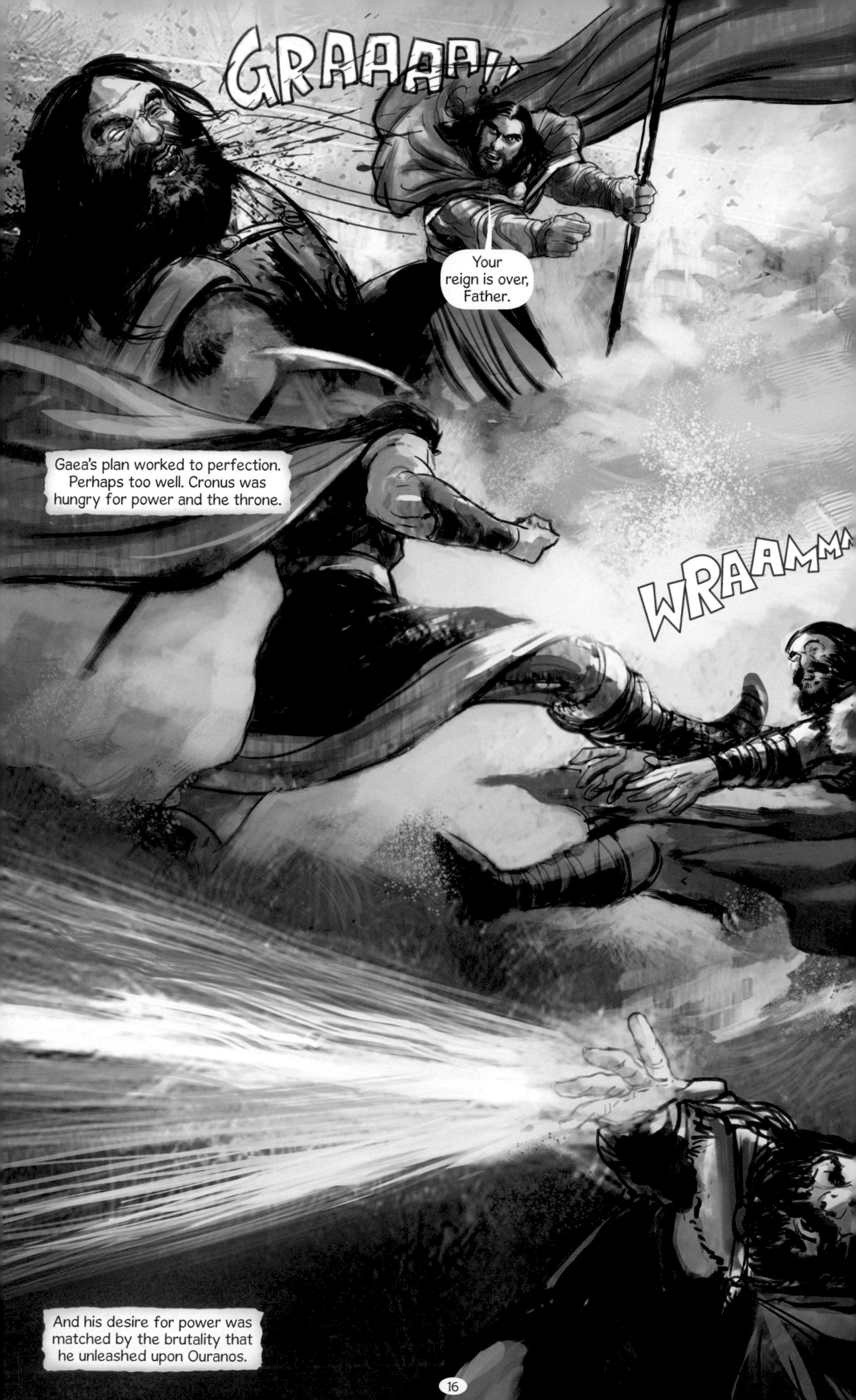
GRAAAAR!!
Your reign is over, Father.
Gaea's plan worked to perfection. Perhaps too well. Cronus was hungry for power and the throne.
WRAAMM
And his desire for power was matched by the brutality that he unleashed upon Ouranos.

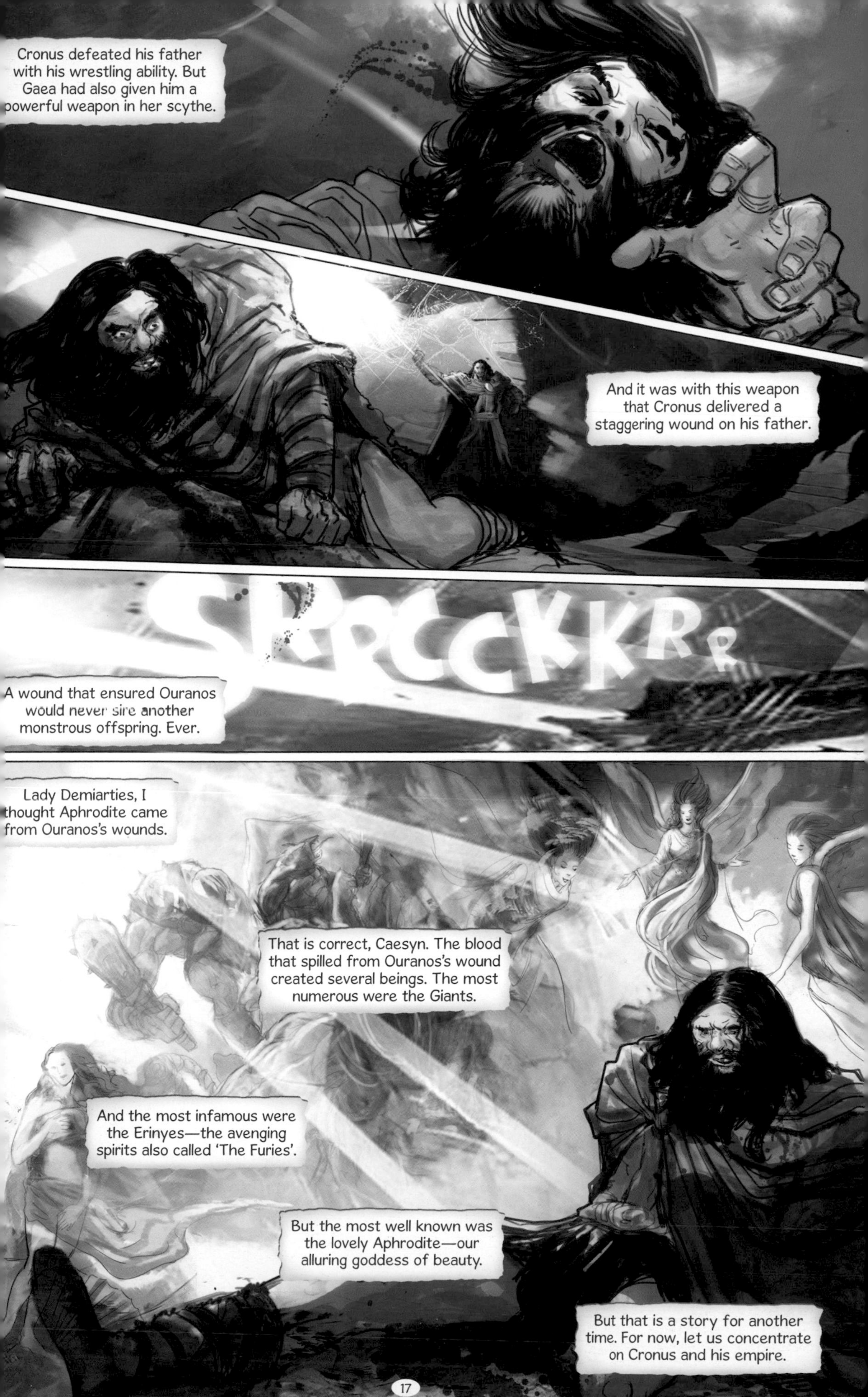

Cronus defeated his father with his wrestling ability. But Gaea had also given him a powerful weapon in her scythe.
And it was with this weapon that Cronus delivered a staggering wound on his father.
SRRCCKKRR
A wound that ensured Ouranos would never sire another monstrous offspring. Ever.
Lady Demiarties, I thought Aphrodite came from Ouranos's wounds.
That is correct, Caesyn. The blood that spilled from Ouranos's wound created several beings. The most numerous were the Giants.
And the most infamous were the Erinyes—the avenging spirits also called 'The Furies'.
But the most well known was the lovely Aphrodite—our alluring goddess of beauty.
But that is a story for another time. For now, let us concentrate on Cronus and his empire.

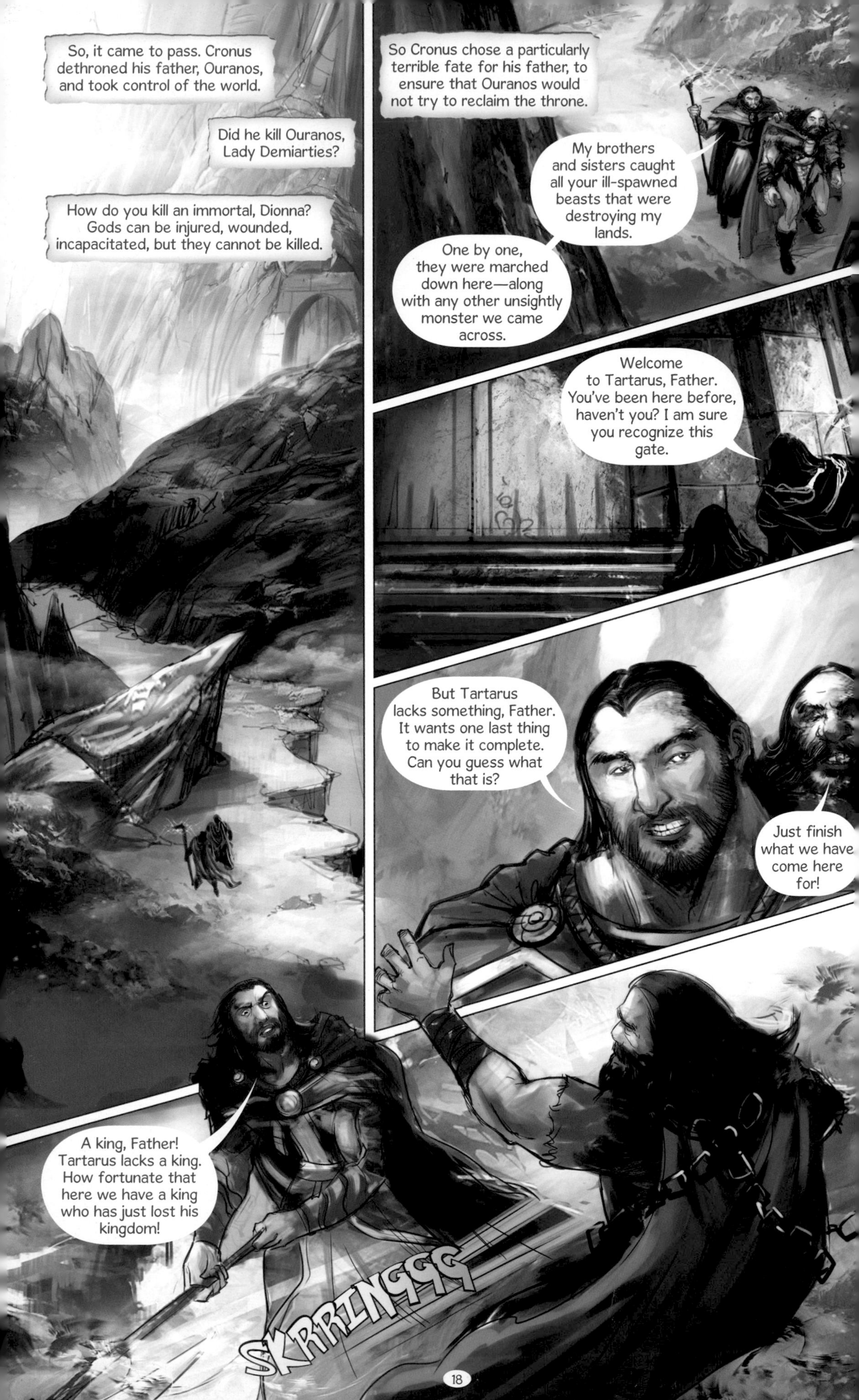
So, it came to pass. Cronus dethroned his father, Ouranos, and took control of the world.
Did he kill Ouranos, Lady Demiarties?
How do you kill an immortal, Dionna? Gods can be injured, wounded, incapacitated, but they cannot be killed.
So Cronus chose a particularly terrible fate for his father, to ensure that Ouranos would not try to reclaim the throne.
My brothers and sisters caught all your ill-spawned beasts that were destroying my lands.
One by one, they were marched down here—along with any other unsightly monster we came across.
Welcome to Tartarus, Father. You've been here before, haven't you? I am sure you recognize this gate.
But Tartarus lacks something, Father. It wants one last thing to make it complete. Can you guess what that is?
Just finish what we have come here for!
A king, Father! Tartarus lacks a king. How fortunate that here we have a king who has just lost his kingdom!
SKRRINGGG

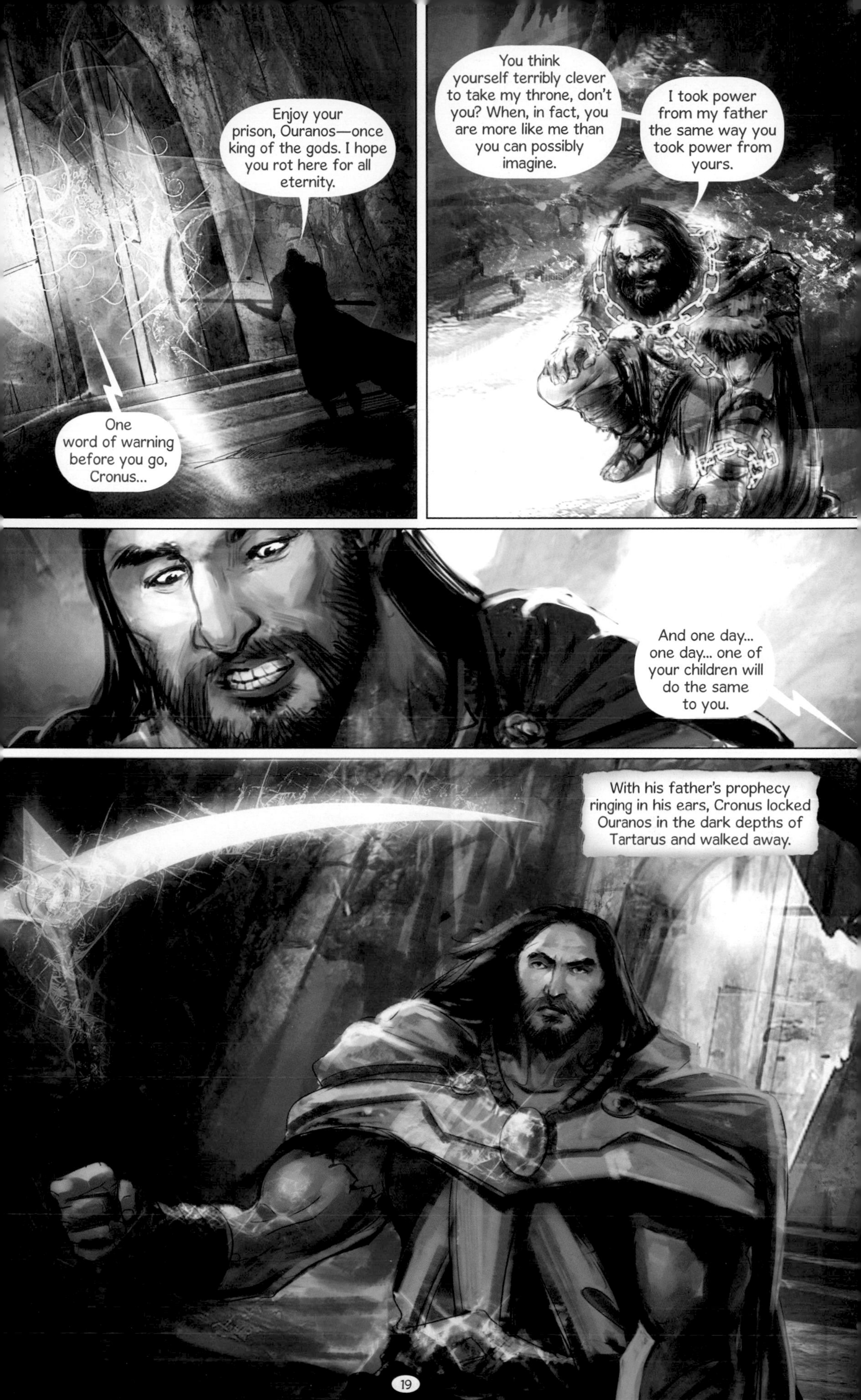
Enjoy your prison, Ouranos—once king of the gods. I hope you rot here for all eternity.
One word of warning before you go, Cronus...
You think yourself terribly clever to take my throne, don't you? When, in fact, you are more like me than you can possibly imagine.
I took power from my father the same way you took power from yours.
And one day... one day... one of your children will do the same to you.
With his father's prophecy ringing in his ears, Cronus locked Ouranos in the dark depths of Tartarus and walked away.

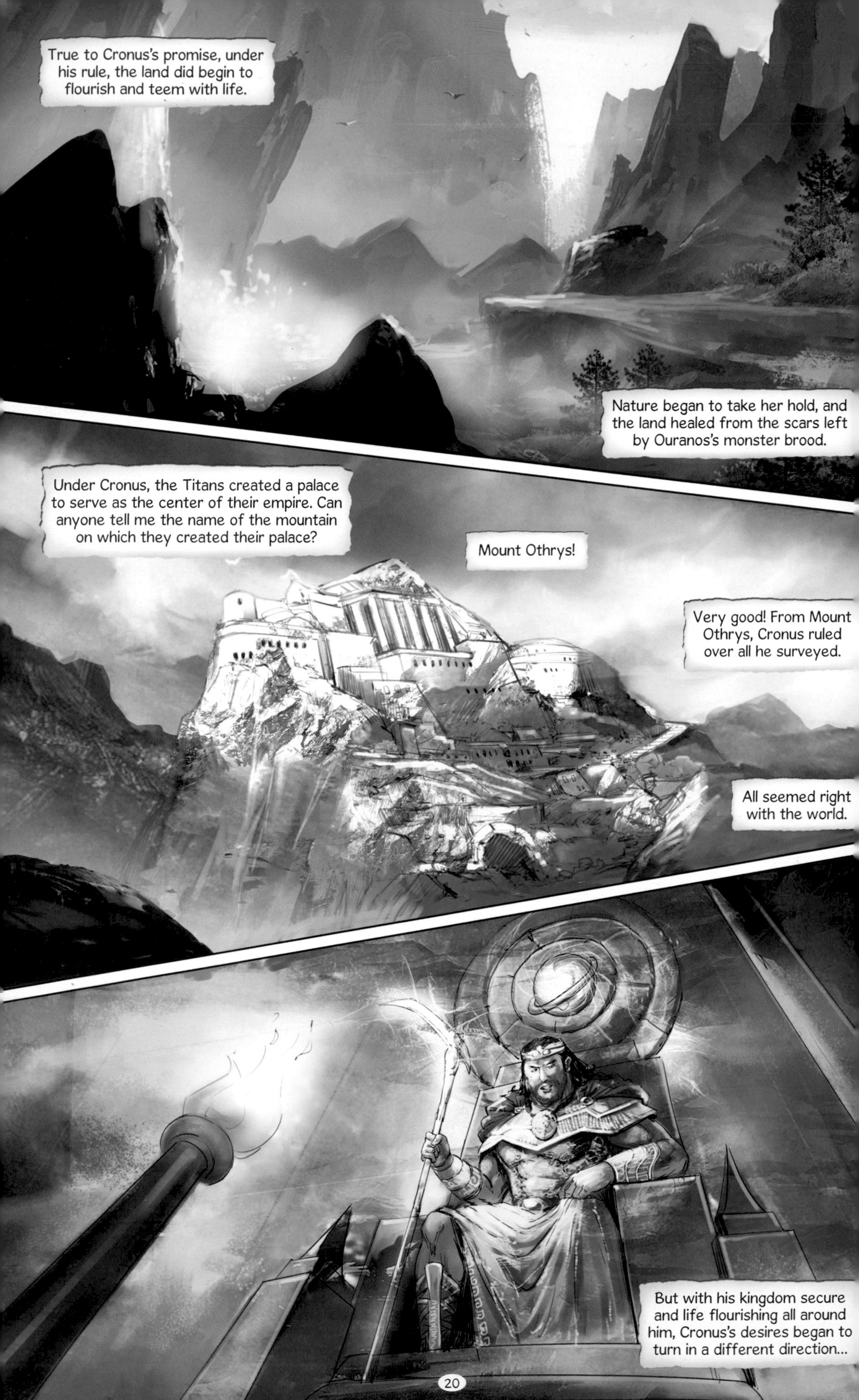
True to Cronus's promise, under his rule, the land did begin to flourish and teem with life.
Nature began to take her hold, and the land healed from the scars left by Ouranos's monster brood.
Under Cronus, the Titans created a palace to serve as the center of their empire. Can anyone tell me the name of the mountain on which they created their palace?
Mount Othrys!
Very good! From Mount Othrys, Cronus ruled over all he surveyed.
All seemed right with the world.
But with his kingdom secure and life flourishing all around him, Cronus's desires began to turn in a different direction...

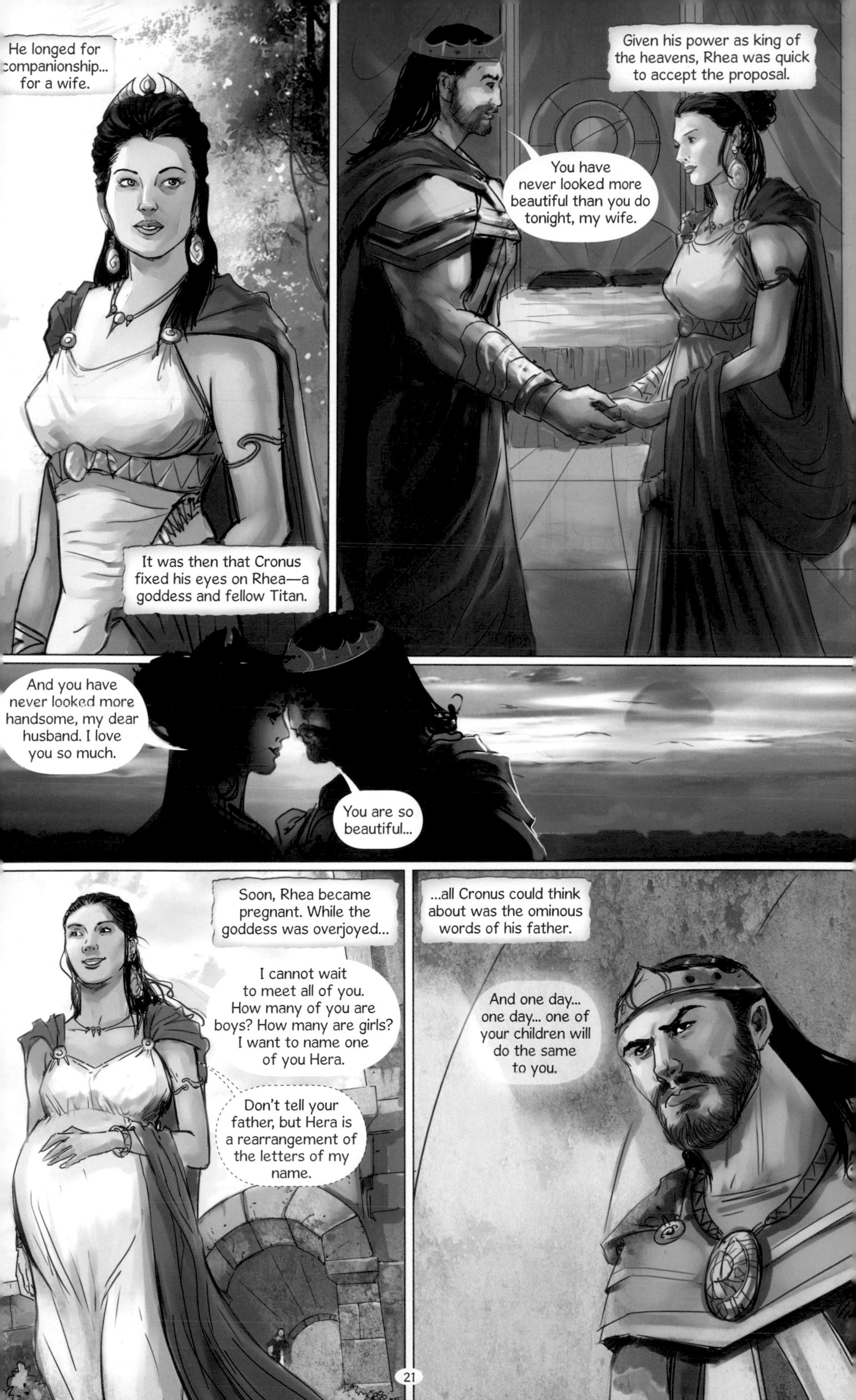
He longed for companionship... for a wife.
It was then that Cronus fixed his eyes on Rhea—a goddess and fellow Titan.
Given his power as king of the heavens, Rhea was quick to accept the proposal.
You have never looked more beautiful than you do tonight, my wife.
And you have never looked more handsome, my dear husband. I love you so much.
You are so beautiful...
Soon, Rhea became pregnant. While the goddess was overjoyed...
I cannot wait to meet all of you. How many of you are boys? How many are girls? I want to name one of you Hera.
Don't tell your father, but Hera is a rearrangement of the letters of my name.
...all Cronus could think about was the ominous words of his father.
And one day... one day... one of your children will do the same to you.

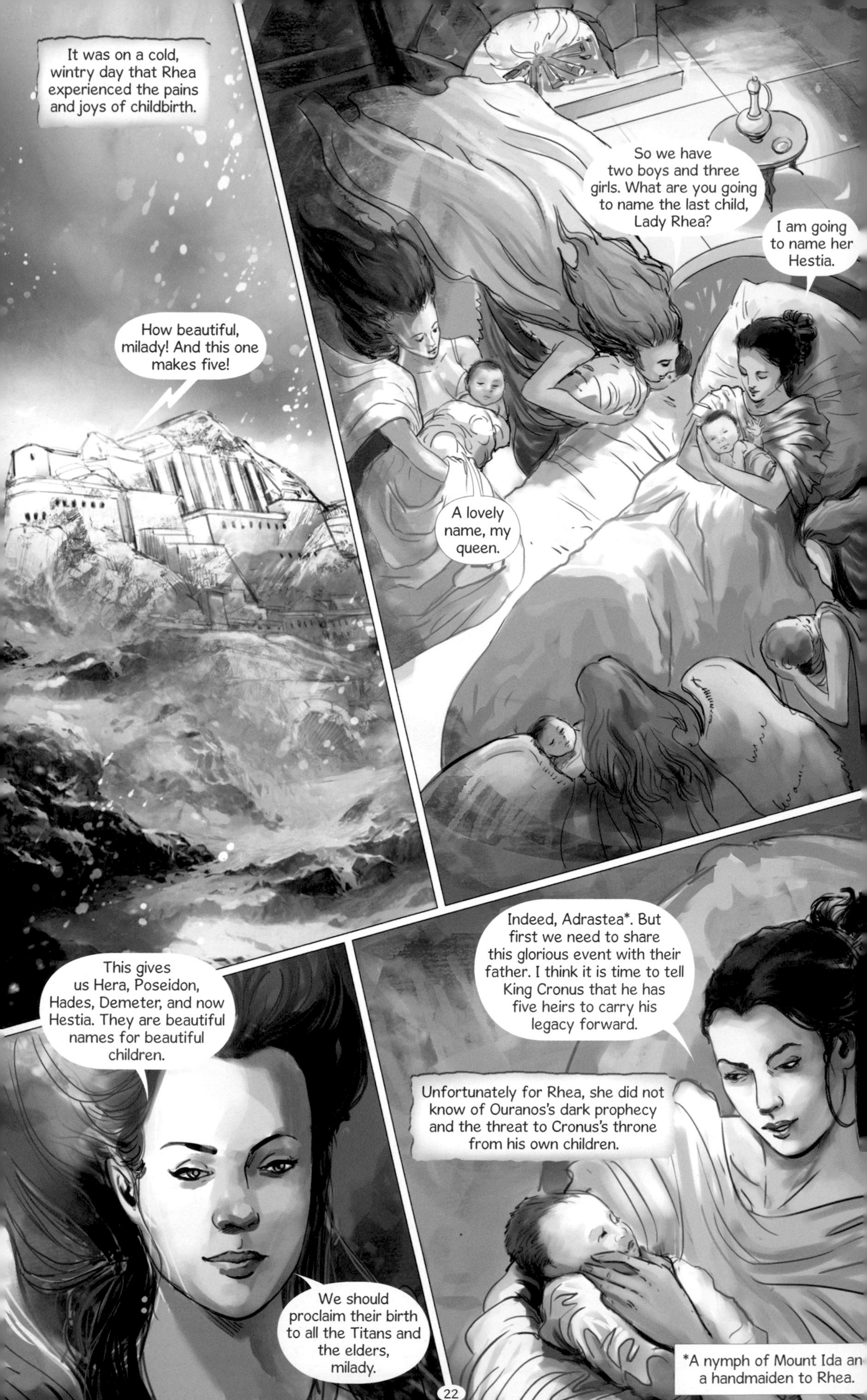
It was on a cold, wintry day that Rhea experienced the pains and joys of childbirth.
How beautiful, milady! And this one makes five!
So we have two boys and three girls. What are you going to name the last child, Lady Rhea?
I am going to name her Hestia.
A lovely name, my queen.
This gives us Hera, Poseidon, Hades, Demeter, and now Hestia. They are beautiful names for beautiful children.
We should proclaim their birth to all the Titans and the elders, milady.
Indeed, Adrastea*. But first we need to share this glorious event with their father. I think it is time to tell King Cronus that he has five heirs to carry his legacy forward.
Unfortunately for Rhea, she did not know of Ouranos's dark prophecy and the threat to Cronus's throne from his own children.
*A nymph of Mount Ida an a handmaiden to Rhea.

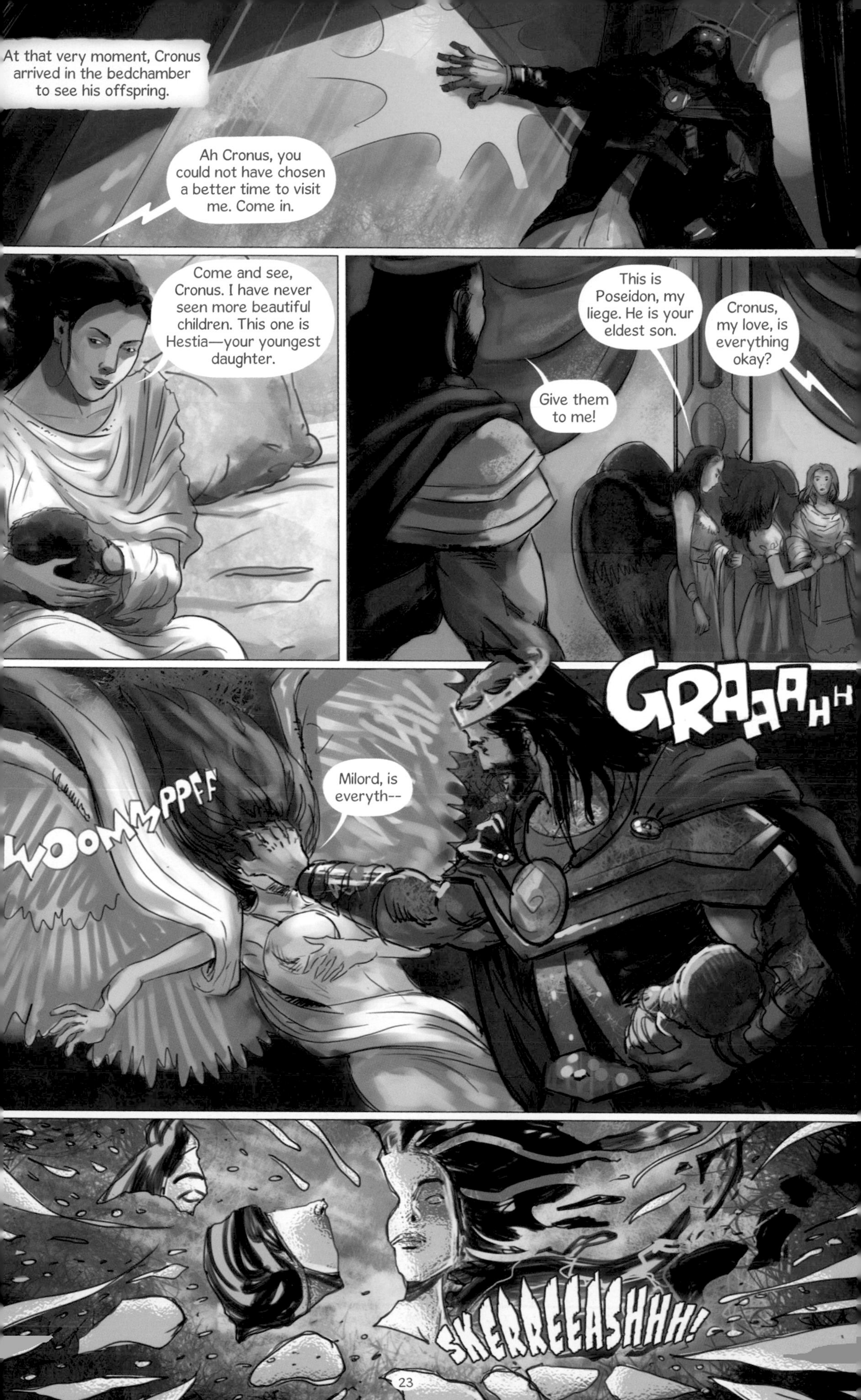
At that very moment, Cronus arrived in the bedchamber to see his offspring.
Ah Cronus, you could not have chosen a better time to visit me. Come in.
Come and see, Cronus. I have never seen more beautiful children. This one is Hestia—your youngest daughter.
Give them to me!
This is Poseidon, my liege. He is your eldest son.
Cronus, my love, is everything okay?
GRAAAHH
WOOMMPPFF
Milord, is everyth--
SKERREEASHHH!

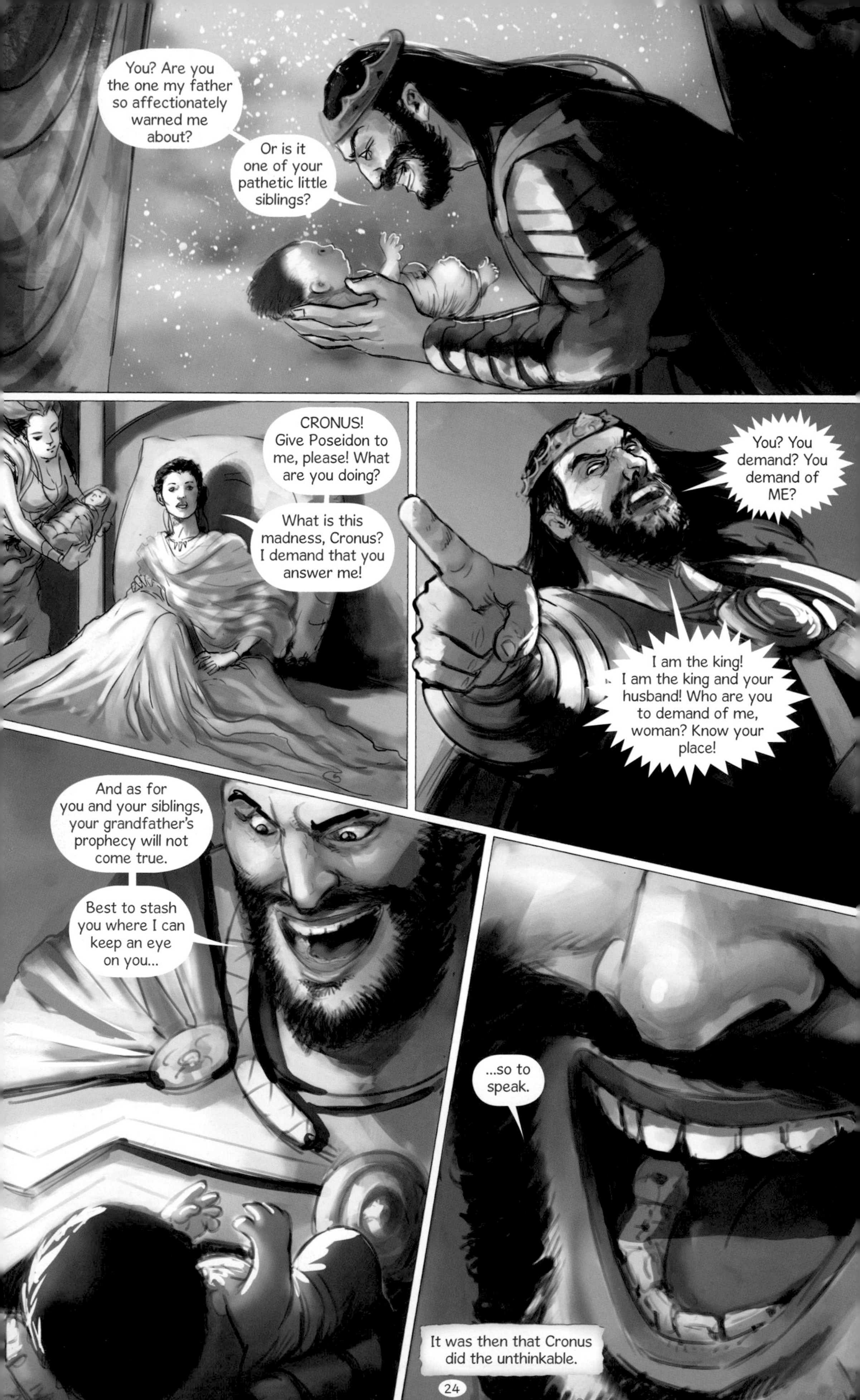
You? Are you the one my father so affectionately warned me about?
Or is it one of your pathetic little siblings?
CRONUS! Give Poseidon to me, please! What are you doing?
What is this madness, Cronus? I demand that you answer me!
You? You demand? You demand of ME?
I am the king! I am the king and your husband! Who are you to demand of me, woman? Know your place!
And as for you and your siblings, your grandfather's prophecy will not come true.
Best to stash you where I can keep an eye on you...
...so to speak.
It was then that Cronus did the unthinkable.

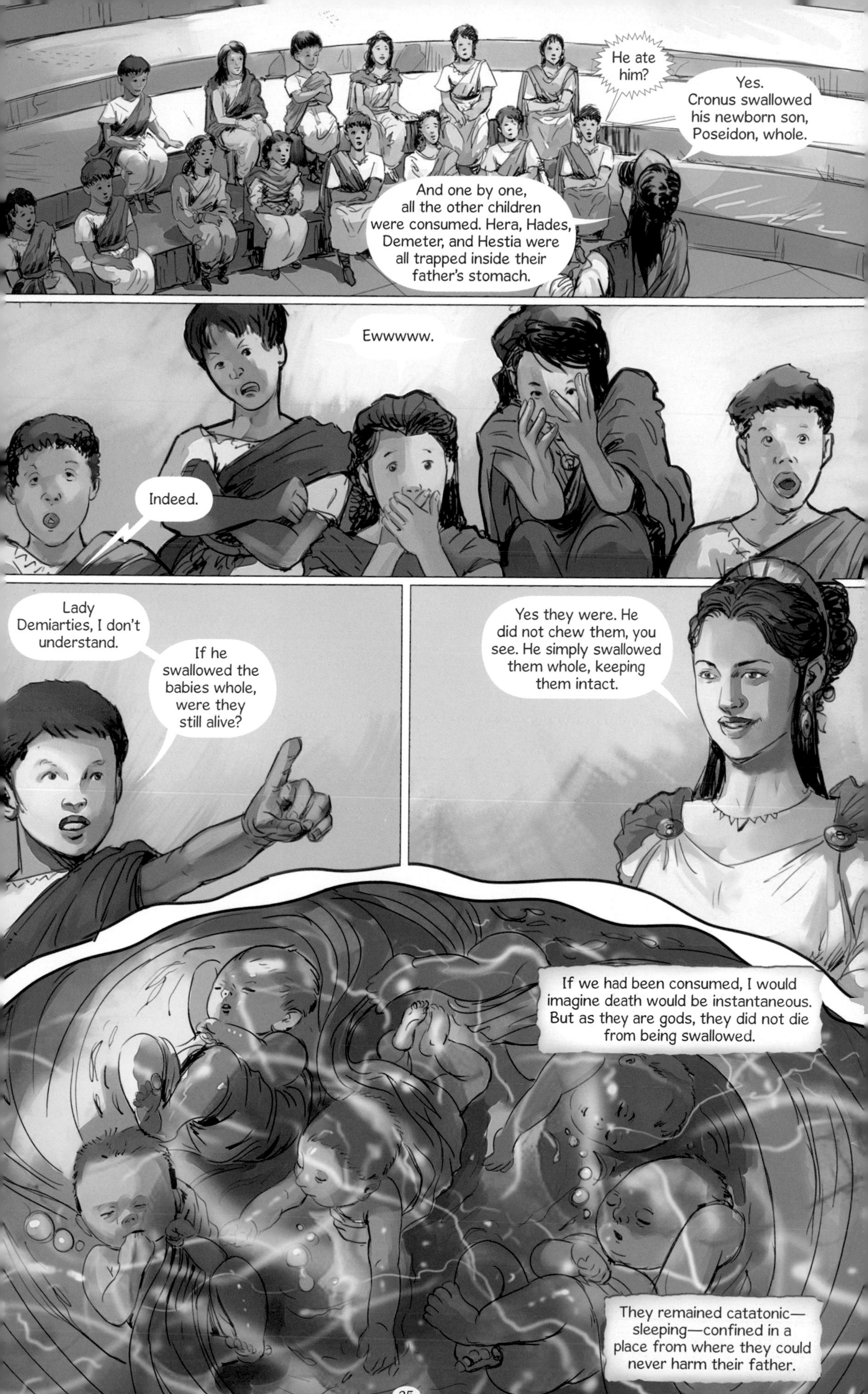
He ate him?
Yes. Cronus swallowed his newborn son, Poseidon, whole.
And one by one, all the other children were consumed. Hera, Hades, Demeter, and Hestia were all trapped inside their father's stomach.
Ewwwww.
Indeed.
Lady Demiarties, I don't understand.
If he swallowed the babies whole, were they still alive?
Yes they were. He did not chew them, you see. He simply swallowed them whole, keeping them intact.
If we had been consumed, I would imagine death would be instantaneous. But as they are gods, they did not die from being swallowed.
They remained catatonic—sleeping—confined in a place from where they could never harm their father.

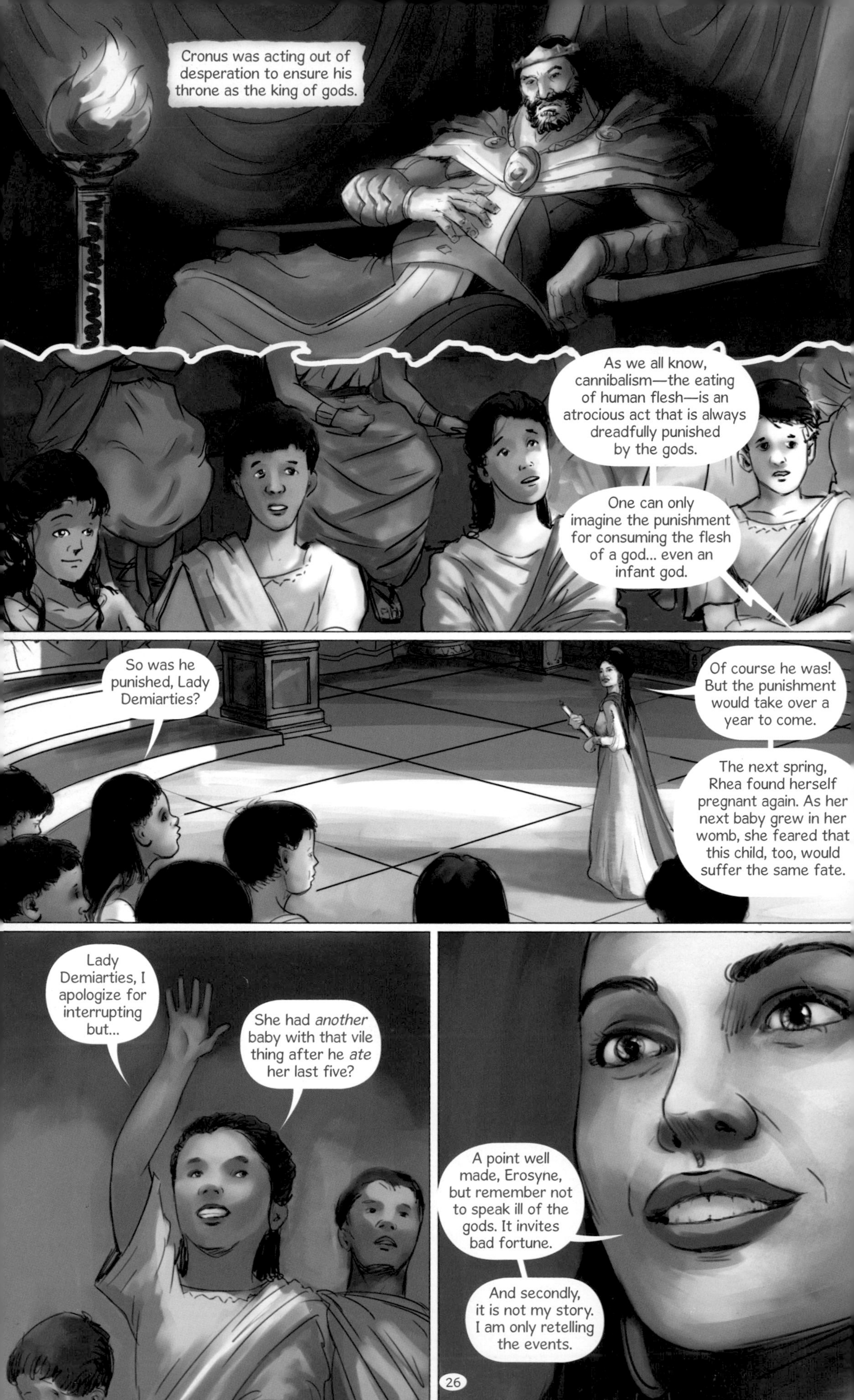
Cronus was acting out of desperation to ensure his throne as the king of gods.
As we all know, cannibalism—the eating of human flesh—is an atrocious act that is always dreadfully punished by the gods.
One can only imagine the punishment for consuming the flesh of a god... even an infant god.
So was he punished, Lady Demiarties?
Of course he was! But the punishment would take over a year to come.
The next spring, Rhea found herself pregnant again. As her next baby grew in her womb, she feared that this child, too, would suffer the same fate.
Lady Demiarties, I apologize for interrupting but...
She had *another* baby with that vile thing after he *ate* her last five?
A point well made, Erosyne, but remember not to speak ill of the gods. It invites bad fortune.
And secondly, it is not my story. I am only retelling the events.

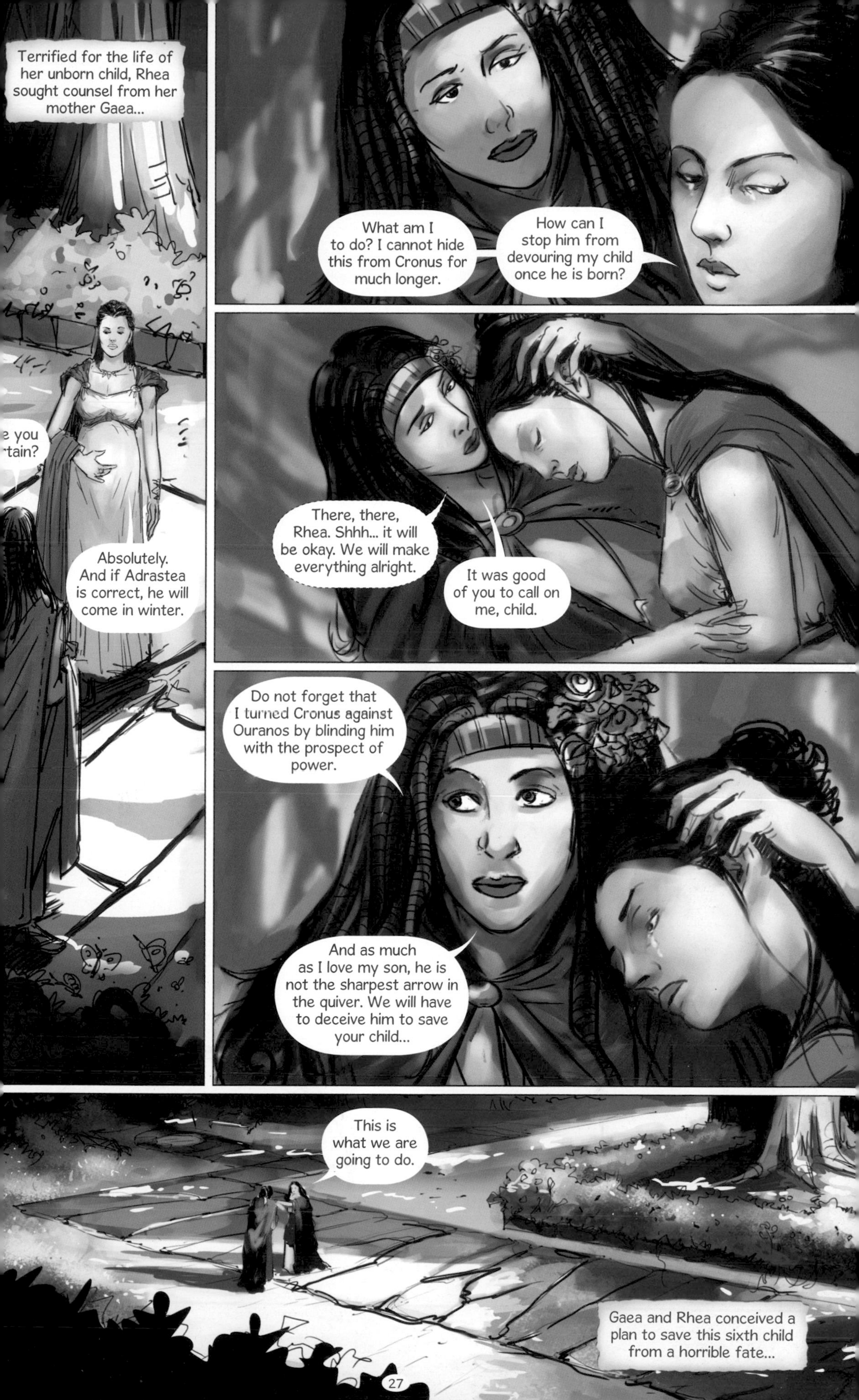

Terrified for the life of her unborn child, Rhea sought counsel from her mother Gaea...
...e you ...rtain?
Absolutely. And if Adrastea is correct, he will come in winter.
What am I to do? I cannot hide this from Cronus for much longer.
How can I stop him from devouring my child once he is born?
There, there, Rhea. Shhh... it will be okay. We will make everything alright.
It was good of you to call on me, child.
Do not forget that I turned Cronus against Ouranos by blinding him with the prospect of power.
And as much as I love my son, he is not the sharpest arrow in the quiver. We will have to deceive him to save your child...
This is what we are going to do.
Gaea and Rhea conceived a plan to save this sixth child from a horrible fate...

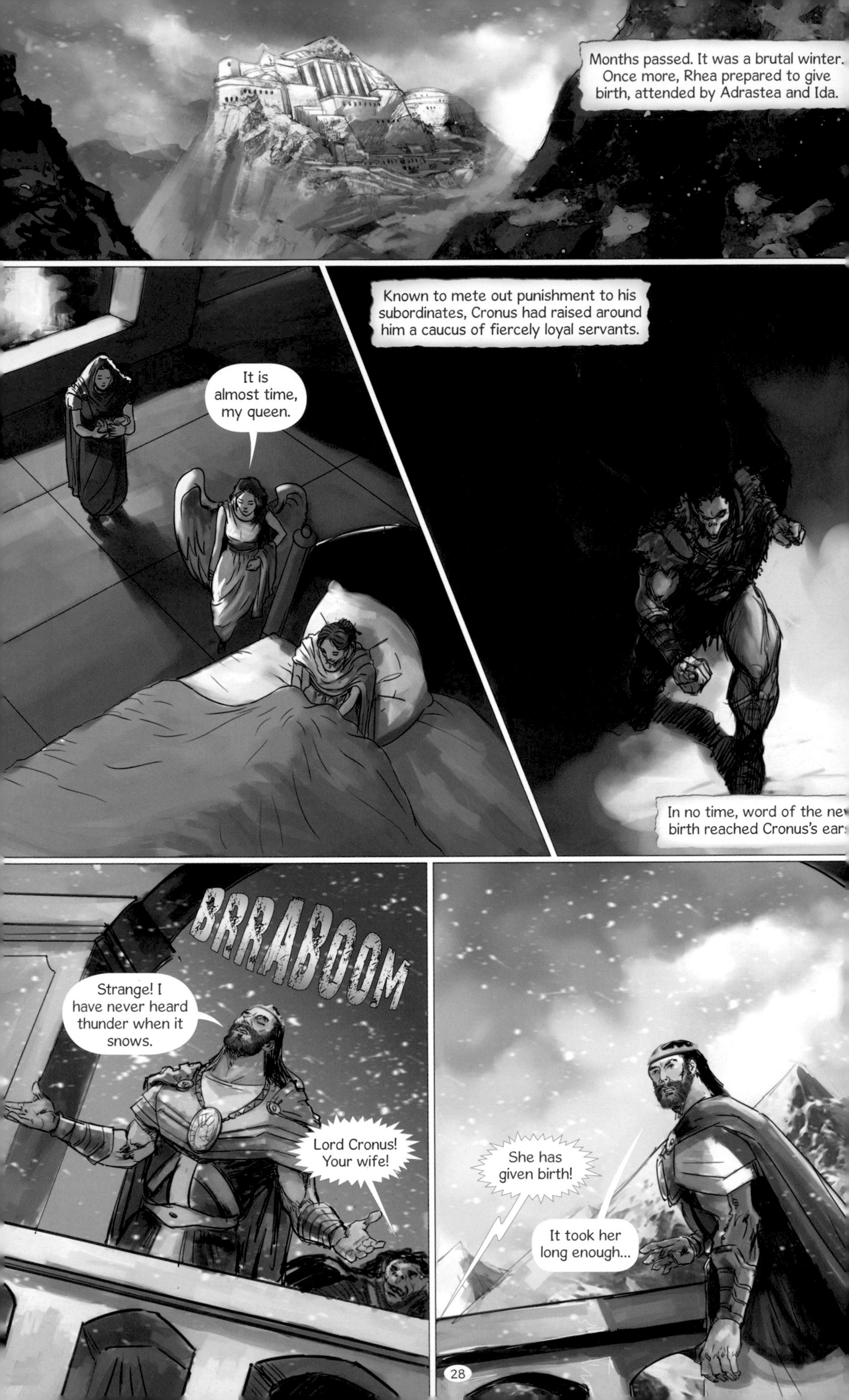

Months passed. It was a brutal winter. Once more, Rhea prepared to give birth, attended by Adrastea and Ida.
It is almost time, my queen.
Known to mete out punishment to his subordinates, Cronus had raised around him a caucus of fiercely loyal servants.
In no time, word of the ne
birth reached Cronus's ear
BRRABOOM
Strange! I have never heard thunder when it snows.
Lord Cronus! Your wife!
She has given birth!
It took her long enough...

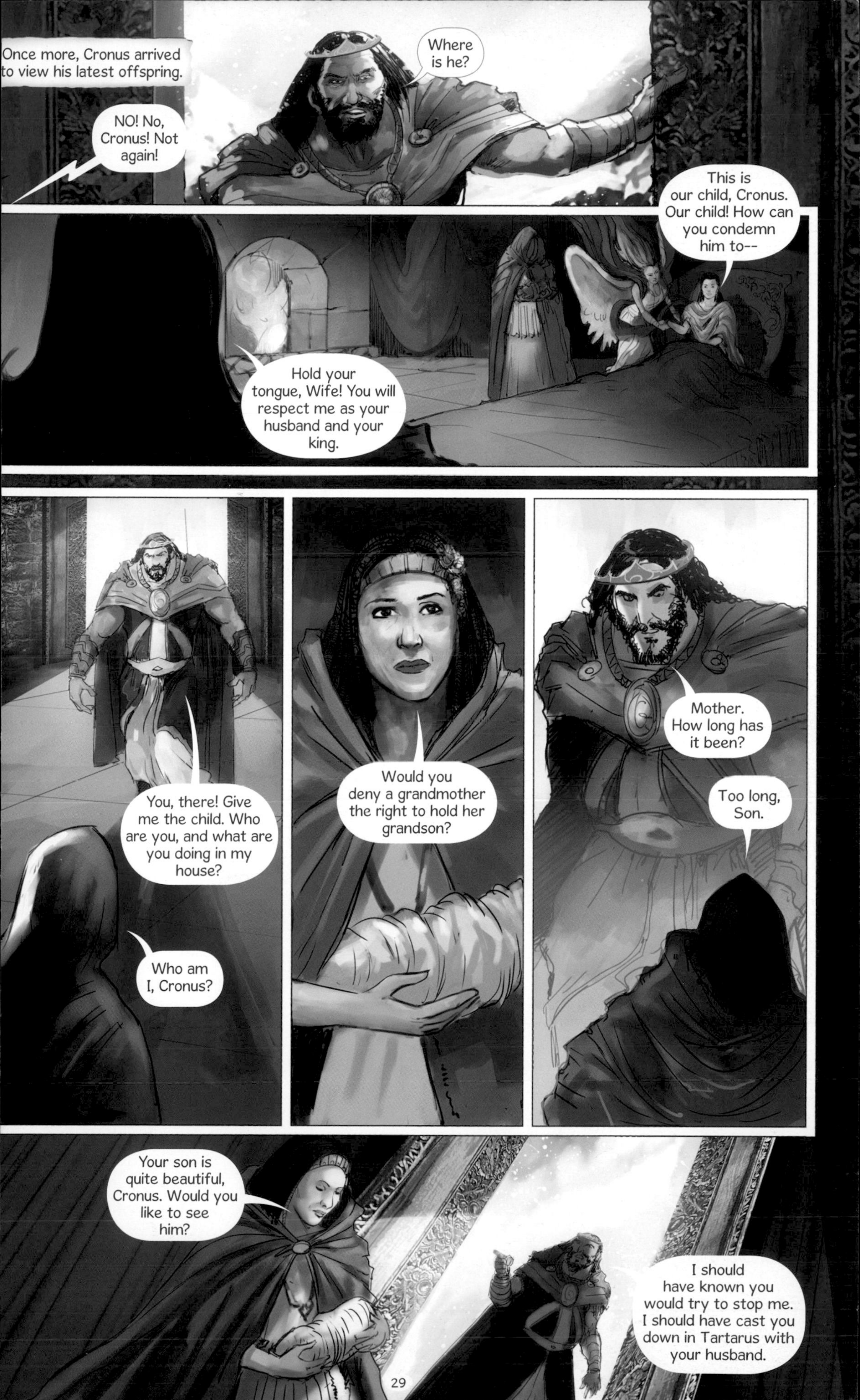
Once more, Cronus arrived to view his latest offspring.
Where is he?
NO! No, Cronus! Not again!
This is our child, Cronus. Our child! How can you condemn him to--
Hold your tongue, Wife! You will respect me as your husband and your king.
You, there! Give me the child. Who are you, and what are you doing in my house?
Who am I, Cronus?
Would you deny a grandmother the right to hold her grandson?
Mother. How long has it been?
Too long, Son.
Your son is quite beautiful, Cronus. Would you like to see him?
I should have known you would try to stop me. I should have cast you down in Tartarus with your husband.

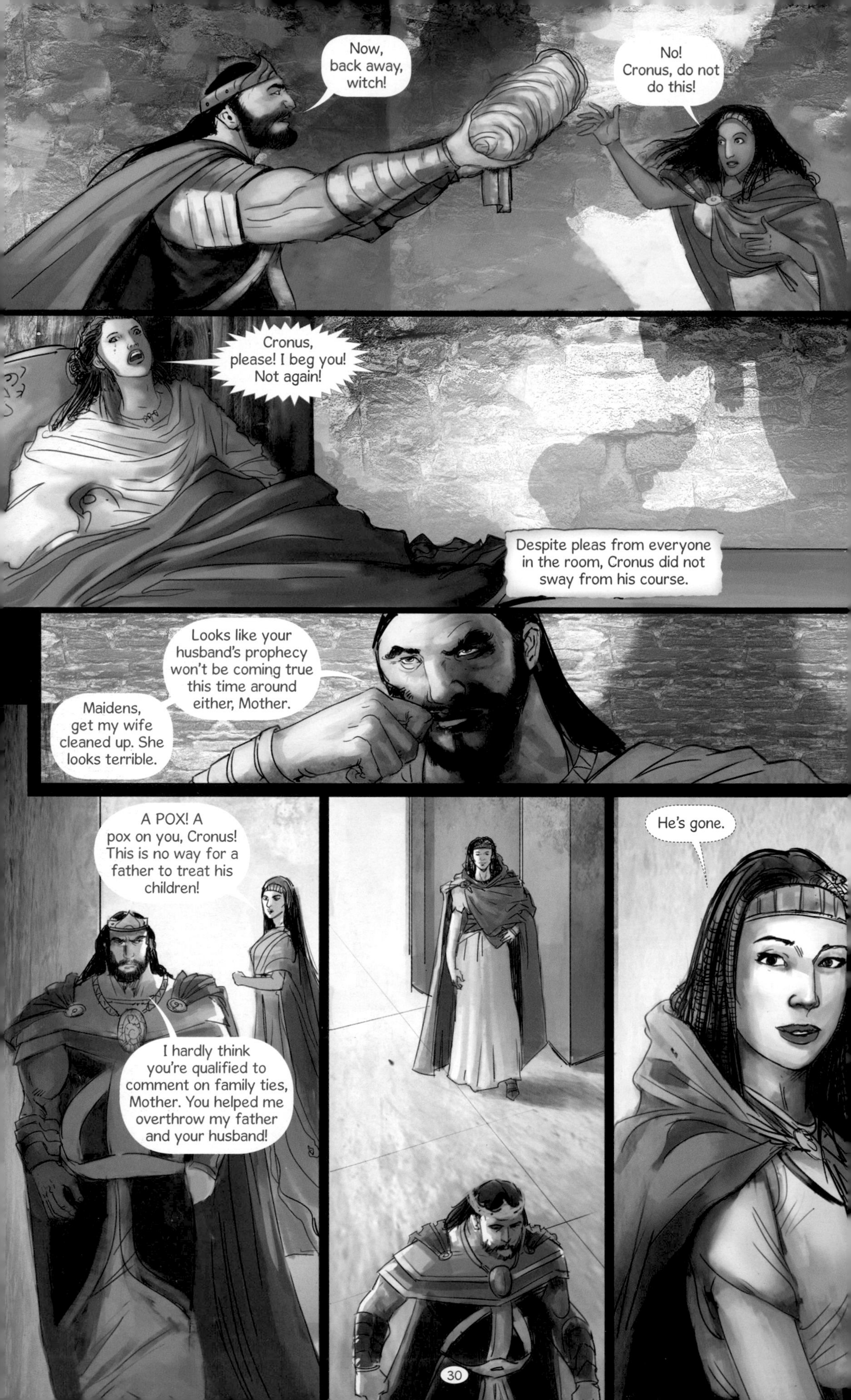

Now, back away, witch!
No! Cronus, do not do this!
Cronus, please! I beg you! Not again!
Despite pleas from everyone in the room, Cronus did not sway from his course.
Looks like your husband's prophecy won't be coming true this time around either, Mother.
Maidens, get my wife cleaned up. She looks terrible.
A POX! A pox on you, Cronus! This is no way for a father to treat his children!
I hardly think you're qualified to comment on family ties, Mother. You helped me overthrow my father and your husband!
He's gone.

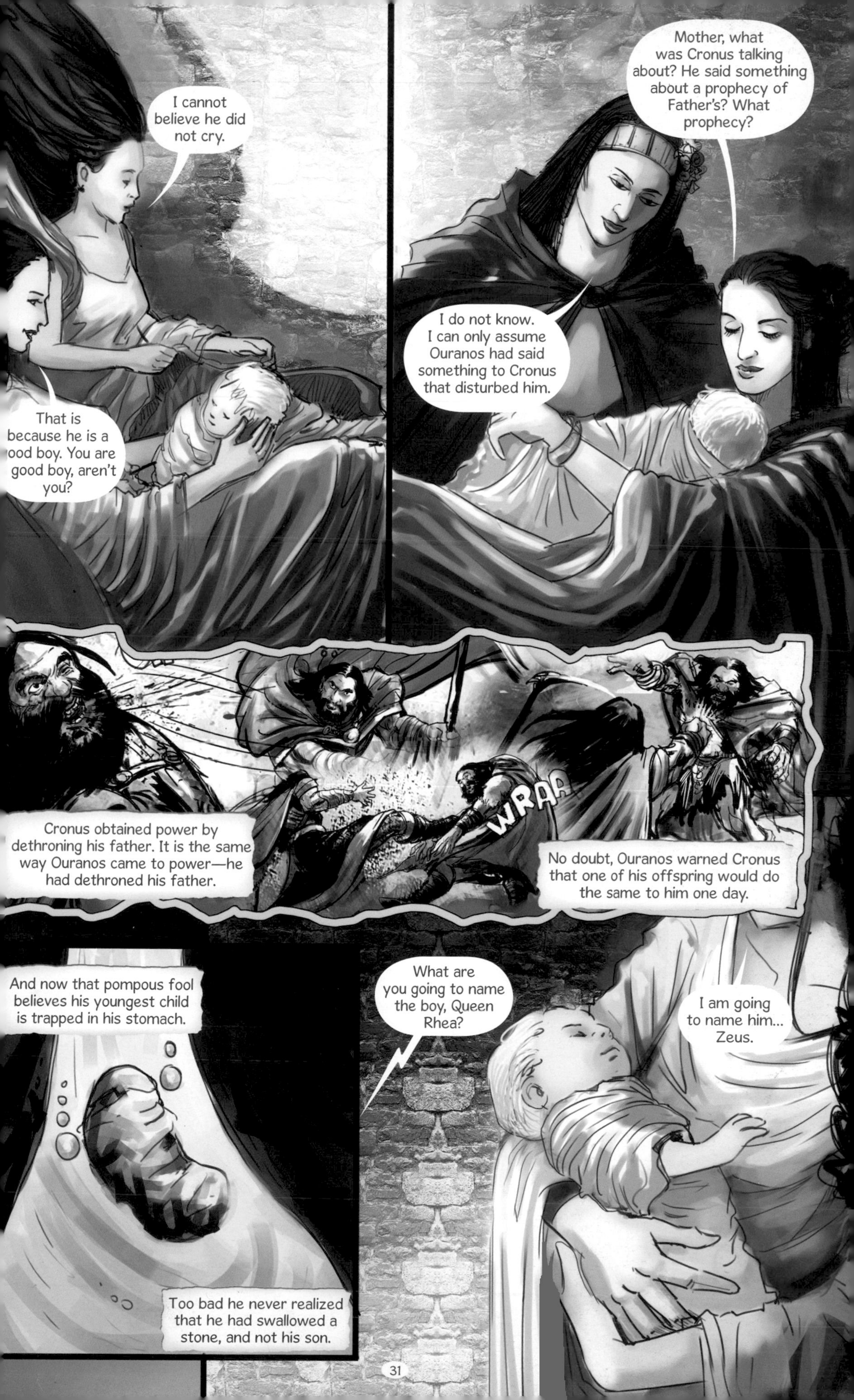

I cannot believe he did not cry.
That is because he is a ood boy. You are good boy, aren't you?
Mother, what was Cronus talking about? He said something about a prophecy of Father's? What prophecy?
I do not know. I can only assume Ouranos had said something to Cronus that disturbed him.
Cronus obtained power by dethroning his father. It is the same way Ouranos came to power—he had dethroned his father.
WRAA
No doubt, Ouranos warned Cronus that one of his offspring would do the same to him one day.
And now that pompous fool believes his youngest child is trapped in his stomach.
Too bad he never realized that he had swallowed a stone, and not his son.
What are you going to name the boy, Queen Rhea?
I am going to name him... Zeus.

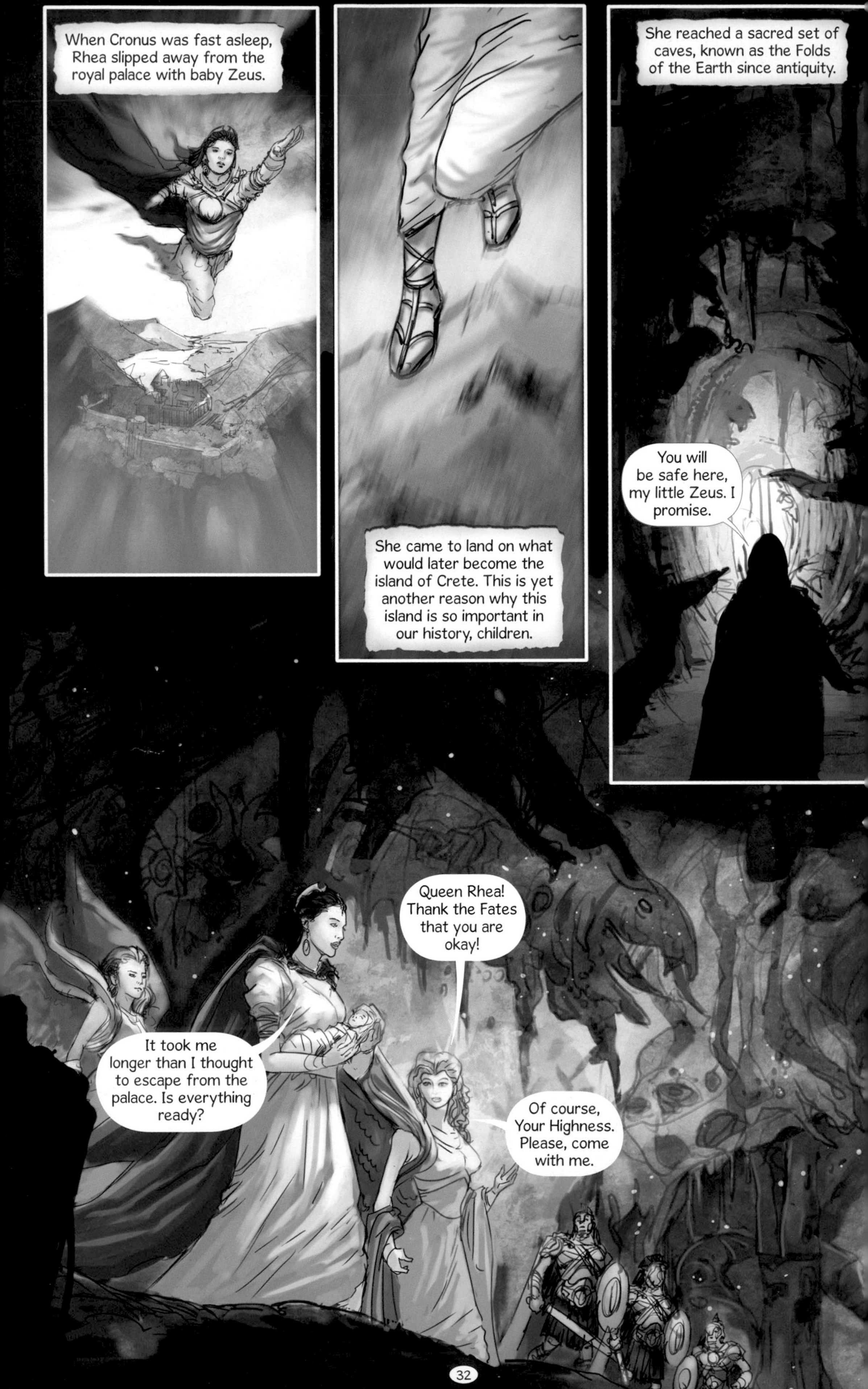
When Cronus was fast asleep, Rhea slipped away from the royal palace with baby Zeus.
She came to land on what would later become the island of Crete. This is yet another reason why this island is so important in our history, children.
She reached a sacred set of caves, known as the Folds of the Earth since antiquity.
You will be safe here, my little Zeus. I promise.
Queen Rhea! Thank the Fates that you are okay!
It took me longer than I thought to escape from the palace. Is everything ready?
Of course, Your Highness. Please, come with me.

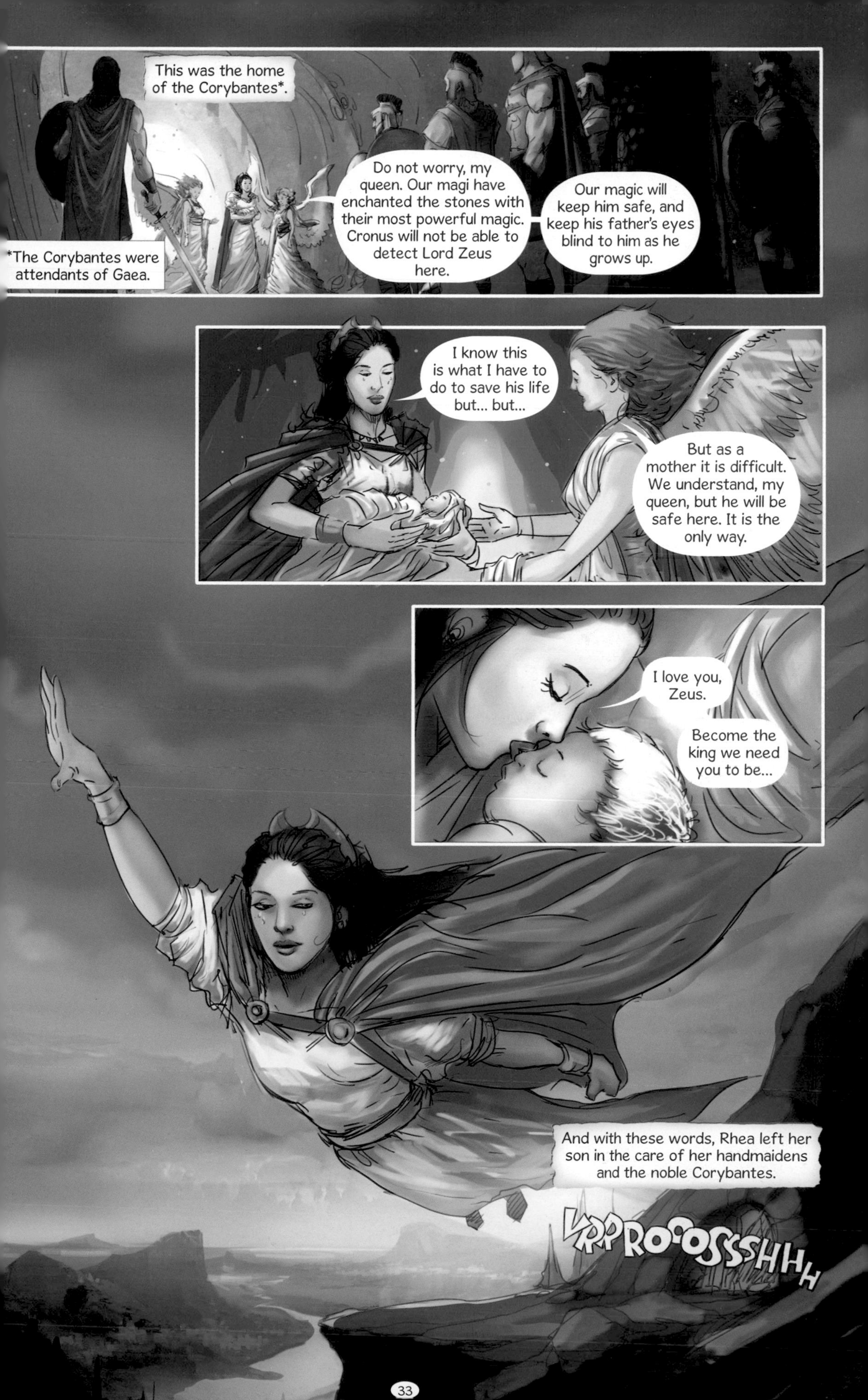
This was the home of the Corybantes*.
*The Corybantes were attendants of Gaea.
Do not worry, my queen. Our magi have enchanted the stones with their most powerful magic. Cronus will not be able to detect Lord Zeus here.
Our magic will keep him safe, and keep his father's eyes blind to him as he grows up.
I know this is what I have to do to save his life but... but...
But as a mother it is difficult. We understand, my queen, but he will be safe here. It is the only way.
I love you, Zeus.
Become the king we need you to be...
And with these words, Rhea left her son in the care of her handmaidens and the noble Corybantes.
VRPROOOSSSHHH

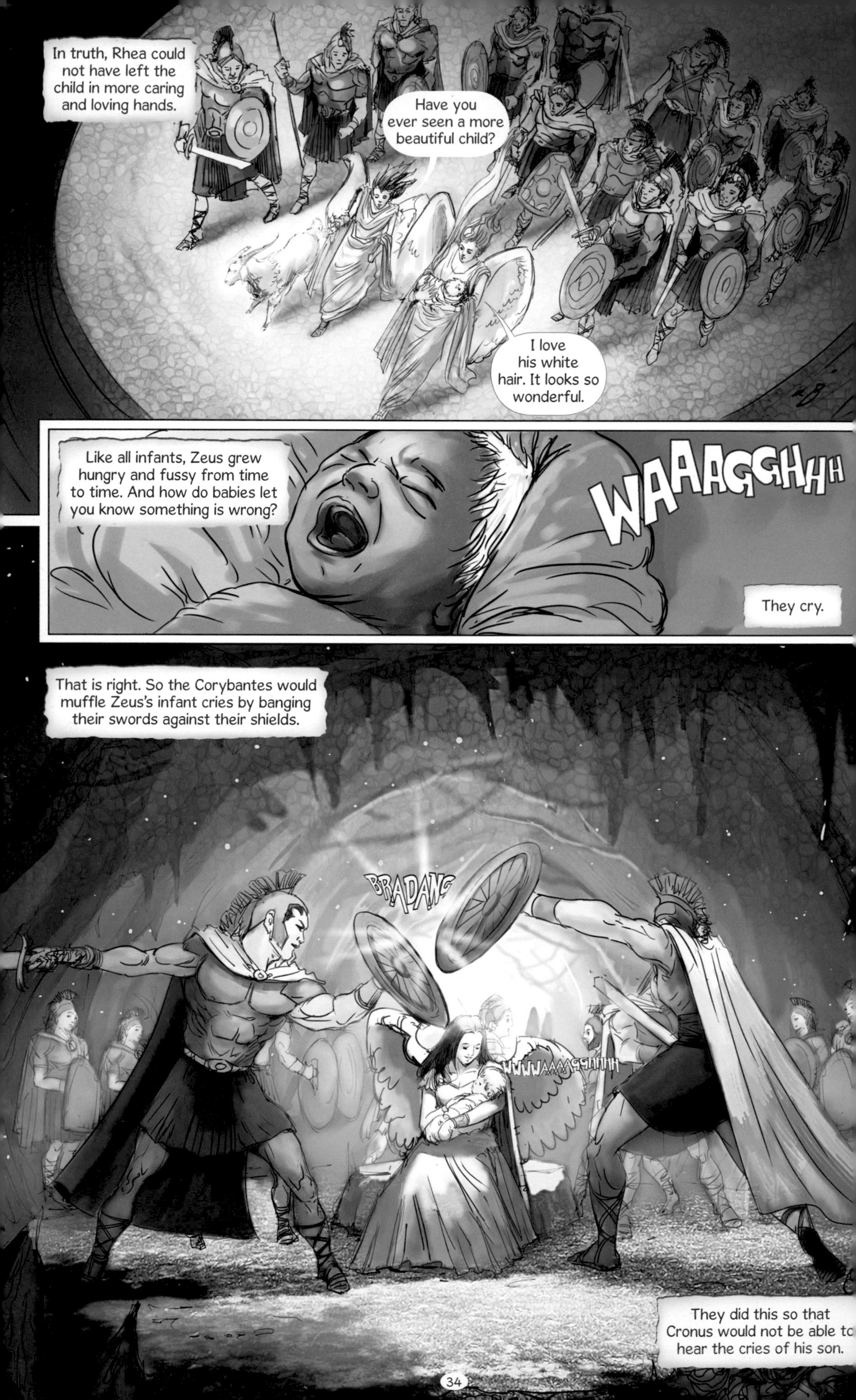

In truth, Rhea could not have left the child in more caring and loving hands.
Have you ever seen a more beautiful child?
I love his white hair. It looks so wonderful.
Like all infants, Zeus grew hungry and fussy from time to time. And how do babies let you know something is wrong?
WAAAGGHHH
They cry.
That is right. So the Corybantes would muffle Zeus's infant cries by banging their swords against their shields.
BRADANG
They did this so that Cronus would not be able to hear the cries of his son.

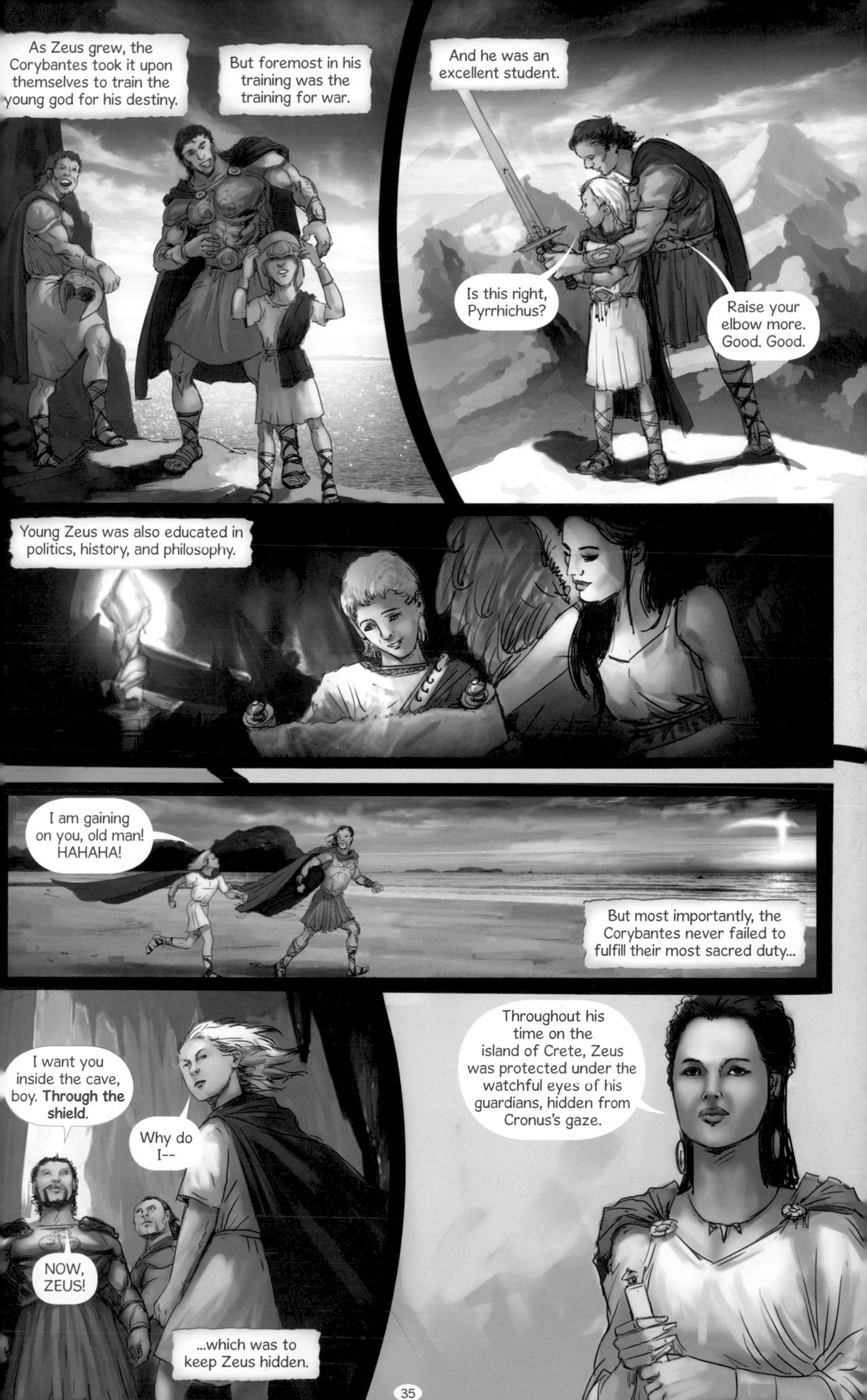
As Zeus grew, the Corybantes took it upon themselves to train the young god for his destiny.
But foremost in his training was the training for war.
And he was an excellent student.
Is this right, Pyrrhichus?
Raise your elbow more. Good. Good.
Young Zeus was also educated in politics, history, and philosophy.
I am gaining on you, old man! HAHAHA!
But most importantly, the Corybantes never failed to fulfill their most sacred duty...
I want you inside the cave, boy. **Through the shield**.
Why do I--
NOW, ZEUS!
...which was to keep Zeus hidden.
Throughout his time on the island of Crete, Zeus was protected under the watchful eyes of his guardians, hidden from Cronus's gaze.

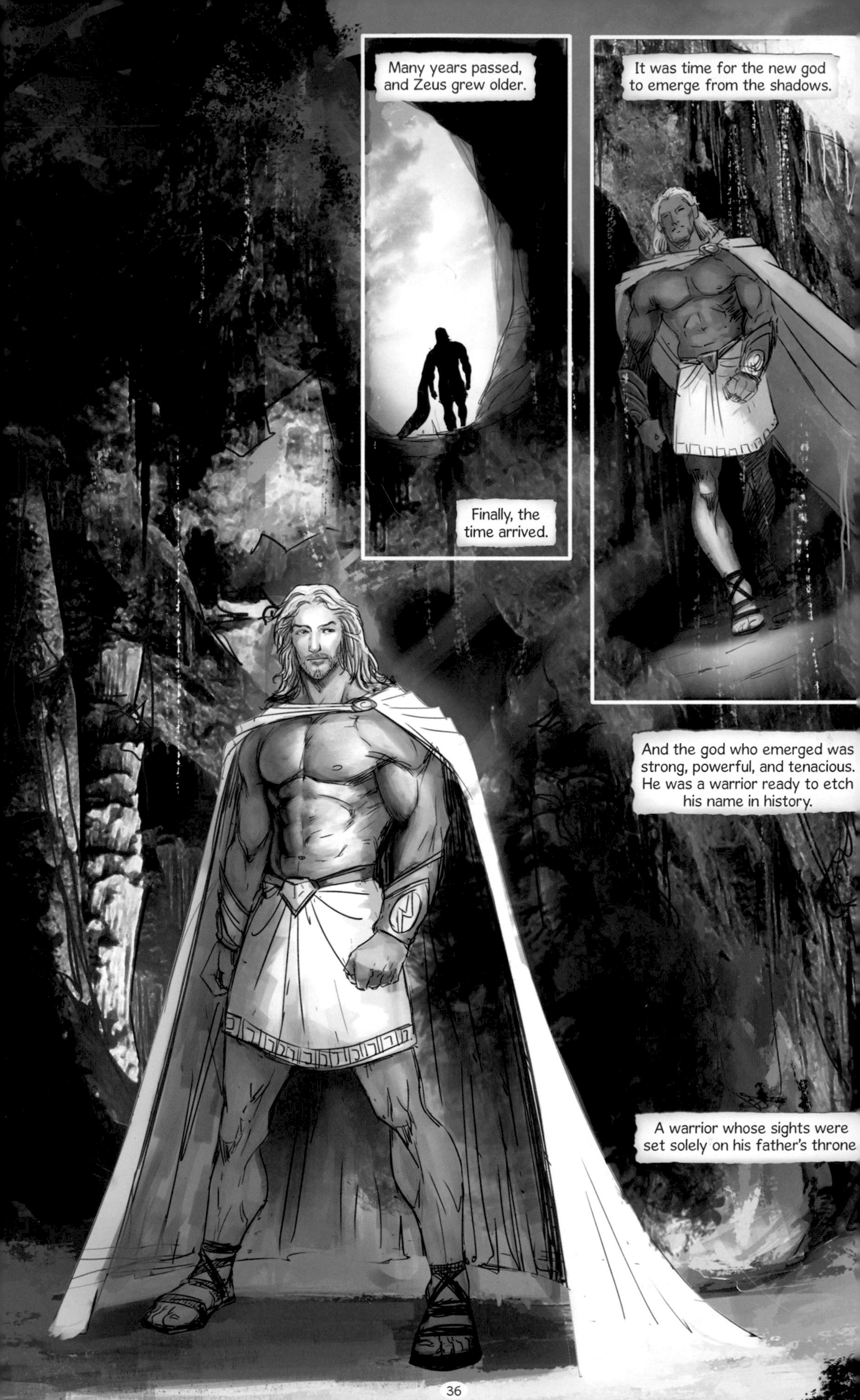
Many years passed, and Zeus grew older.
Finally, the time arrived.
It was time for the new god to emerge from the shadows.
And the god who emerged was strong, powerful, and tenacious. He was a warrior ready to etch his name in history.
A warrior whose sights were set solely on his father's throne

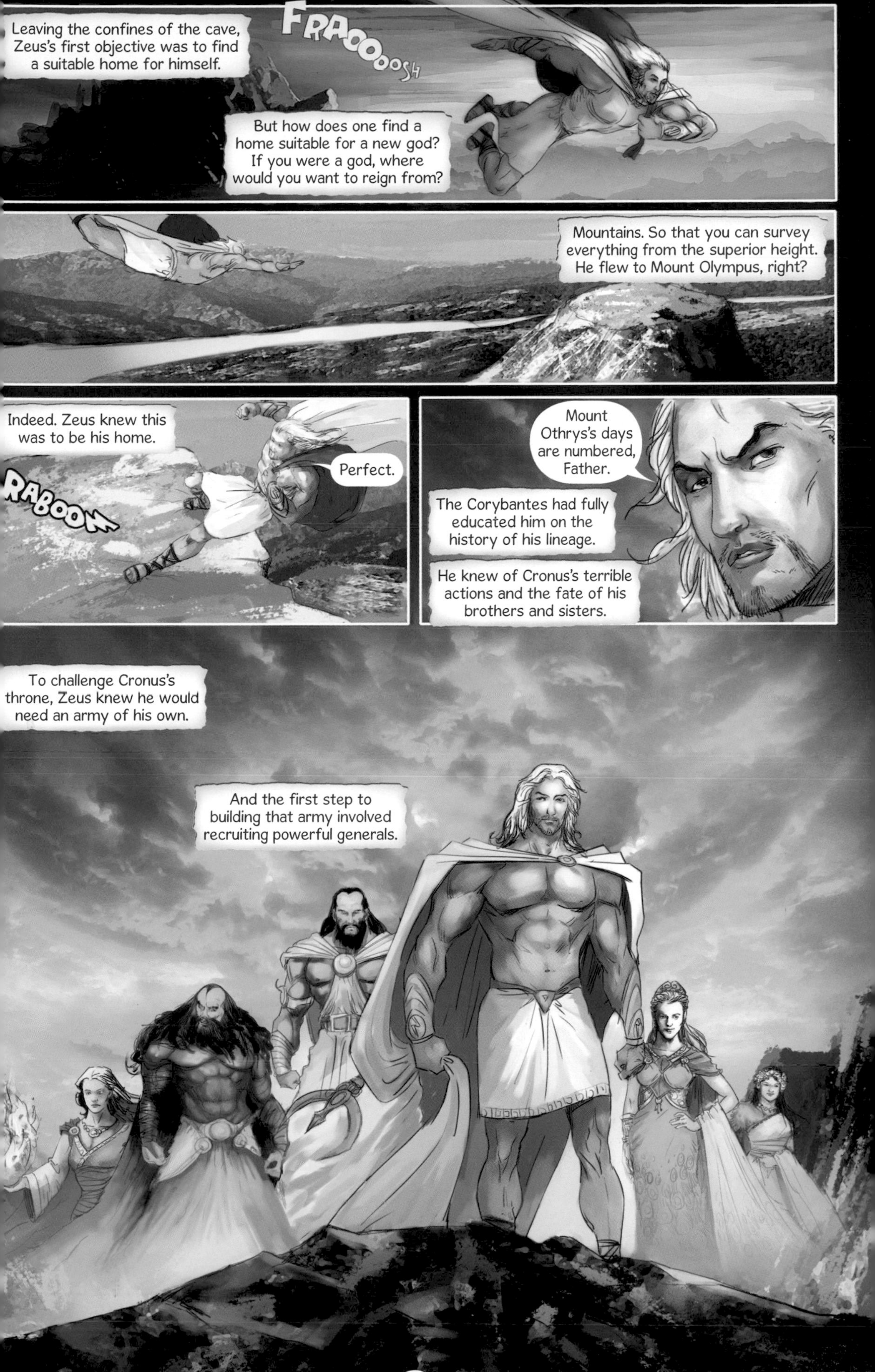
Leaving the confines of the cave, Zeus's first objective was to find a suitable home for himself.
FRAOOOOOSH
But how does one find a home suitable for a new god? If you were a god, where would you want to reign from?
Mountains. So that you can survey everything from the superior height. He flew to Mount Olympus, right?
Indeed. Zeus knew this was to be his home.
Perfect.
RABOOM
Mount Othrys's days are numbered, Father.
The Corybantes had fully educated him on the history of his lineage.
He knew of Cronus's terrible actions and the fate of his brothers and sisters.
To challenge Cronus's throne, Zeus knew he would need an army of his own.
And the first step to building that army involved recruiting powerful generals.

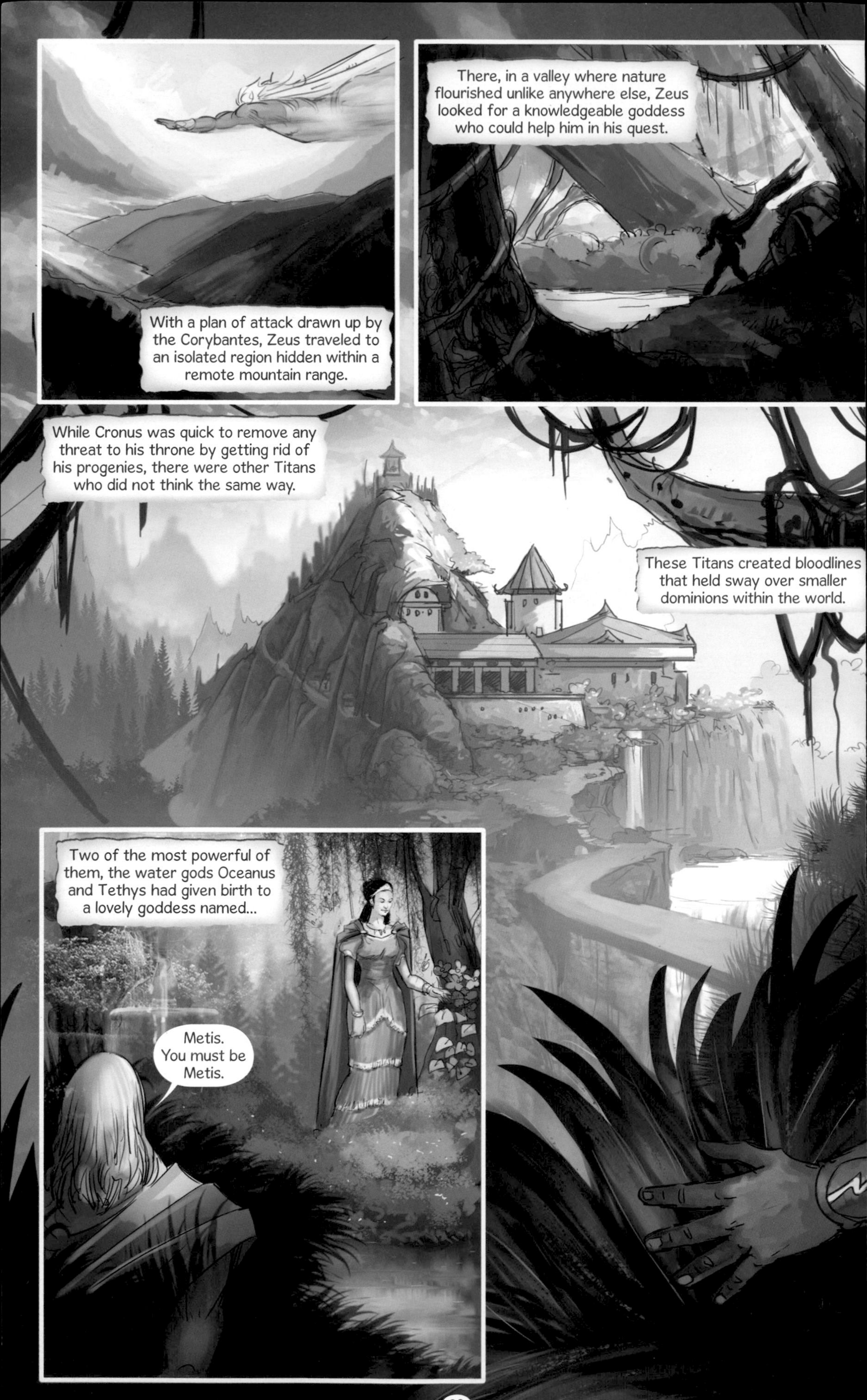
With a plan of attack drawn up by the Corybantes, Zeus traveled to an isolated region hidden within a remote mountain range.
There, in a valley where nature flourished unlike anywhere else, Zeus looked for a knowledgeable goddess who could help him in his quest.
While Cronus was quick to remove any threat to his throne by getting rid of his progenies, there were other Titans who did not think the same way.
These Titans created bloodlines that held sway over smaller dominions within the world.
Two of the most powerful of them, the water gods Oceanus and Tethys had given birth to a lovely goddess named...
Metis. You must be Metis.

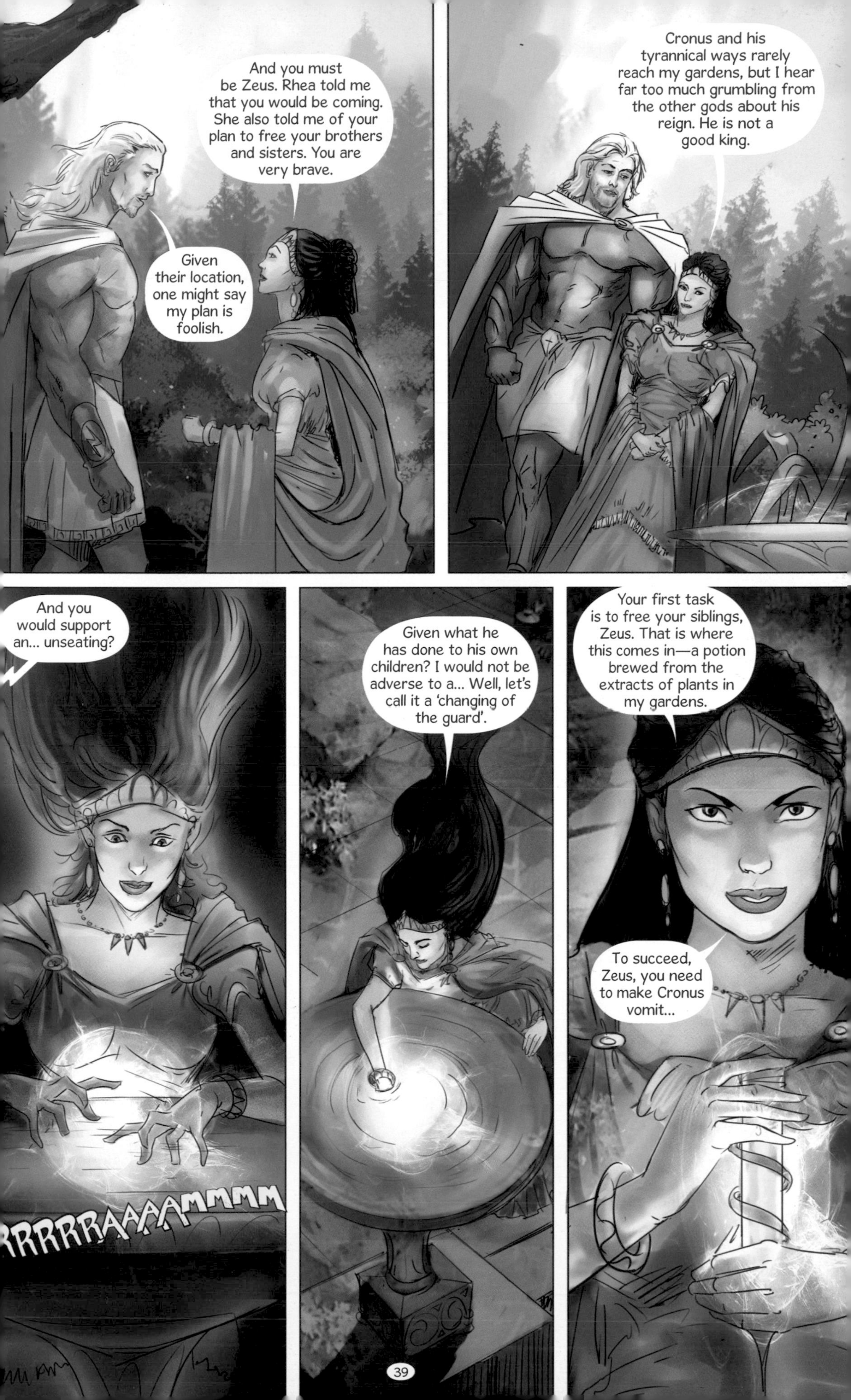
And you must be Zeus. Rhea told me that you would be coming. She also told me of your plan to free your brothers and sisters. You are very brave.
Given their location, one might say my plan is foolish.
Cronus and his tyrannical ways rarely reach my gardens, but I hear far too much grumbling from the other gods about his reign. He is not a good king.
And you would support an... unseating?
RRRRRAAAAMMMM
Given what he has done to his own children? I would not be adverse to a... Well, let's call it a 'changing of the guard'.
Your first task is to free your siblings, Zeus. That is where this comes in—a potion brewed from the extracts of plants in my gardens.
To succeed, Zeus, you need to make Cronus vomit...

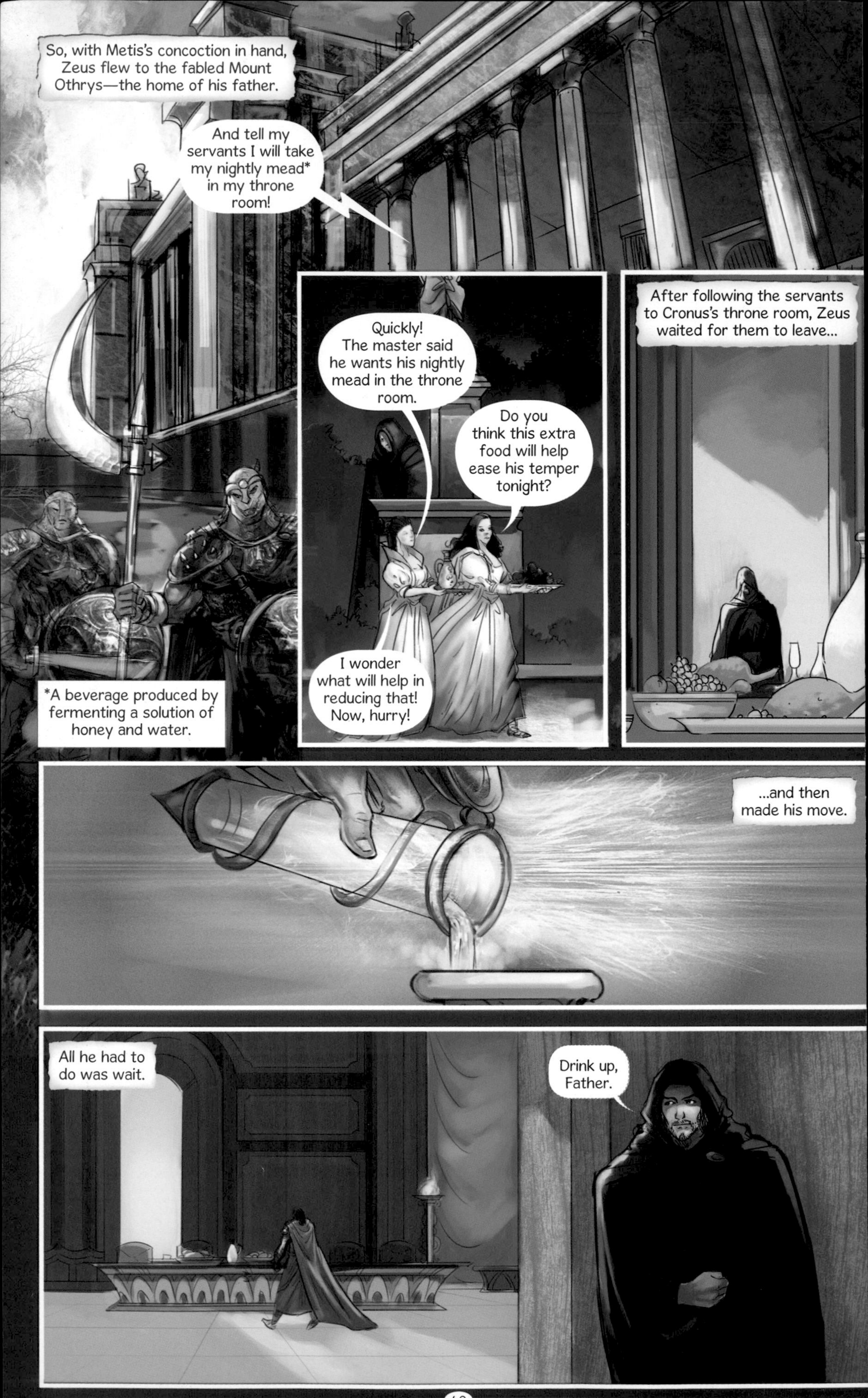
So, with Metis's concoction in hand, Zeus flew to the fabled Mount Othrys—the home of his father.
And tell my servants I will take my nightly mead* in my throne room!
*A beverage produced by fermenting a solution of honey and water.
Quickly! The master said he wants his nightly mead in the throne room.
Do you think this extra food will help ease his temper tonight?
I wonder what will help in reducing that! Now, hurry!
After following the servants to Cronus's throne room, Zeus waited for them to leave...
...and then made his move.
All he had to do was wait.
Drink up, Father.

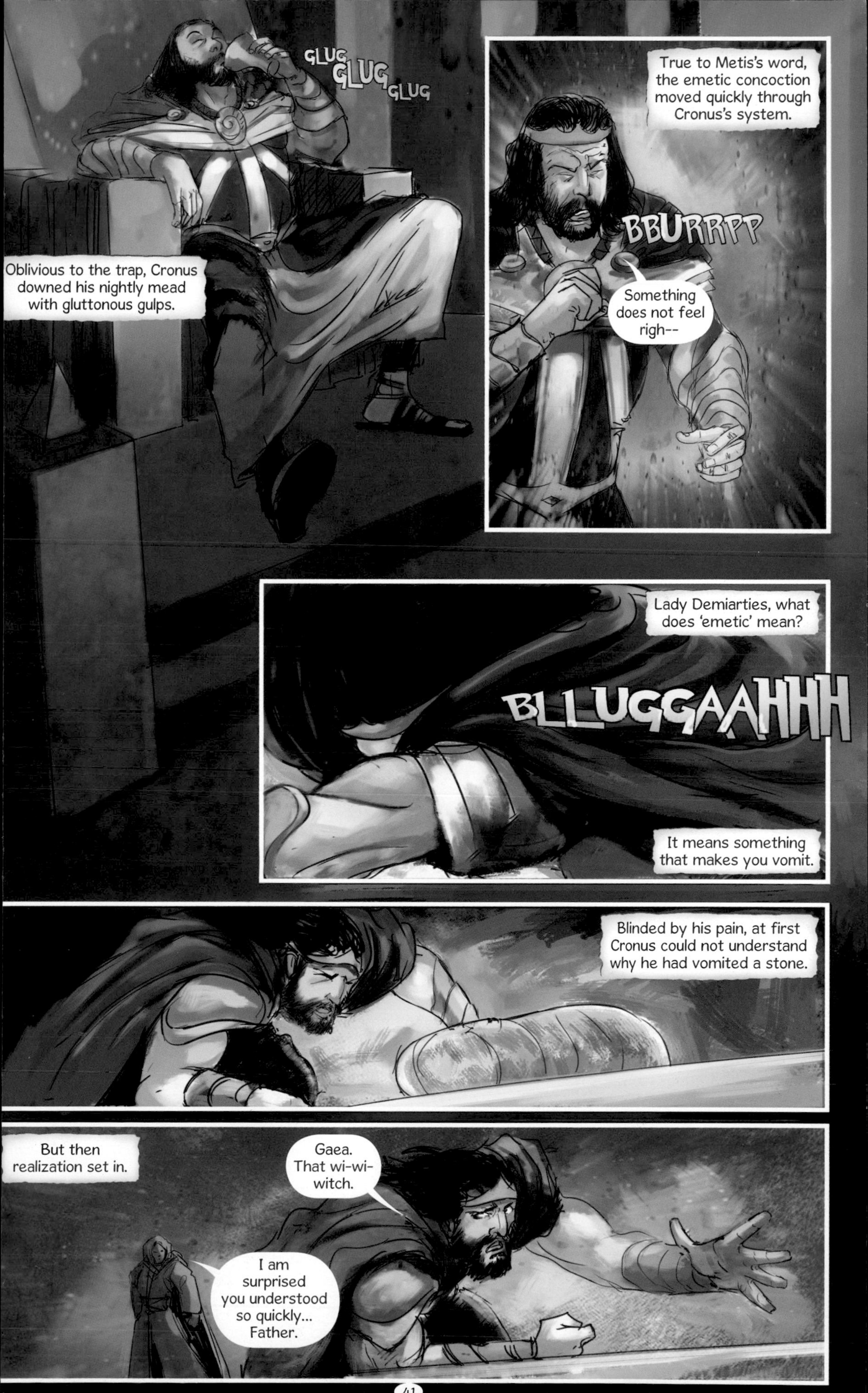
GLUG GLUG GLUG
Oblivious to the trap, Cronus downed his nightly mead with gluttonous gulps.
True to Metis's word, the emetic concoction moved quickly through Cronus's system.
BBURRPP
Something does not feel righ--
Lady Demiarties, what does 'emetic' mean?
BLLUGGAAHHH
It means something that makes you vomit.
Blinded by his pain, at first Cronus could not understand why he had vomited a stone.
But then realization set in.
Gaea. That wi-wi-witch.
I am surprised you understood so quickly... Father.

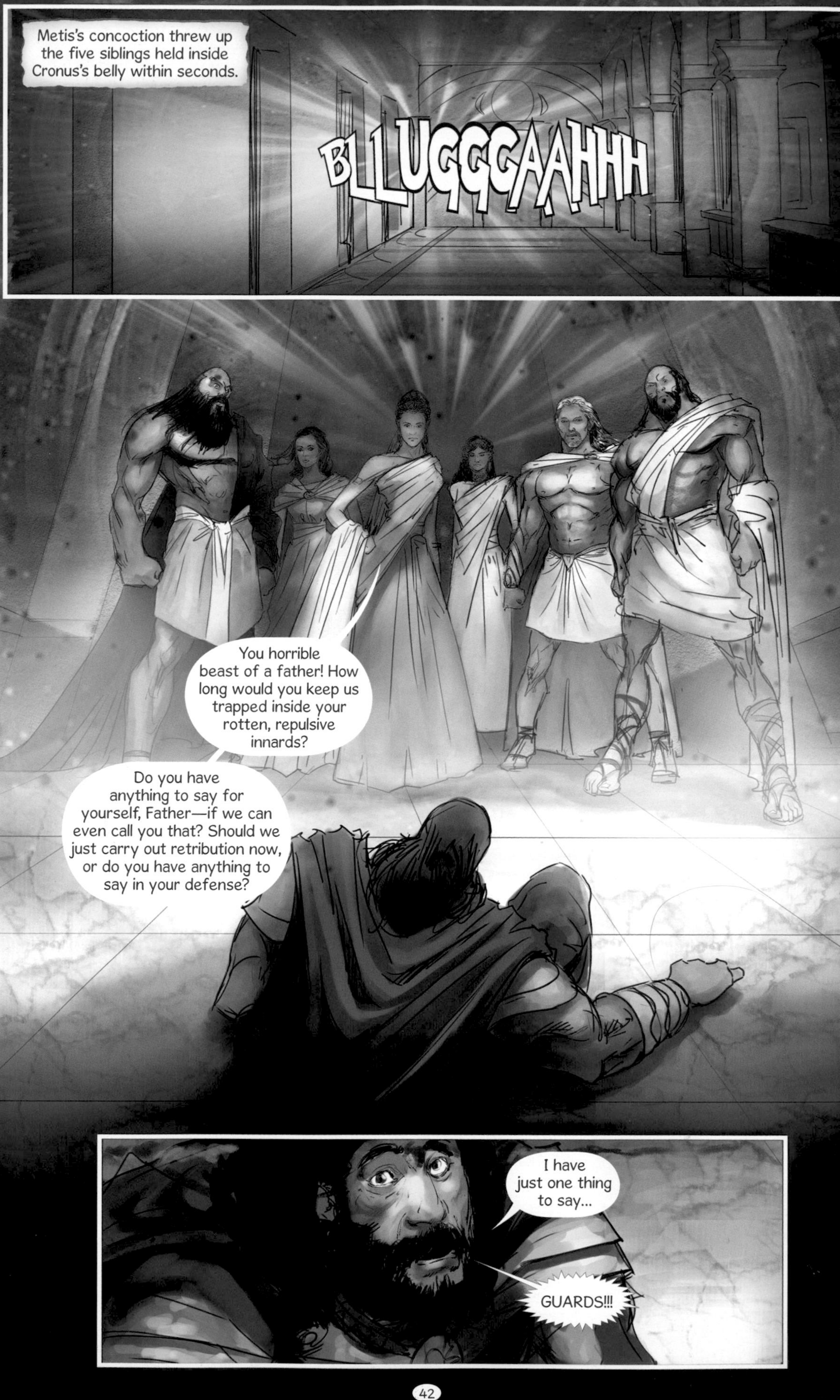
Metis's concoction threw up the five siblings held inside Cronus's belly within seconds.
BLLUGGGAAHHH
You horrible beast of a father! How long would you keep us trapped inside your rotten, repulsive innards?
Do you have anything to say for yourself, Father—if we can even call you that? Should we just carry out retribution now, or do you have anything to say in your defense?
I have just one thing to say...
GUARDS!!!

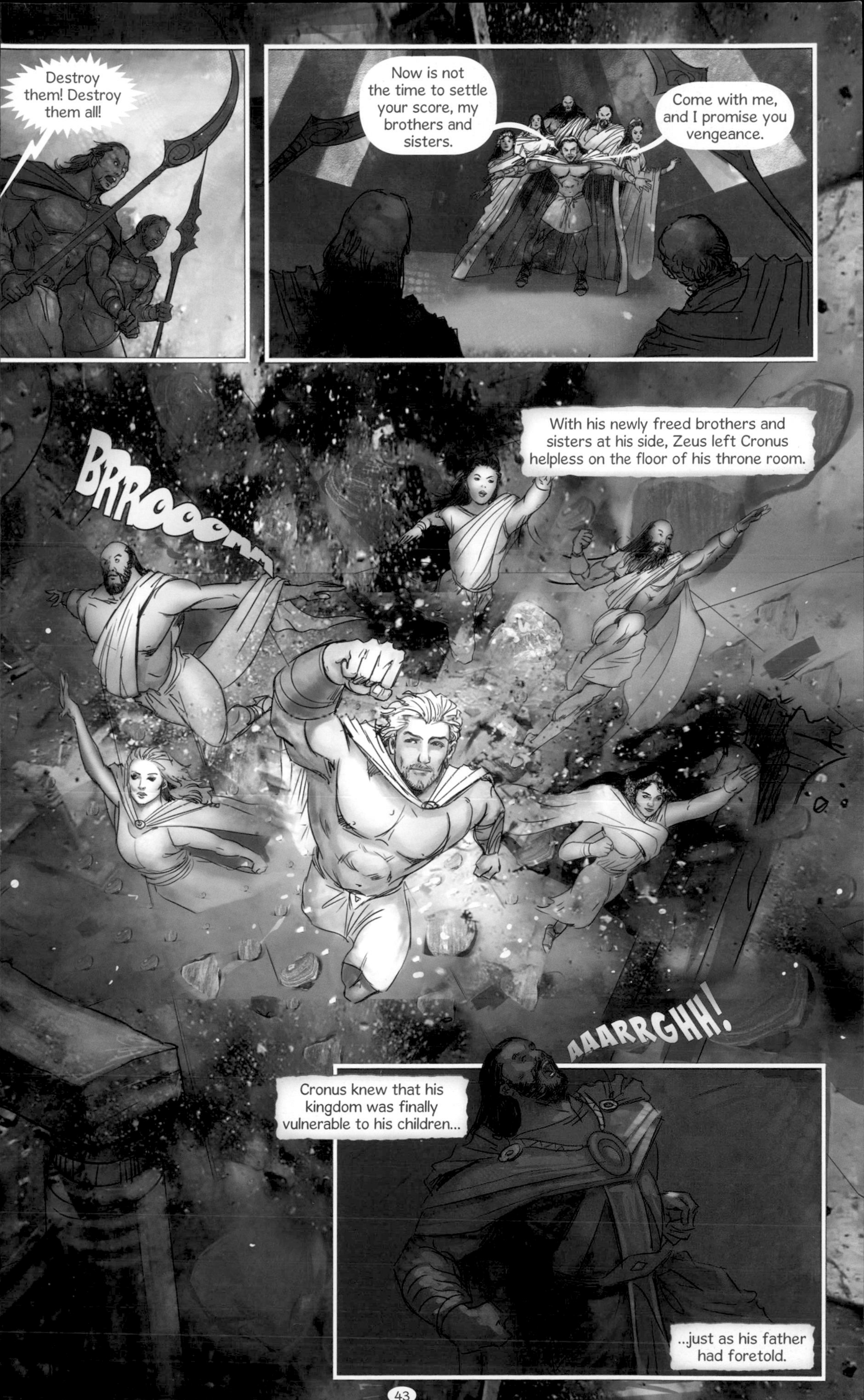
Destroy them! Destroy them all!
Now is not the time to settle your score, my brothers and sisters.
Come with me, and I promise you vengeance.
With his newly freed brothers and sisters at his side, Zeus left Cronus helpless on the floor of his throne room.
BRROOOOM
AAARRGHH!
Cronus knew that his kingdom was finally vulnerable to his children...
...just as his father had foretold.

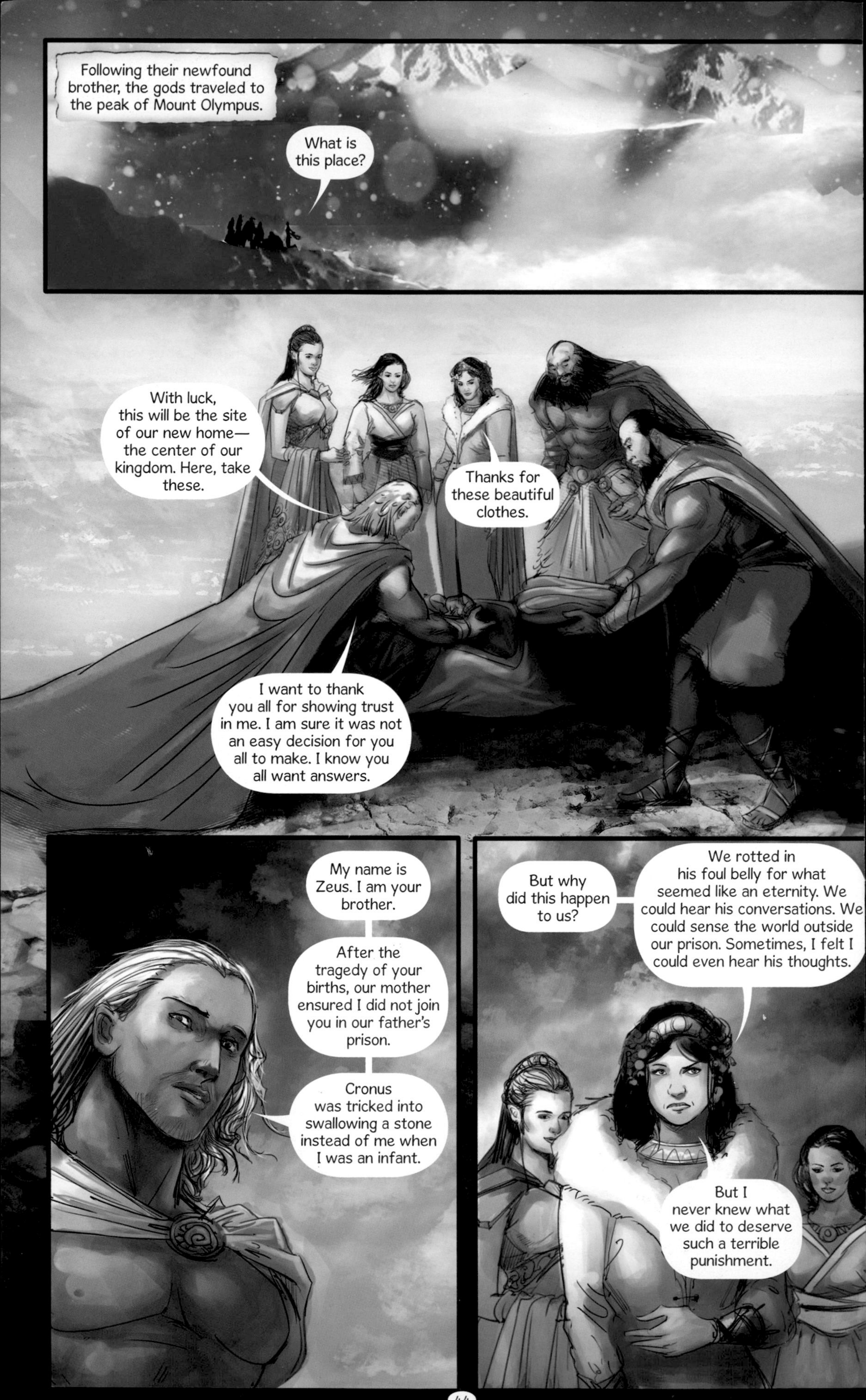
Following their newfound brother, the gods traveled to the peak of Mount Olympus.
What is this place?
With luck, this will be the site of our new home—the center of our kingdom. Here, take these.
Thanks for these beautiful clothes.
I want to thank you all for showing trust in me. I am sure it was not an easy decision for you all to make. I know you all want answers.
My name is Zeus. I am your brother.
After the tragedy of your births, our mother ensured I did not join you in our father's prison.
Cronus was tricked into swallowing a stone instead of me when I was an infant.
But why did this happen to us?
We rotted in his foul belly for what seemed like an eternity. We could hear his conversations. We could sense the world outside our prison. Sometimes, I felt I could even hear his thoughts.
But I never knew what we did to deserve such a terrible punishment.

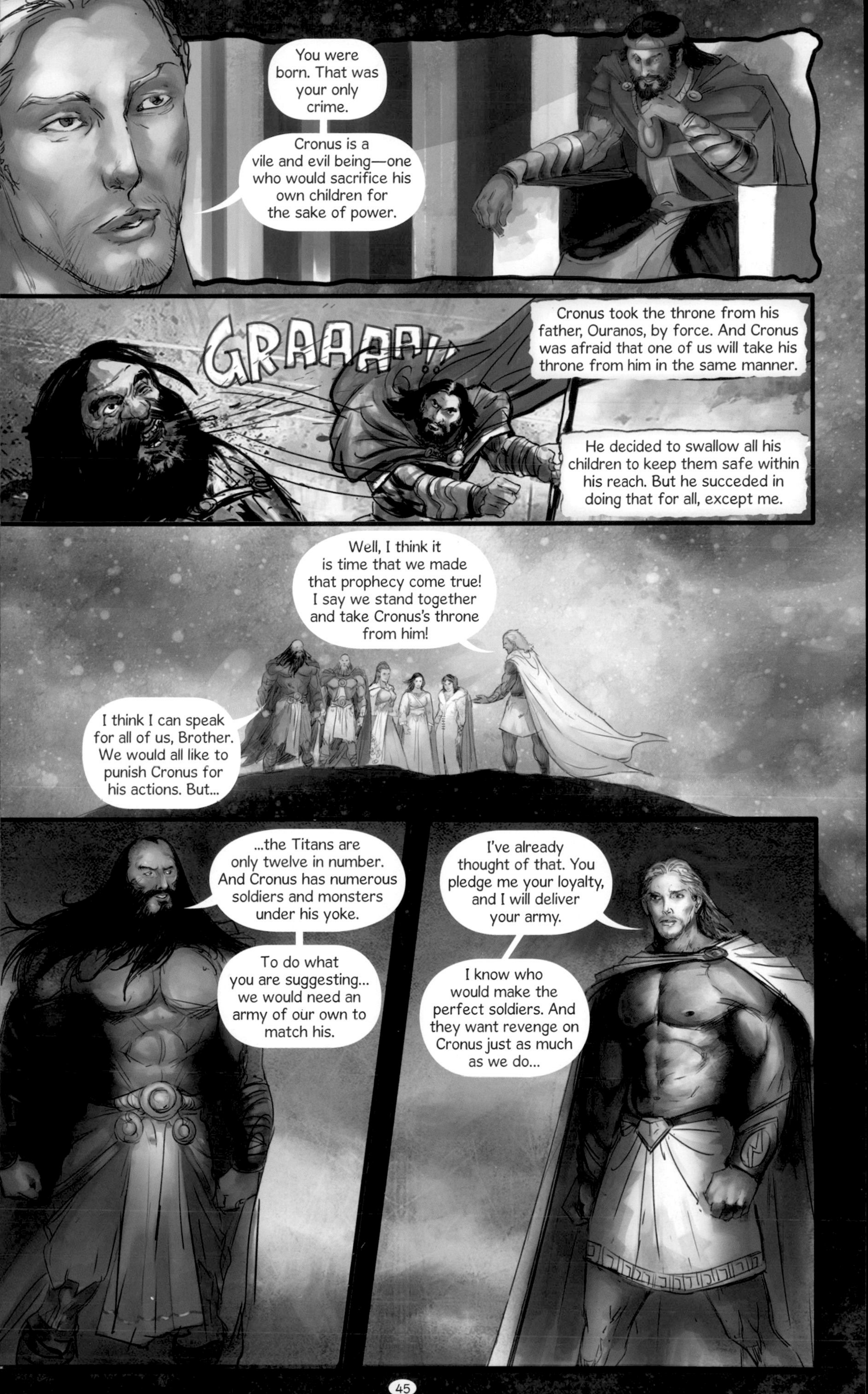
You were born. That was your only crime.
Cronus is a vile and evil being—one who would sacrifice his own children for the sake of power.
GRAAAA!!
Cronus took the throne from his father, Ouranos, by force. And Cronus was afraid that one of us will take his throne from him in the same manner.
He decided to swallow all his children to keep them safe within his reach. But he succeded in doing that for all, except me.
Well, I think it is time that we made that prophecy come true! I say we stand together and take Cronus's throne from him!
I think I can speak for all of us, Brother. We would all like to punish Cronus for his actions. But...
...the Titans are only twelve in number. And Cronus has numerous soldiers and monsters under his yoke.
To do what you are suggesting... we would need an army of our own to match his.
I've already thought of that. You pledge me your loyalty, and I will deliver your army.
I know who would make the perfect soldiers. And they want revenge on Cronus just as much as we do...

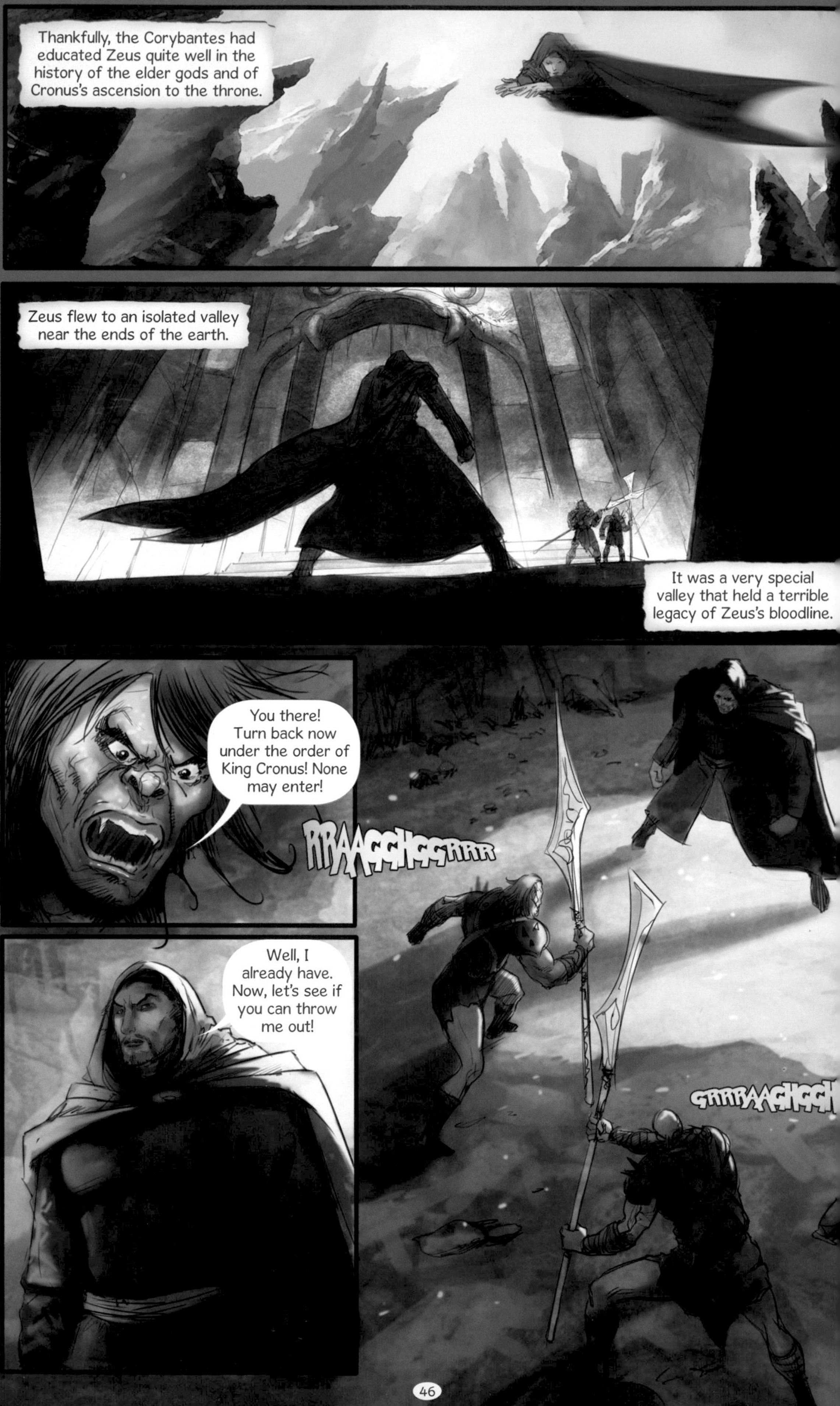
Thankfully, the Corybantes had educated Zeus quite well in the history of the elder gods and of Cronus's ascension to the throne.
Zeus flew to an isolated valley near the ends of the earth.
It was a very special valley that held a terrible legacy of Zeus's bloodline.
You there! Turn back now under the order of King Cronus! None may enter!
RRAAGGHGGRRR
Well, I already have. Now, let's see if you can throw me out!
GRRRAAGHGGH

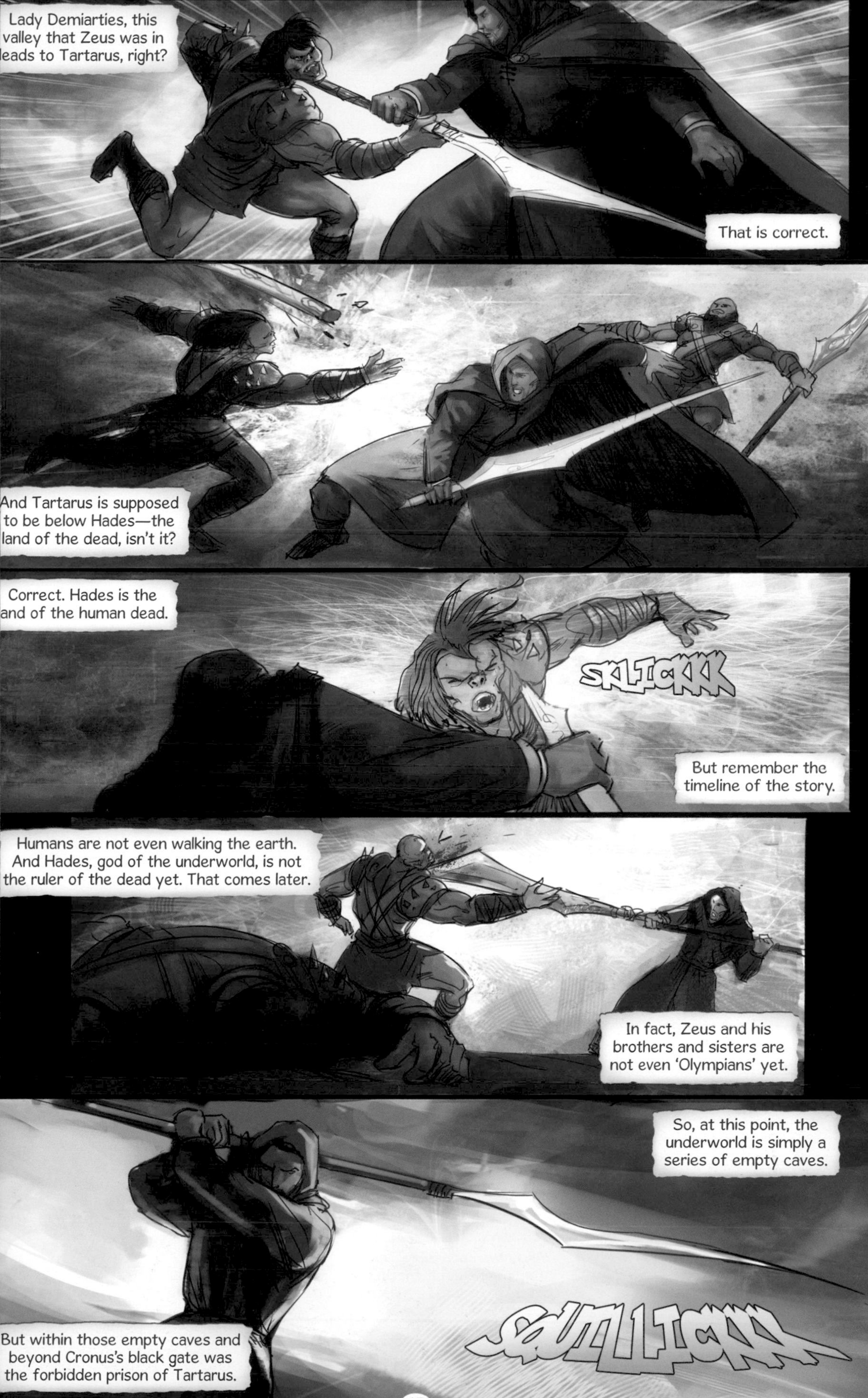

Lady Demiarties, this valley that Zeus was in leads to Tartarus, right?
That is correct.
And Tartarus is supposed to be below Hades—the land of the dead, isn't it?
Correct. Hades is the land of the human dead.
SKLICKKK
But remember the timeline of the story.
Humans are not even walking the earth. And Hades, god of the underworld, is not the ruler of the dead yet. That comes later.
In fact, Zeus and his brothers and sisters are not even 'Olympians' yet.
So, at this point, the underworld is simply a series of empty caves.
But within those empty caves and beyond Cronus's black gate was the forbidden prison of Tartarus.

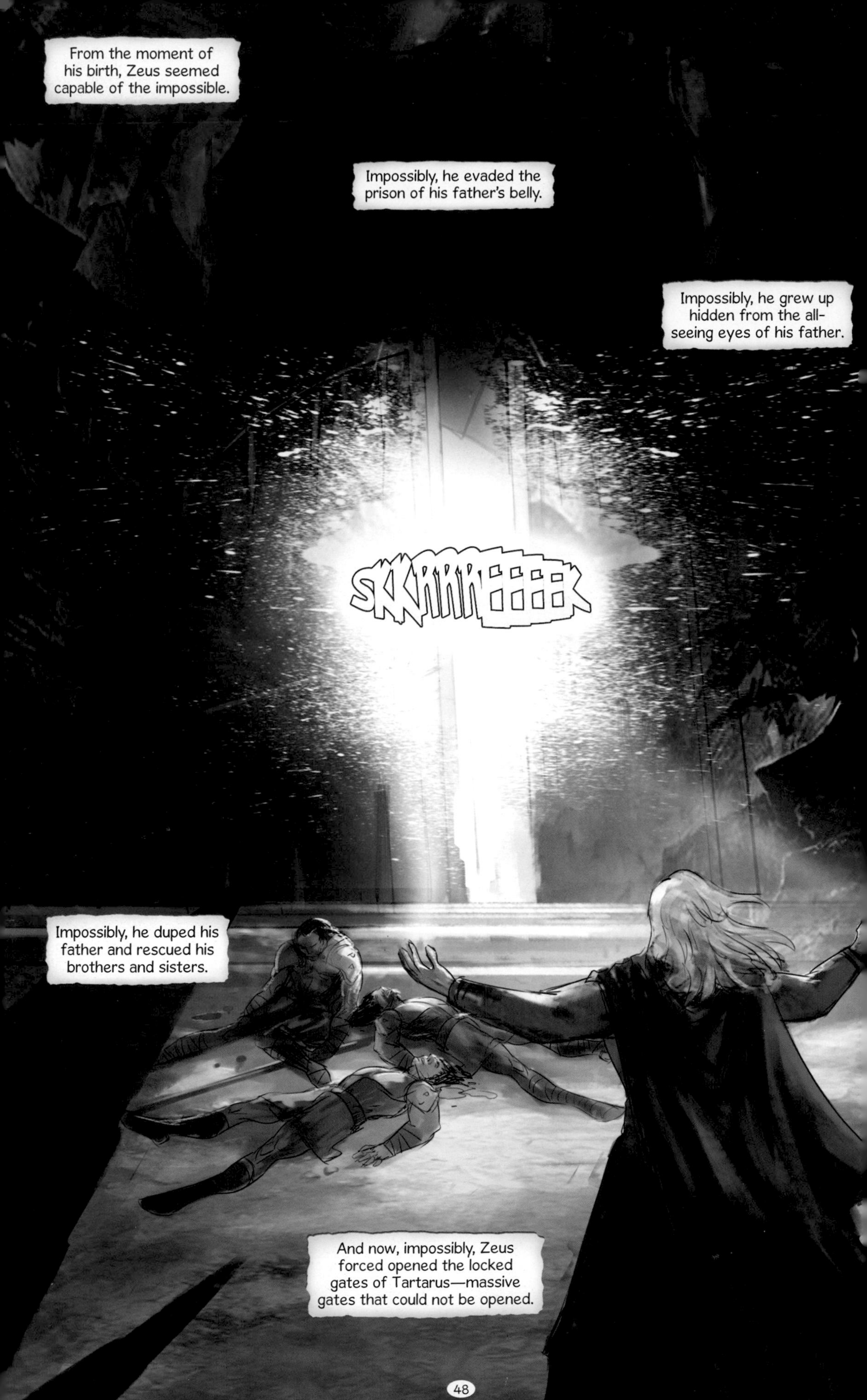
From the moment of his birth, Zeus seemed capable of the impossible.
Impossibly, he evaded the prison of his father's belly.
Impossibly, he grew up hidden from the all-seeing eyes of his father.
SKKRRREEEEK
Impossibly, he duped his father and rescued his brothers and sisters.
And now, impossibly, Zeus forced opened the locked gates of Tartarus—massive gates that could not be opened.

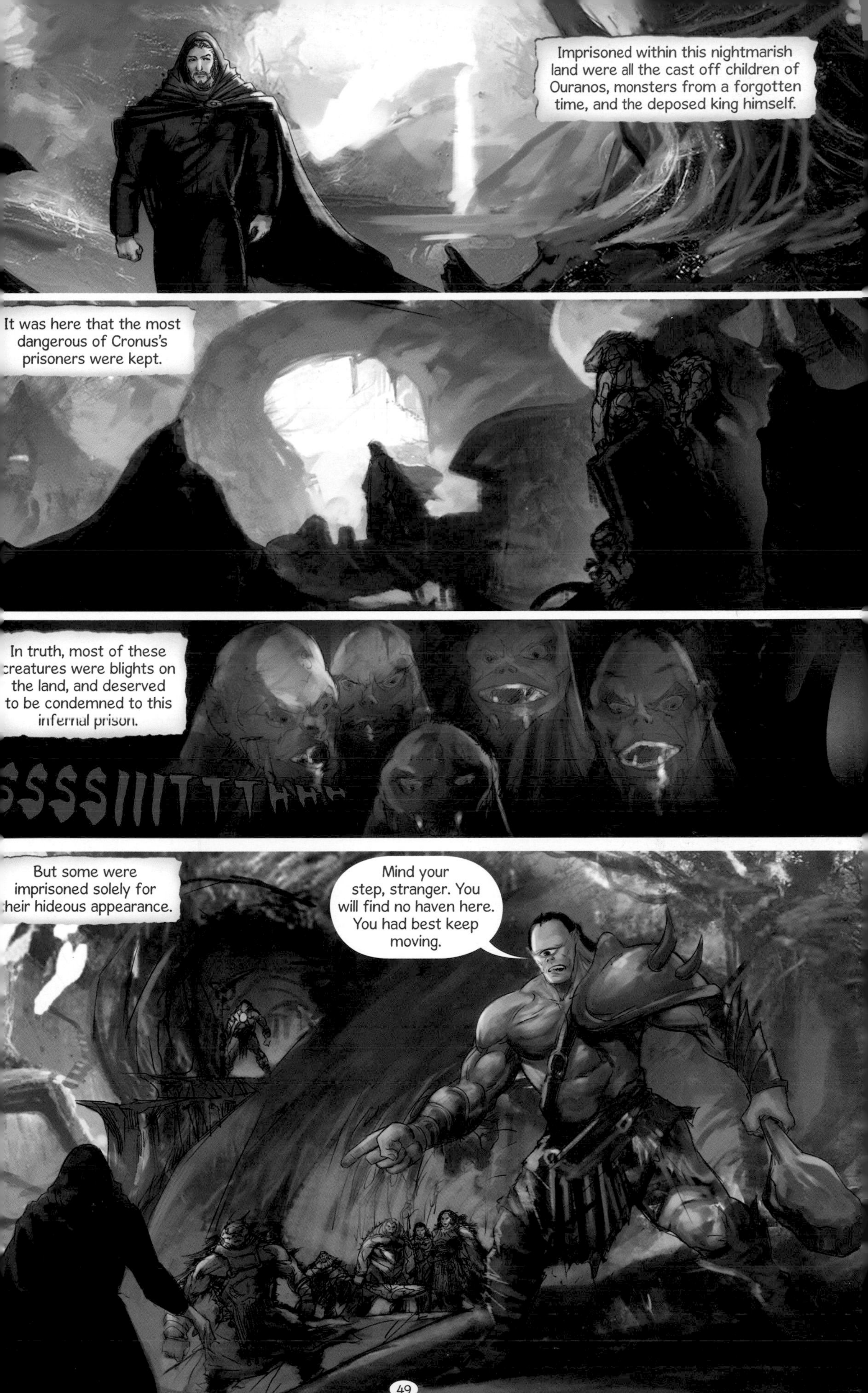
Imprisoned within this nightmarish land were all the cast off children of Ouranos, monsters from a forgotten time, and the deposed king himself.
It was here that the most dangerous of Cronus's prisoners were kept.
In truth, most of these creatures were blights on the land, and deserved to be condemned to this infernal prison.
SSSSIIITTT
But some were imprisoned solely for their hideous appearance.
Mind your step, stranger. You will find no haven here. You had best keep moving.

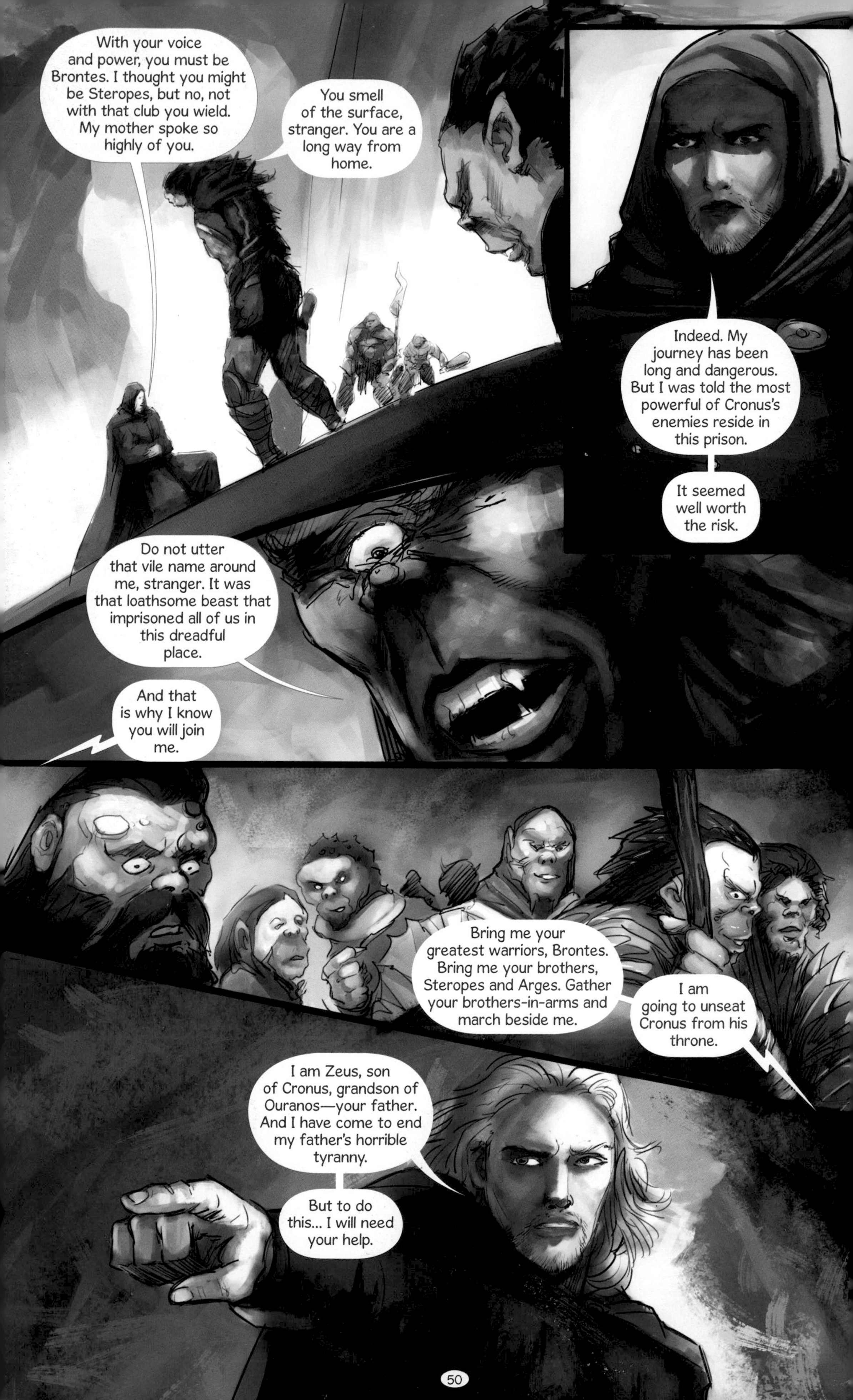
With your voice and power, you must be Brontes. I thought you might be Steropes, but no, not with that club you wield. My mother spoke so highly of you.
You smell of the surface, stranger. You are a long way from home.
Indeed. My journey has been long and dangerous. But I was told the most powerful of Cronus's enemies reside in this prison.
It seemed well worth the risk.
Do not utter that vile name around me, stranger. It was that loathsome beast that imprisoned all of us in this dreadful place.
And that is why I know you will join me.
Bring me your greatest warriors, Brontes. Bring me your brothers, Steropes and Arges. Gather your brothers-in-arms and march beside me.
I am going to unseat Cronus from his throne.
I am Zeus, son of Cronus, grandson of Ouranos—your father. And I have come to end my father's horrible tyranny.
But to do this... I will need your help.

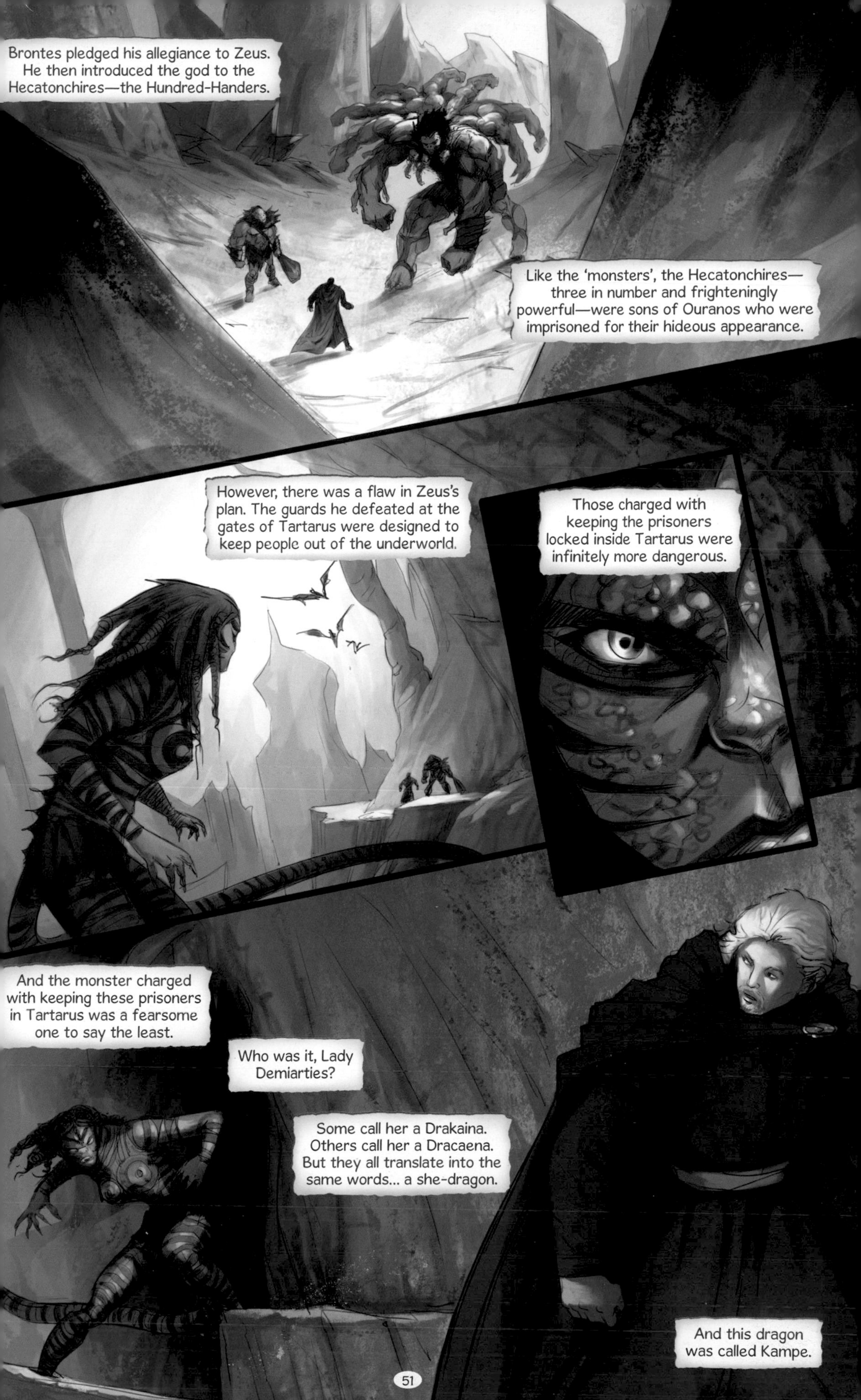
Brontes pledged his allegiance to Zeus. He then introduced the god to the Hecatonchires—the Hundred-Handers.
Like the 'monsters', the Hecatonchires—three in number and frighteningly powerful—were sons of Ouranos who were imprisoned for their hideous appearance.
However, there was a flaw in Zeus's plan. The guards he defeated at the gates of Tartarus were designed to keep people out of the underworld.
Those charged with keeping the prisoners locked inside Tartarus were infinitely more dangerous.
And the monster charged with keeping these prisoners in Tartarus was a fearsome one to say the least.
Who was it, Lady Demiarties?
Some call her a Drakaina. Others call her a Dracaena. But they all translate into the same words... a she-dragon.
And this dragon was called Kampe.

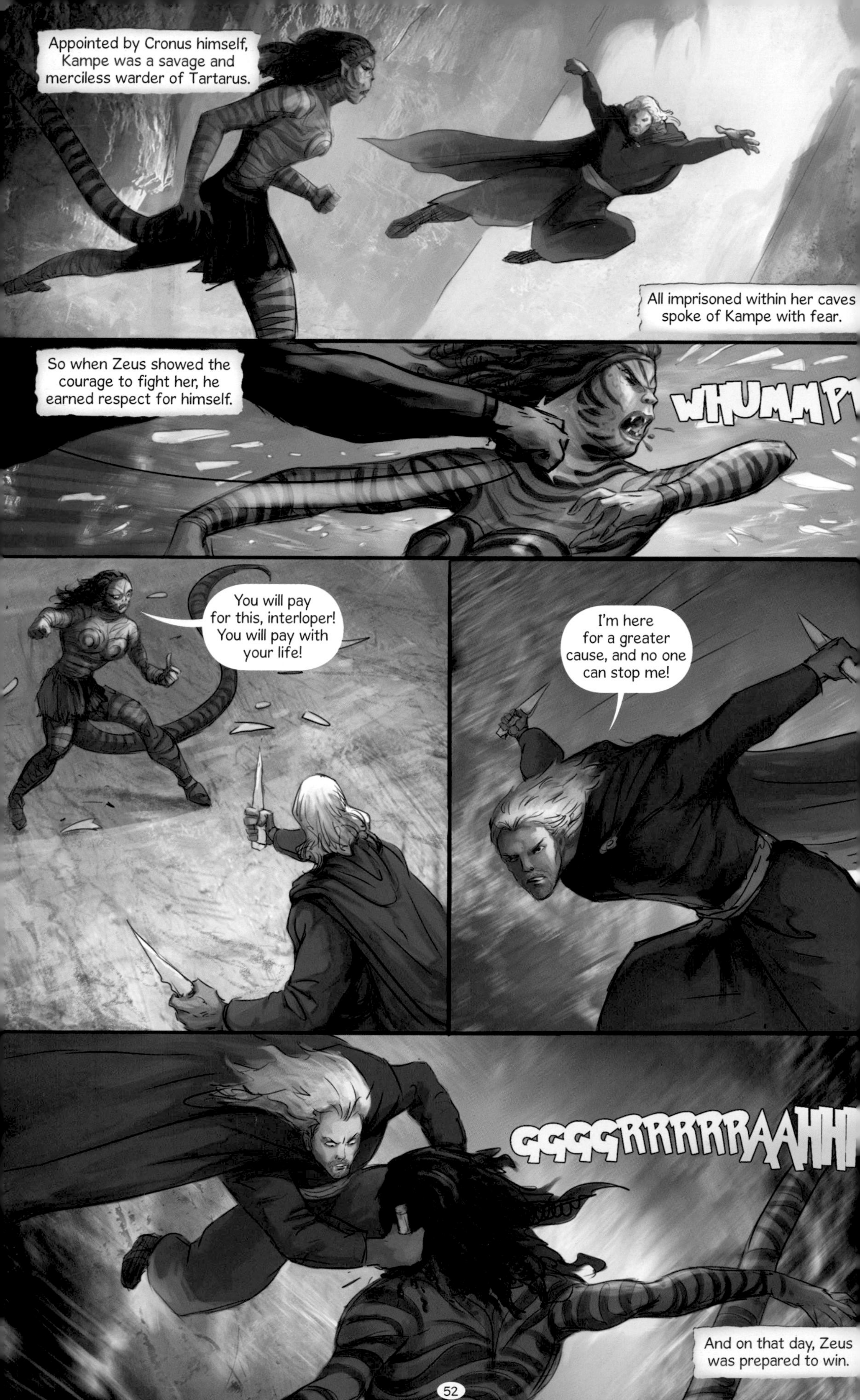

Appointed by Cronus himself, Kampe was a savage and merciless warder of Tartarus.
All imprisoned within her caves spoke of Kampe with fear.
So when Zeus showed the courage to fight her, he earned respect for himself.
WHUMMP!
You will pay for this, interloper! You will pay with your life!
I'm here for a greater cause, and no one can stop me!
GGGGRRRRRRAAHH
And on that day, Zeus was prepared to win.

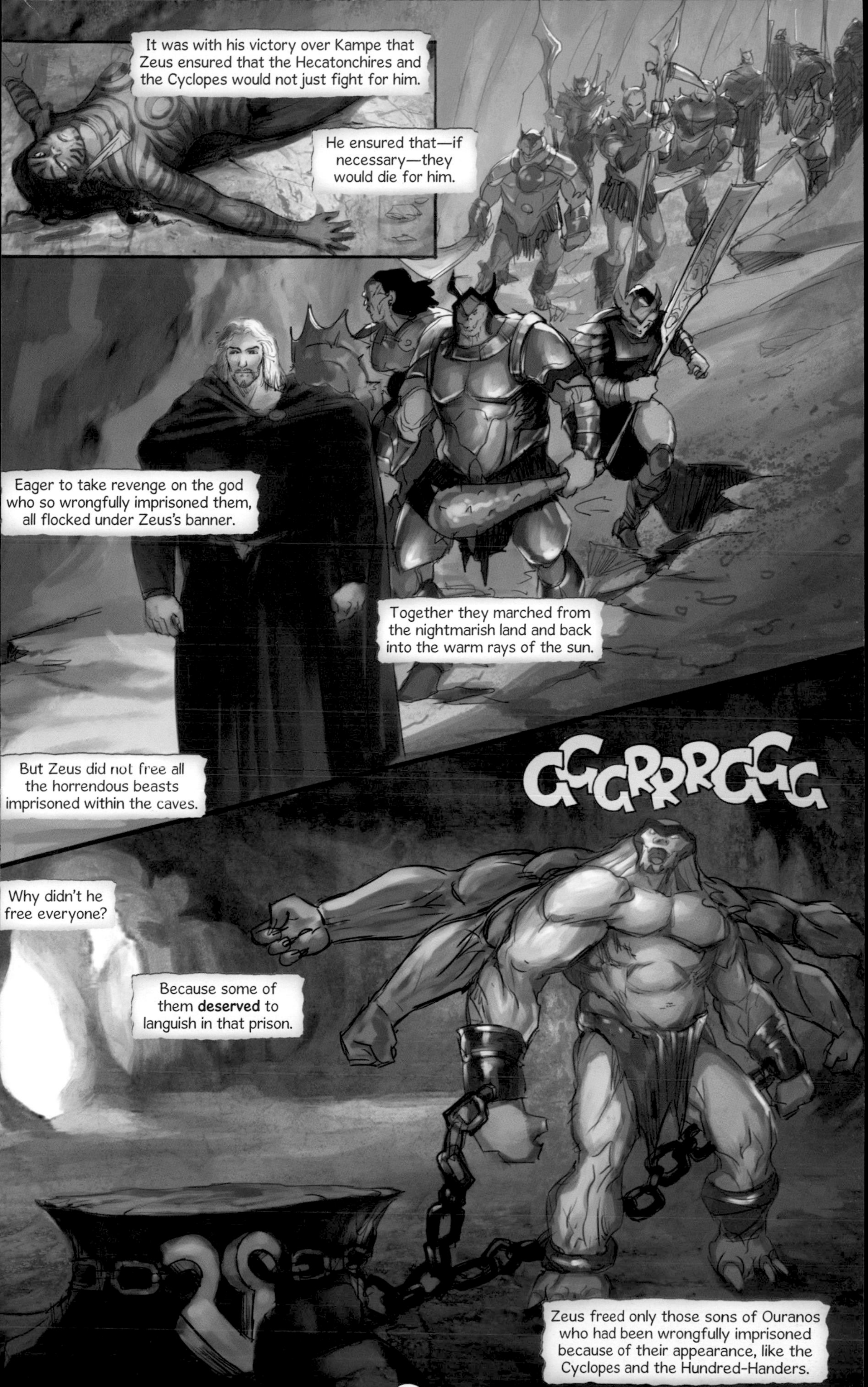
It was with his victory over Kampe that Zeus ensured that the Hecatonchires and the Cyclopes would not just fight for him.
He ensured that—if necessary—they would die for him.
Eager to take revenge on the god who so wrongfully imprisoned them, all flocked under Zeus's banner.
Together they marched from the nightmarish land and back into the warm rays of the sun.
But Zeus did not free all the horrendous beasts imprisoned within the caves.
GGGRRRGGG
Why didn't he free everyone?
Because some of them **deserved** to languish in that prison.
Zeus freed only those sons of Ouranos who had been wrongfully imprisoned because of their appearance, like the Cyclopes and the Hundred-Handers.

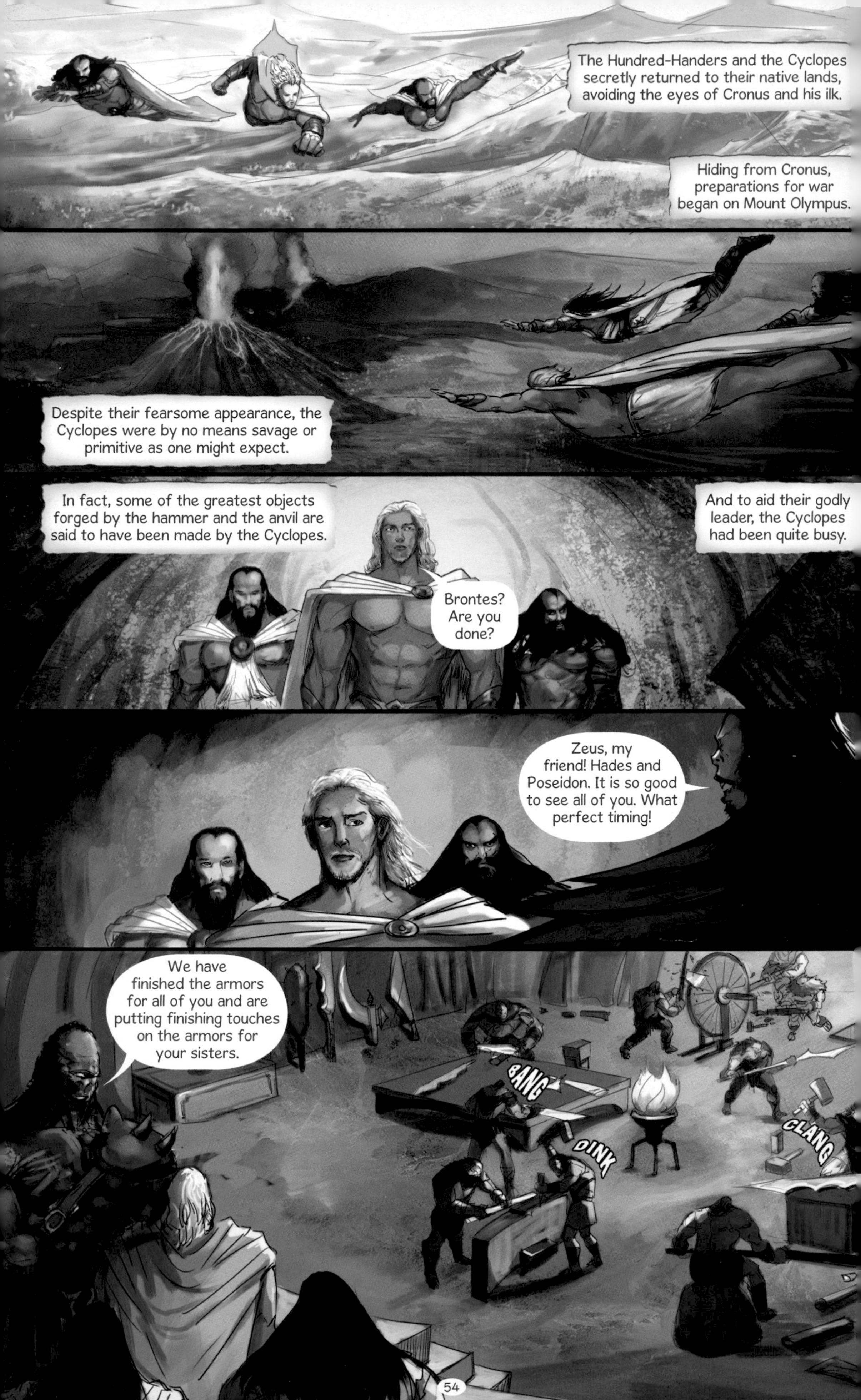

The Hundred-Handers and the Cyclopes secretly returned to their native lands, avoiding the eyes of Cronus and his ilk.
Hiding from Cronus, preparations for war began on Mount Olympus.
Despite their fearsome appearance, the Cyclopes were by no means savage or primitive as one might expect.
In fact, some of the greatest objects forged by the hammer and the anvil are said to have been made by the Cyclopes.
And to aid their godly leader, the Cyclopes had been quite busy.
Brontes? Are you done?
Zeus, my friend! Hades and Poseidon. It is so good to see all of you. What perfect timing!
We have finished the armors for all of you and are putting finishing touches on the armors for your sisters.
BANG
DINK
CLANG

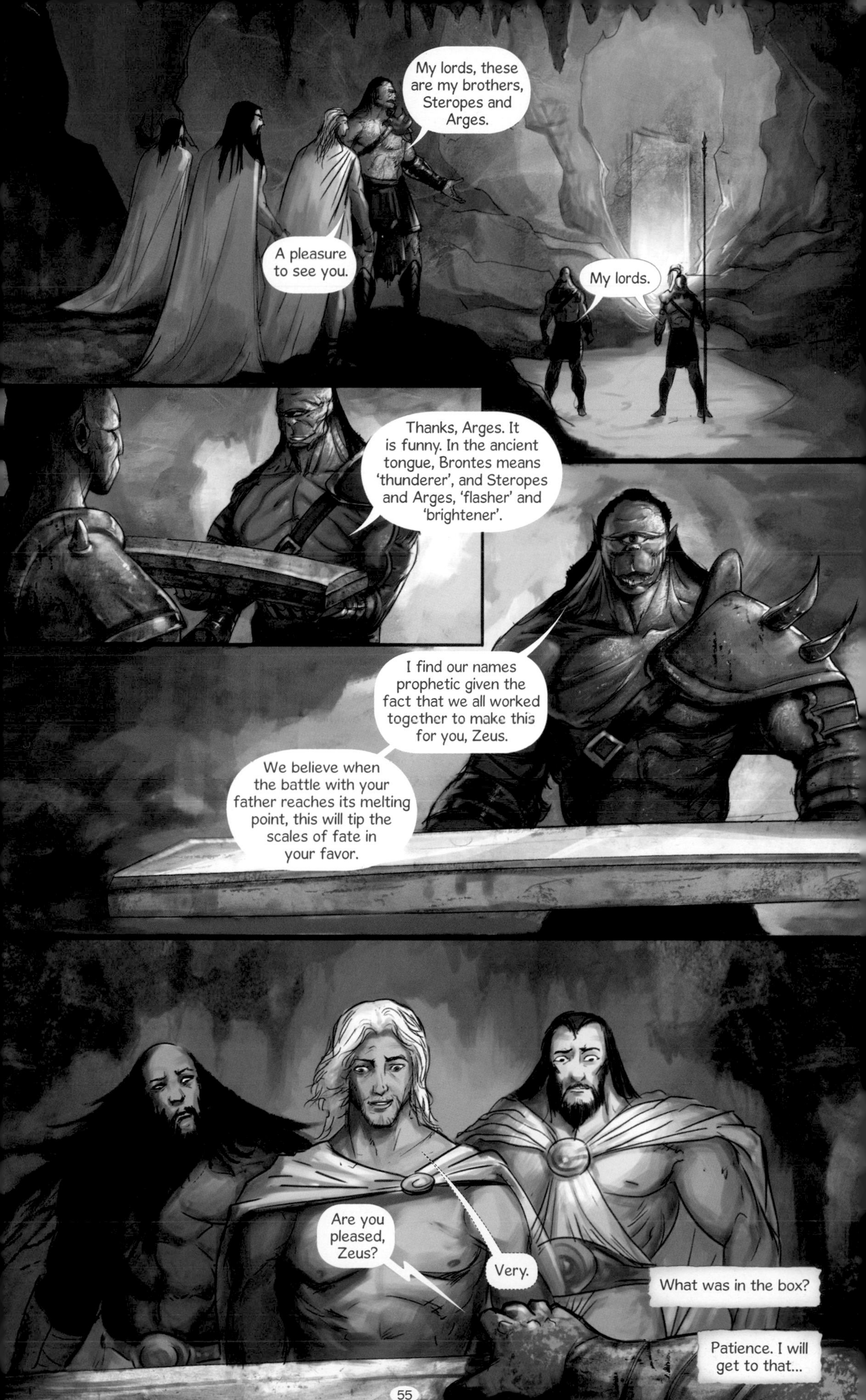
My lords, these are my brothers, Steropes and Arges.
A pleasure to see you.
My lords.
Thanks, Arges. It is funny. In the ancient tongue, Brontes means 'thunderer', and Steropes and Arges, 'flasher' and 'brightener'.
I find our names prophetic given the fact that we all worked together to make this for you, Zeus.
We believe when the battle with your father reaches its melting point, this will tip the scales of fate in your favor.
Are you pleased, Zeus?
Very.
What was in the box?
Patience. I will get to that...

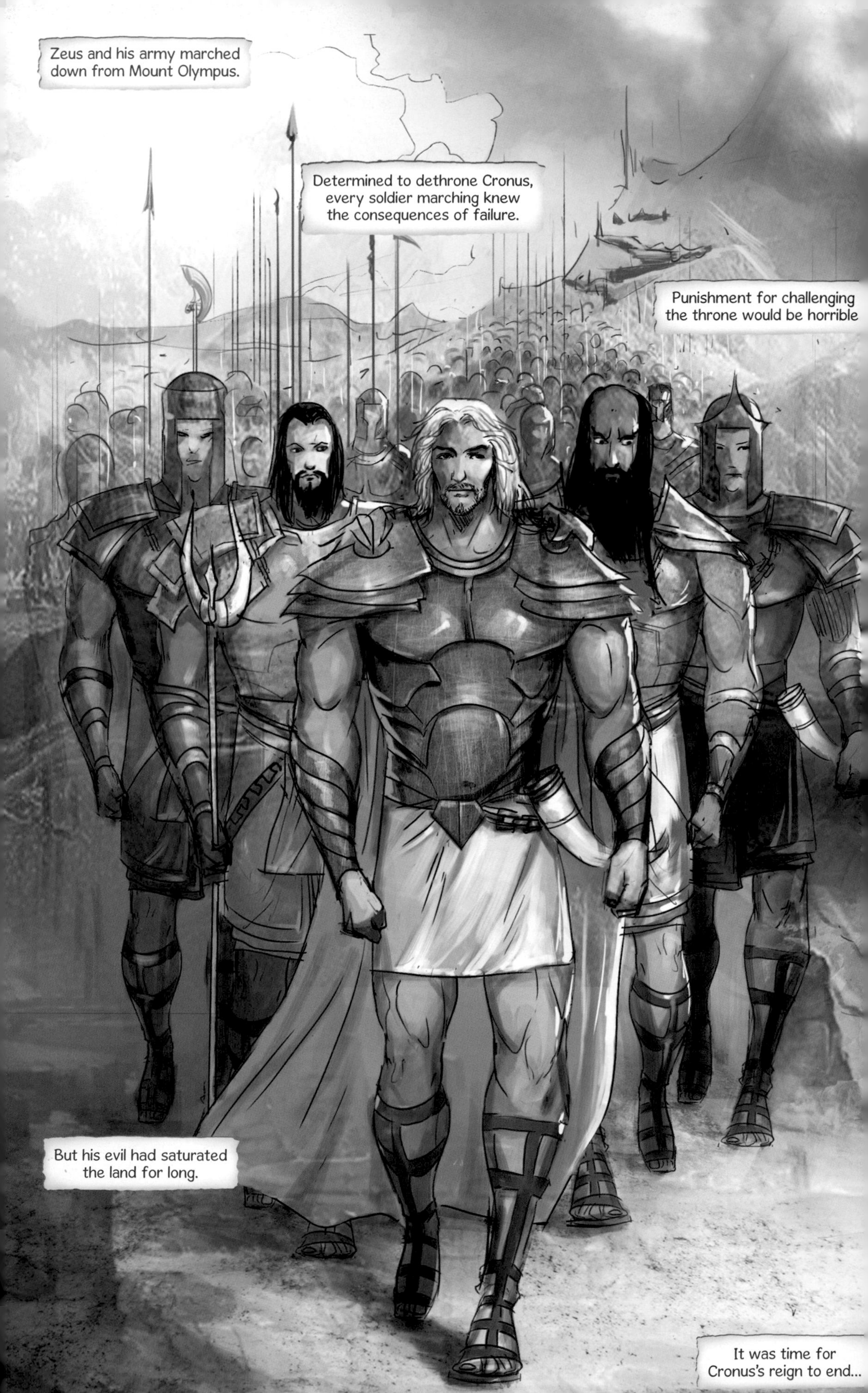
Zeus and his army marched down from Mount Olympus.
Determined to dethrone Cronus, every soldier marching knew the consequences of failure.
Punishment for challenging the throne would be horrible
But his evil had saturated the land for long.
It was time for Cronus's reign to end...

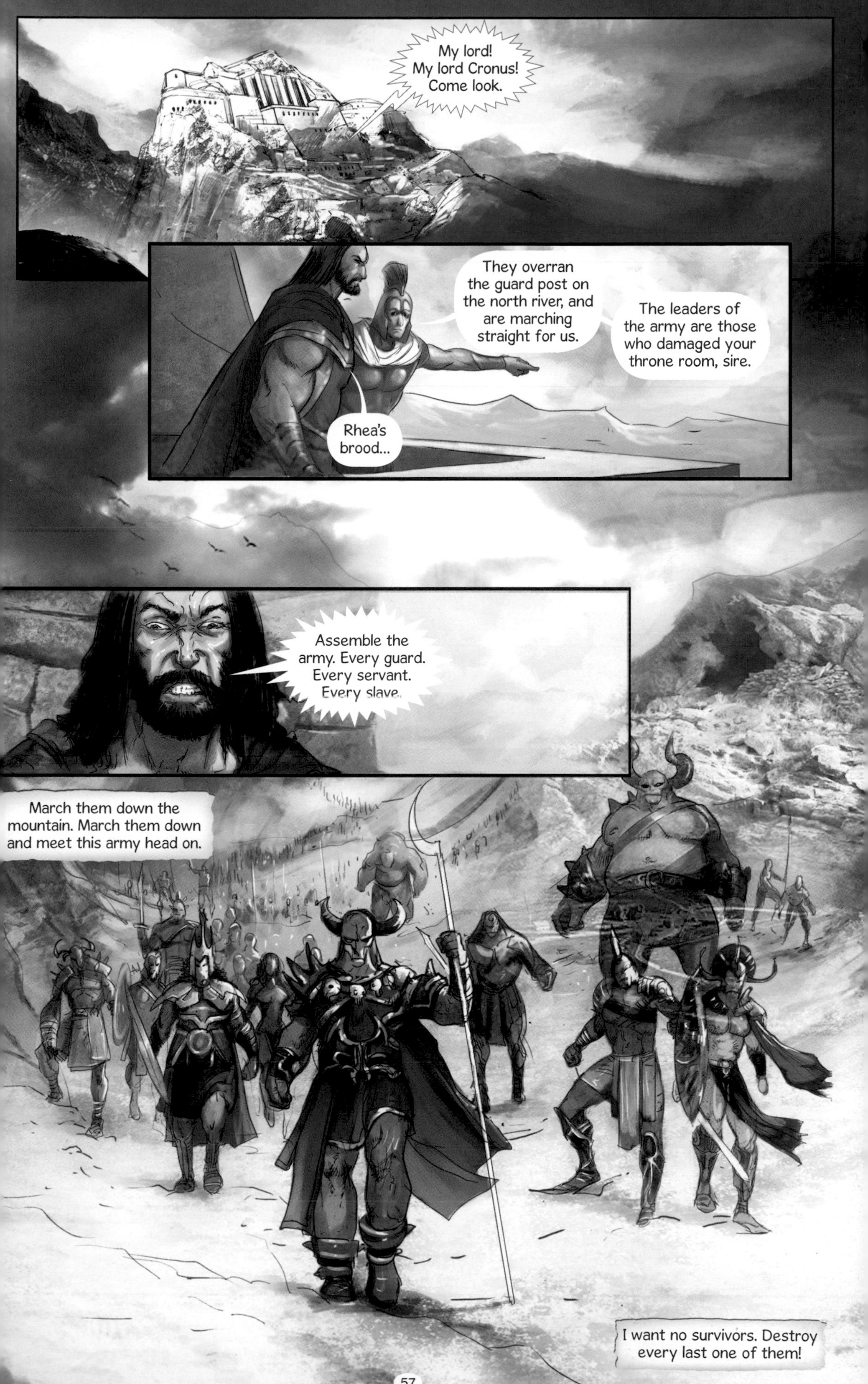

My lord! My lord Cronus! Come look.
They overran the guard post on the north river, and are marching straight for us.
The leaders of the army are those who damaged your throne room, sire.
Rhea's brood...
Assemble the army. Every guard. Every servant. Every slave.
March them down the mountain. March them down and meet this army head on.
I want no survivors. Destroy every last one of them!

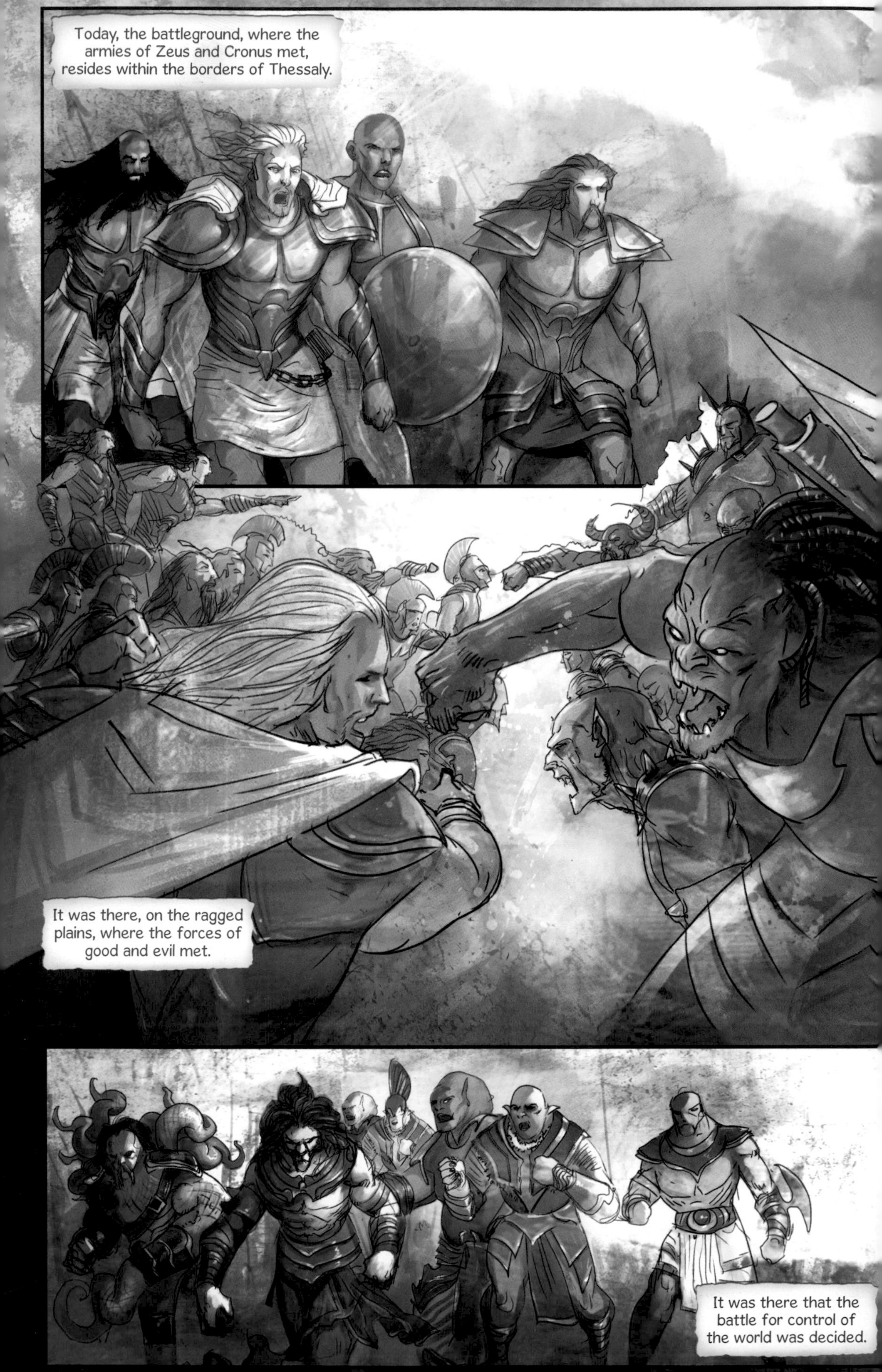
Today, the battleground, where the armies of Zeus and Cronus met, resides within the borders of Thessaly.
It was there, on the ragged plains, where the forces of good and evil met.
It was there that the battle for control of the world was decided.

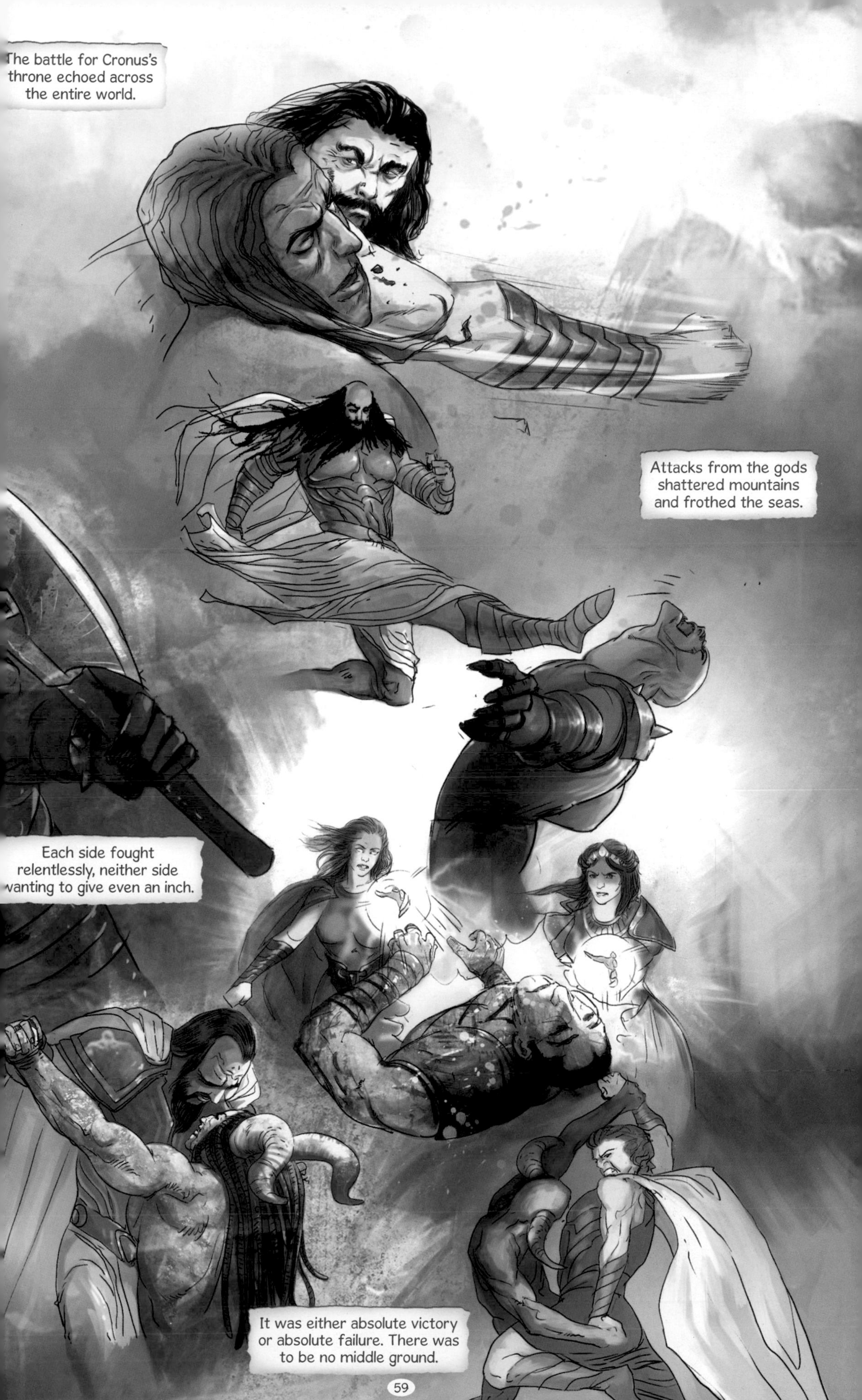

The battle for Cronus's throne echoed across the entire world.
Attacks from the gods shattered mountains and frothed the seas.
Each side fought relentlessly, neither side wanting to give even an inch.
It was either absolute victory or absolute failure. There was to be no middle ground.

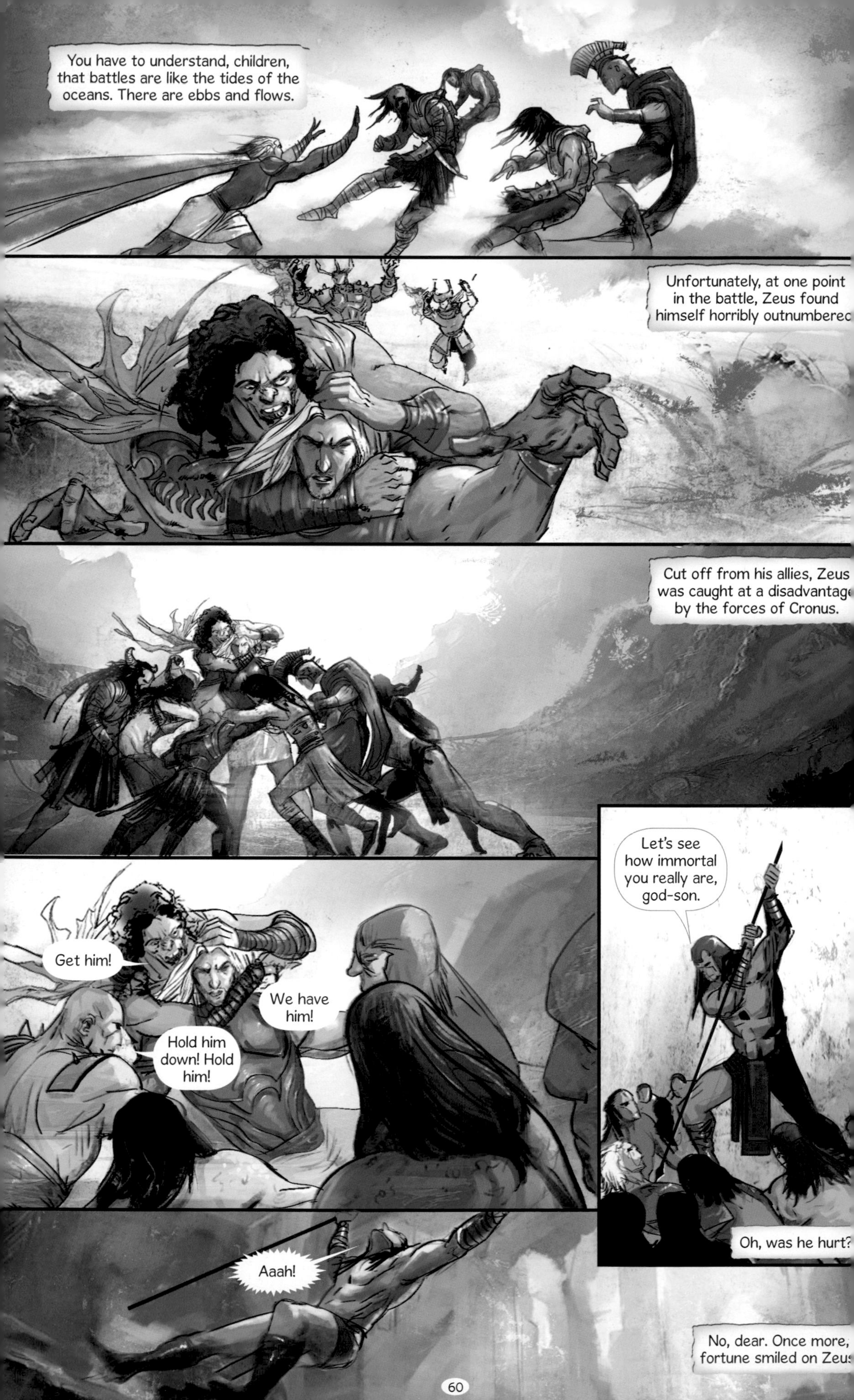

You have to understand, children, that battles are like the tides of the oceans. There are ebbs and flows.
Unfortunately, at one point in the battle, Zeus found himself horribly outnumbered
Cut off from his allies, Zeus was caught at a disadvantage by the forces of Cronus.
Get him!
We have him!
Hold him down! Hold him!
Let's see how immortal you really are, god-son.
Oh, was he hurt?
Aaah!
No, dear. Once more, fortune smiled on Zeus

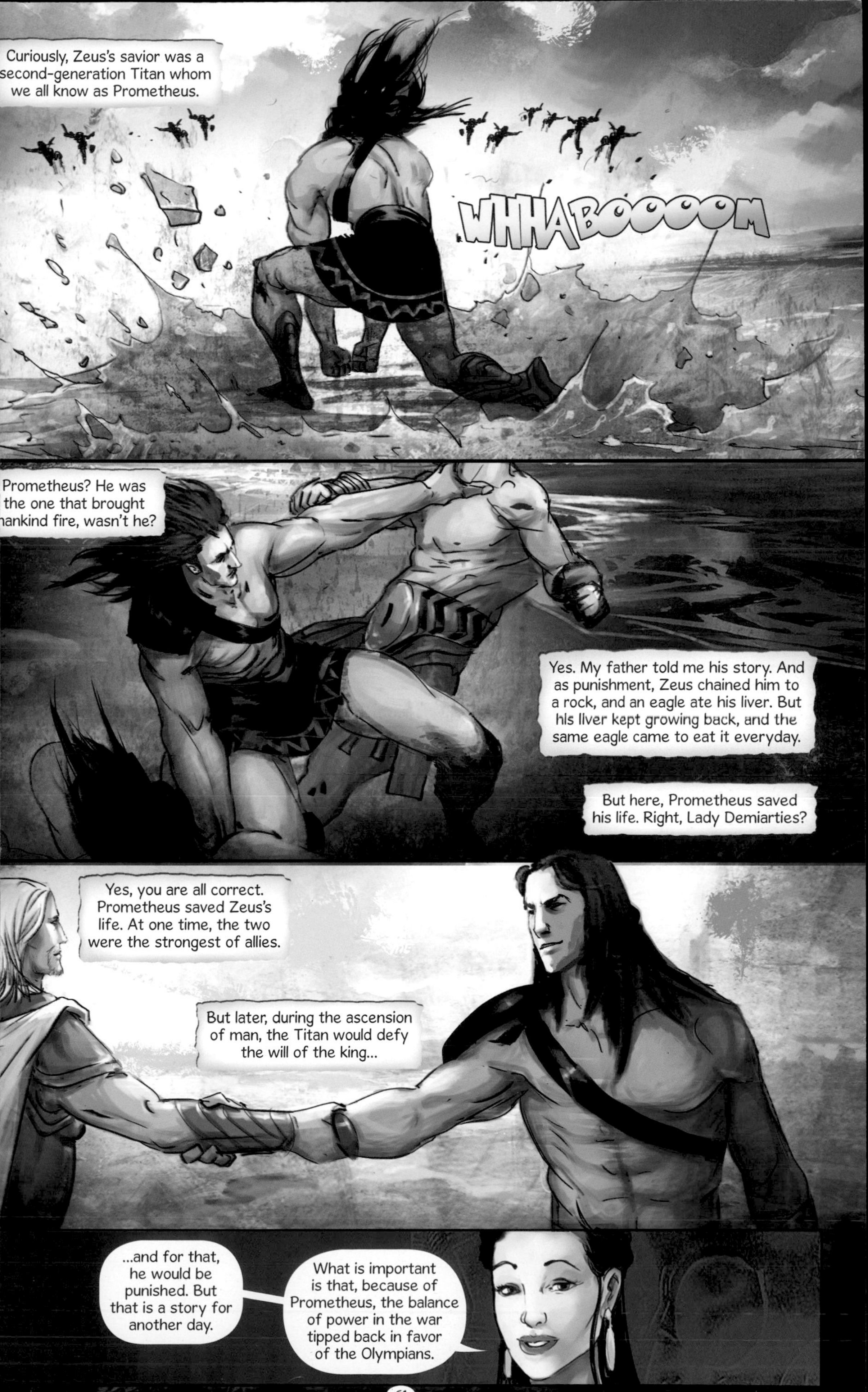
Curiously, Zeus's savior was a second-generation Titan whom we all know as Prometheus.
WHHABOOOOM
Prometheus? He was the one that brought mankind fire, wasn't he?
Yes. My father told me his story. And as punishment, Zeus chained him to a rock, and an eagle ate his liver. But his liver kept growing back, and the same eagle came to eat it everyday.
But here, Prometheus saved his life. Right, Lady Demiarties?
Yes, you are all correct. Prometheus saved Zeus's life. At one time, the two were the strongest of allies.
But later, during the ascension of man, the Titan would defy the will of the king...
...and for that, he would be punished. But that is a story for another day.
What is important is that, because of Prometheus, the balance of power in the war tipped back in favor of the Olympians.

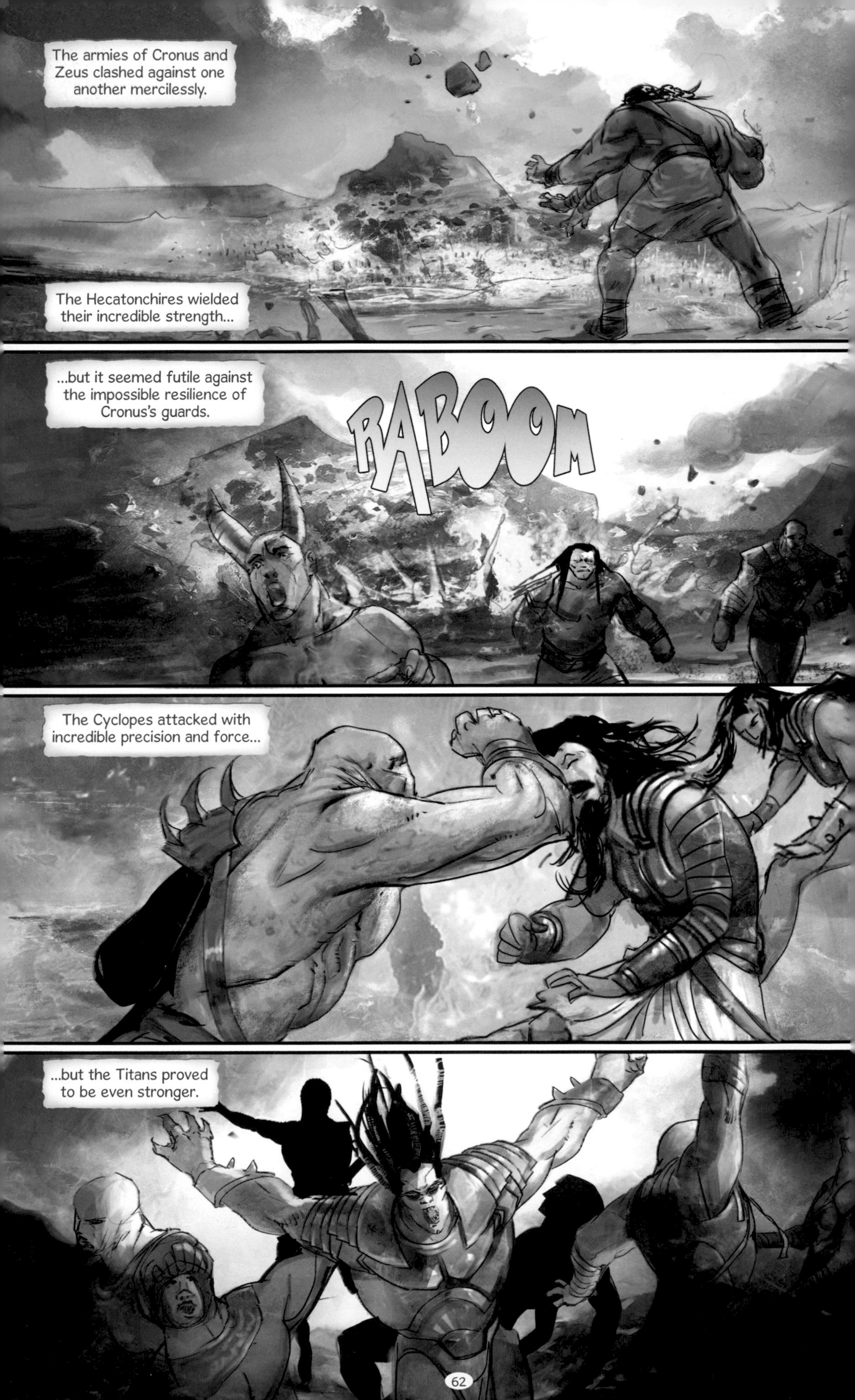
The armies of Cronus and Zeus clashed against one another mercilessly.
The Hecatonchires wielded their incredible strength...
...but it seemed futile against the impossible resilience of Cronus's guards.
RABOOM
The Cyclopes attacked with incredible precision and force...
...but the Titans proved to be even stronger.

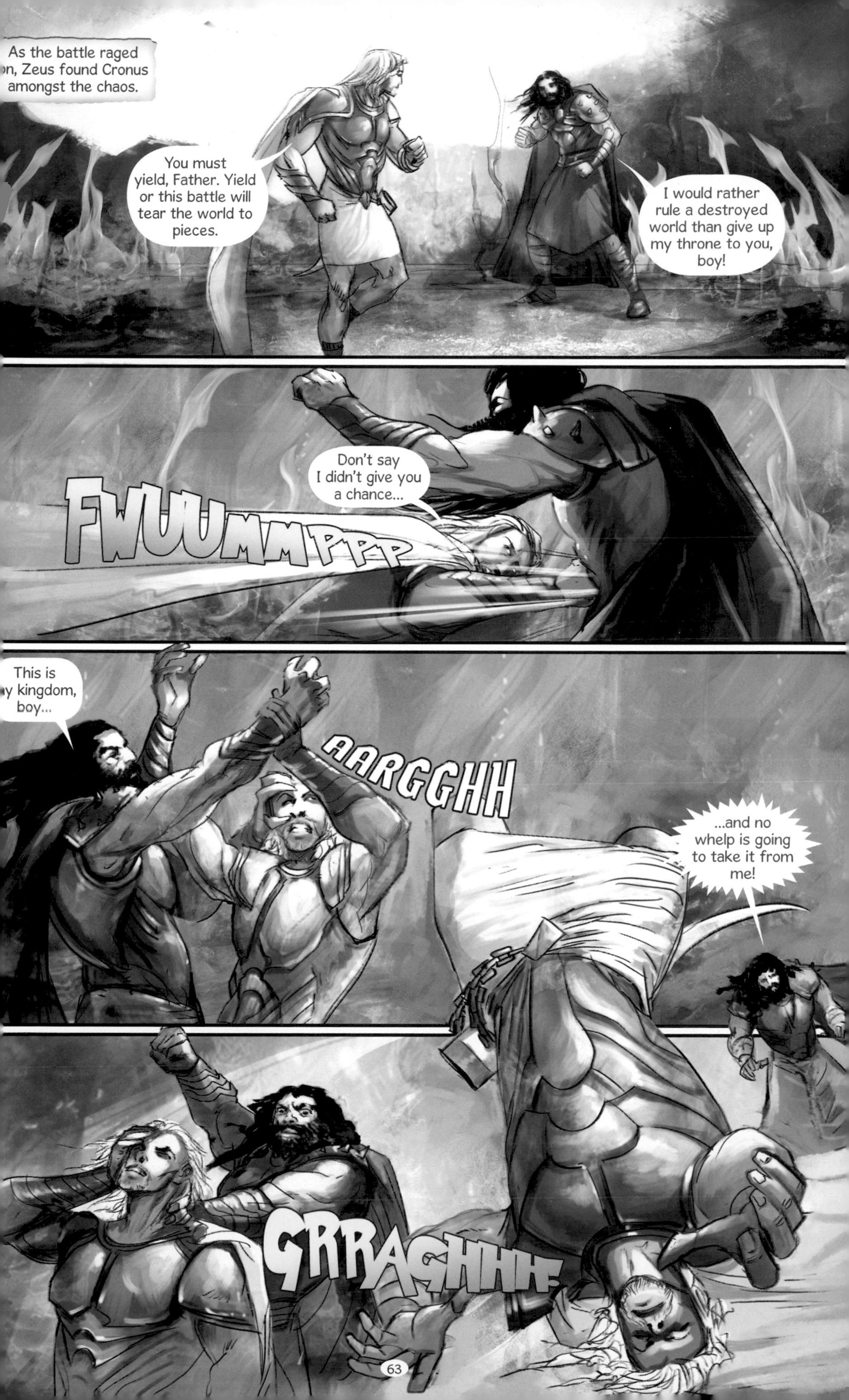
As the battle raged on, Zeus found Cronus amongst the chaos.
You must yield, Father. Yield or this battle will tear the world to pieces.
I would rather rule a destroyed world than give up my throne to you, boy!
Don't say I didn't give you a chance...
FWUUMMPPP
This is my kingdom, boy...
AARGGHH
...and no whelp is going to take it from me!
GRRAGHHH!

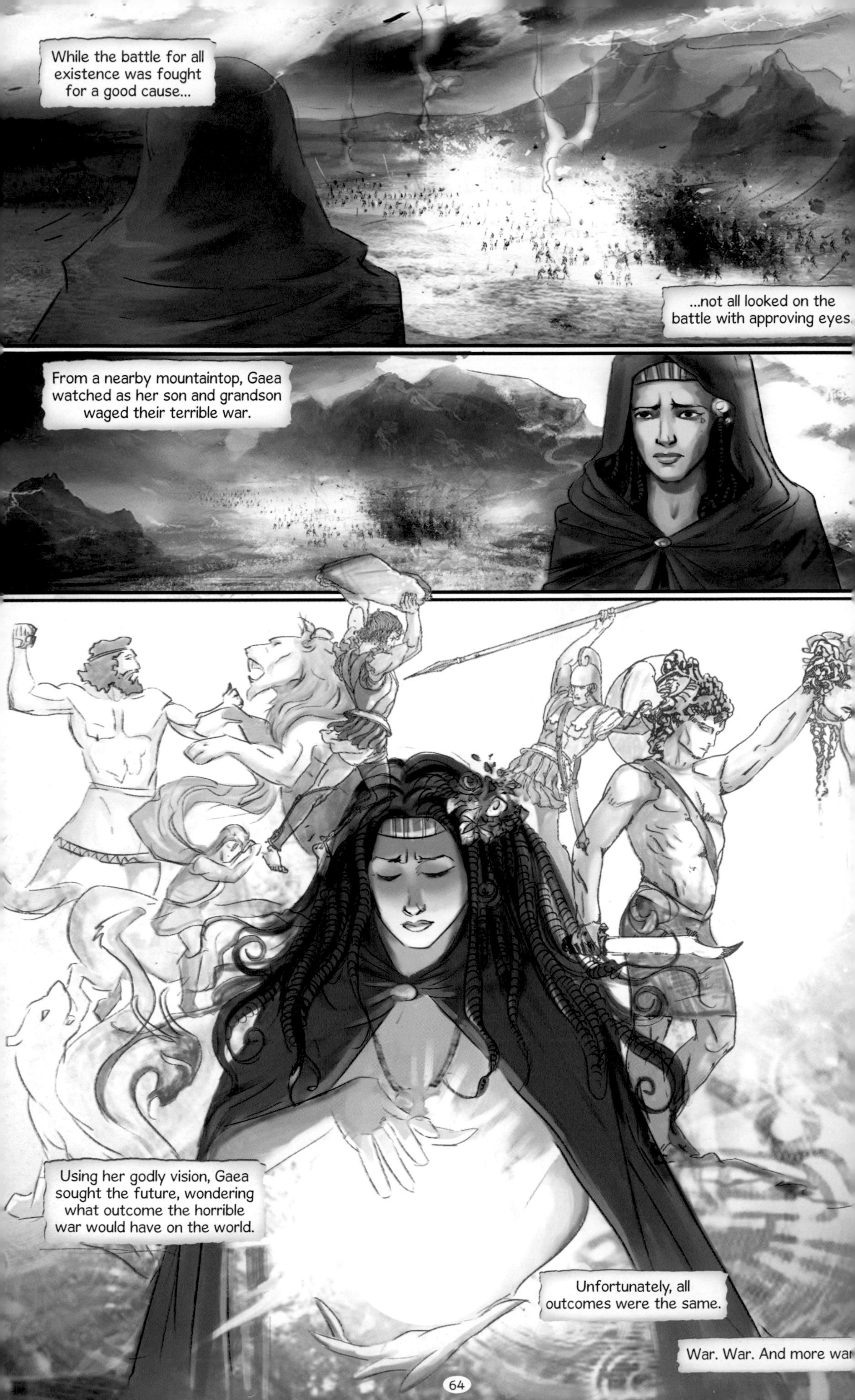
While the battle for all existence was fought for a good cause...
...not all looked on the battle with approving eyes.
From a nearby mountaintop, Gaea watched as her son and grandson waged their terrible war.
Using her godly vision, Gaea sought the future, wondering what outcome the horrible war would have on the world.
Unfortunately, all outcomes were the same.
War. War. And more war

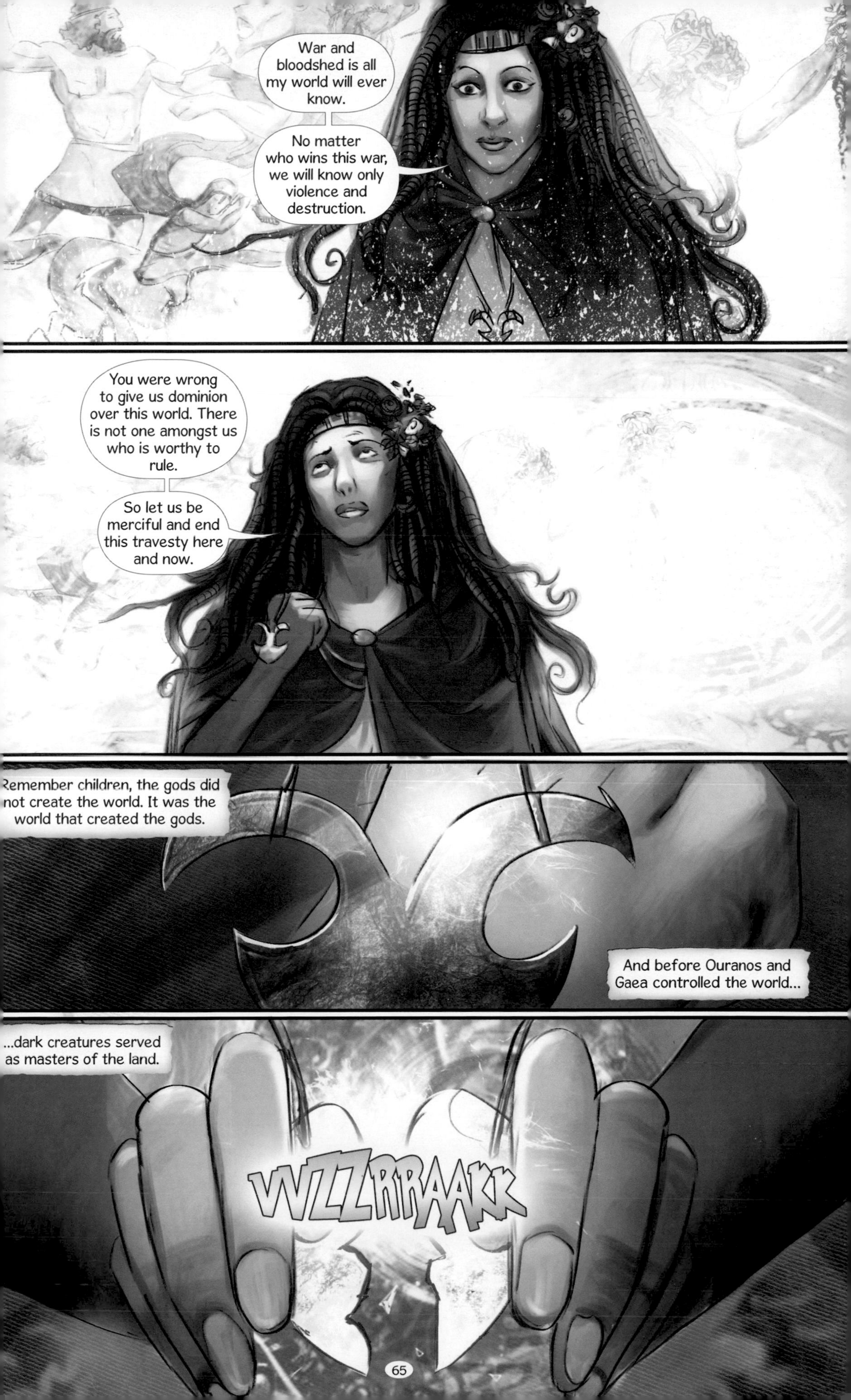
War and bloodshed is all my world will ever know.
No matter who wins this war, we will know only violence and destruction.
You were wrong to give us dominion over this world. There is not one amongst us who is worthy to rule.
So let us be merciful and end this travesty here and now.
Remember children, the gods did not create the world. It was the world that created the gods.
And before Ouranos and Gaea controlled the world...
...dark creatures served as masters of the land.
VVZZRRAAKK

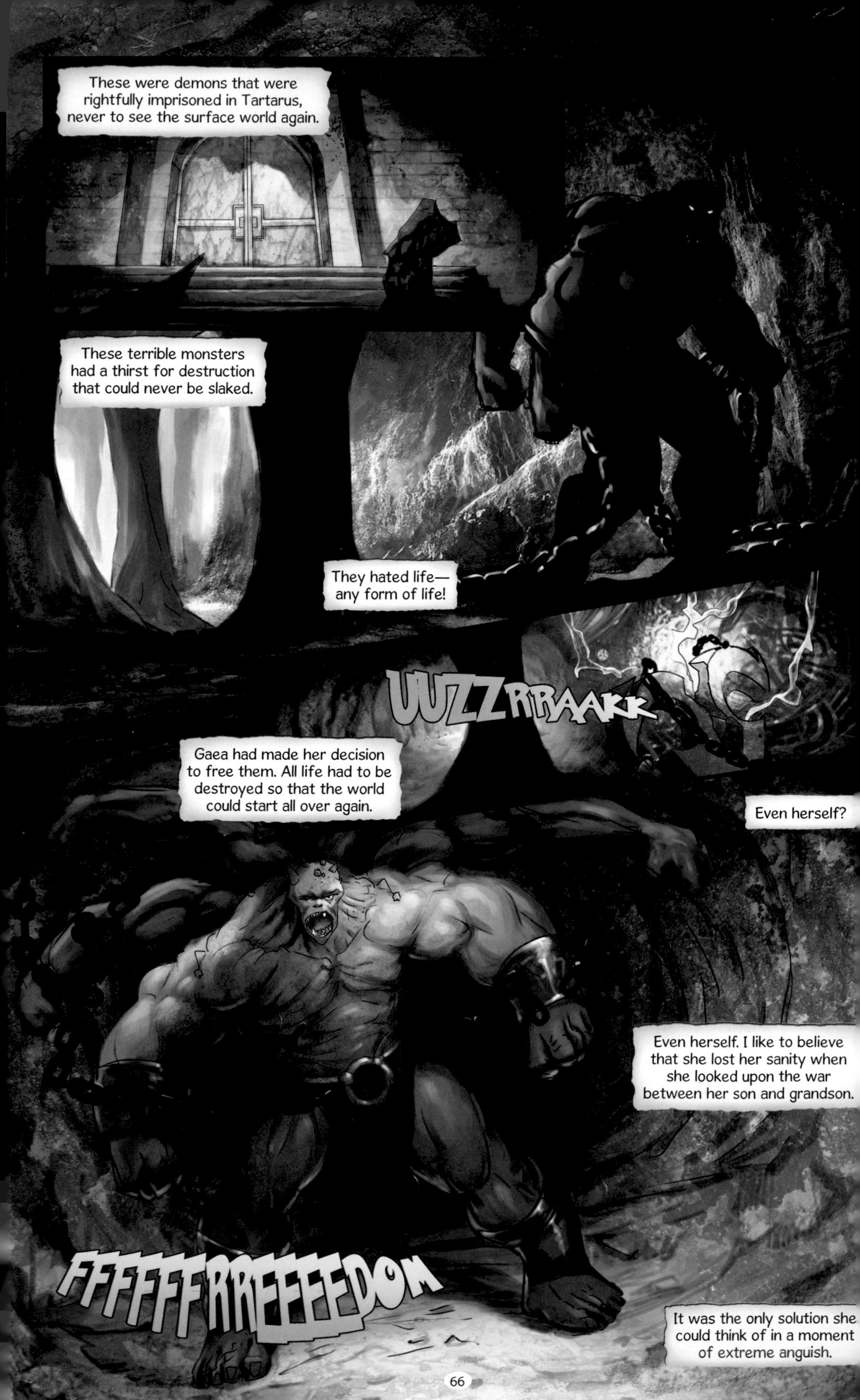
These were demons that were rightfully imprisoned in Tartarus, never to see the surface world again.
These terrible monsters had a thirst for destruction that could never be slaked.
They hated life—any form of life!
UUZZRRRAAKK
Gaea had made her decision to free them. All life had to be destroyed so that the world could start all over again.
Even herself?
Even herself. I like to believe that she lost her sanity when she looked upon the war between her son and grandson.
FFFFFFRREEEEDOM
It was the only solution she could think of in a moment of extreme anguish.

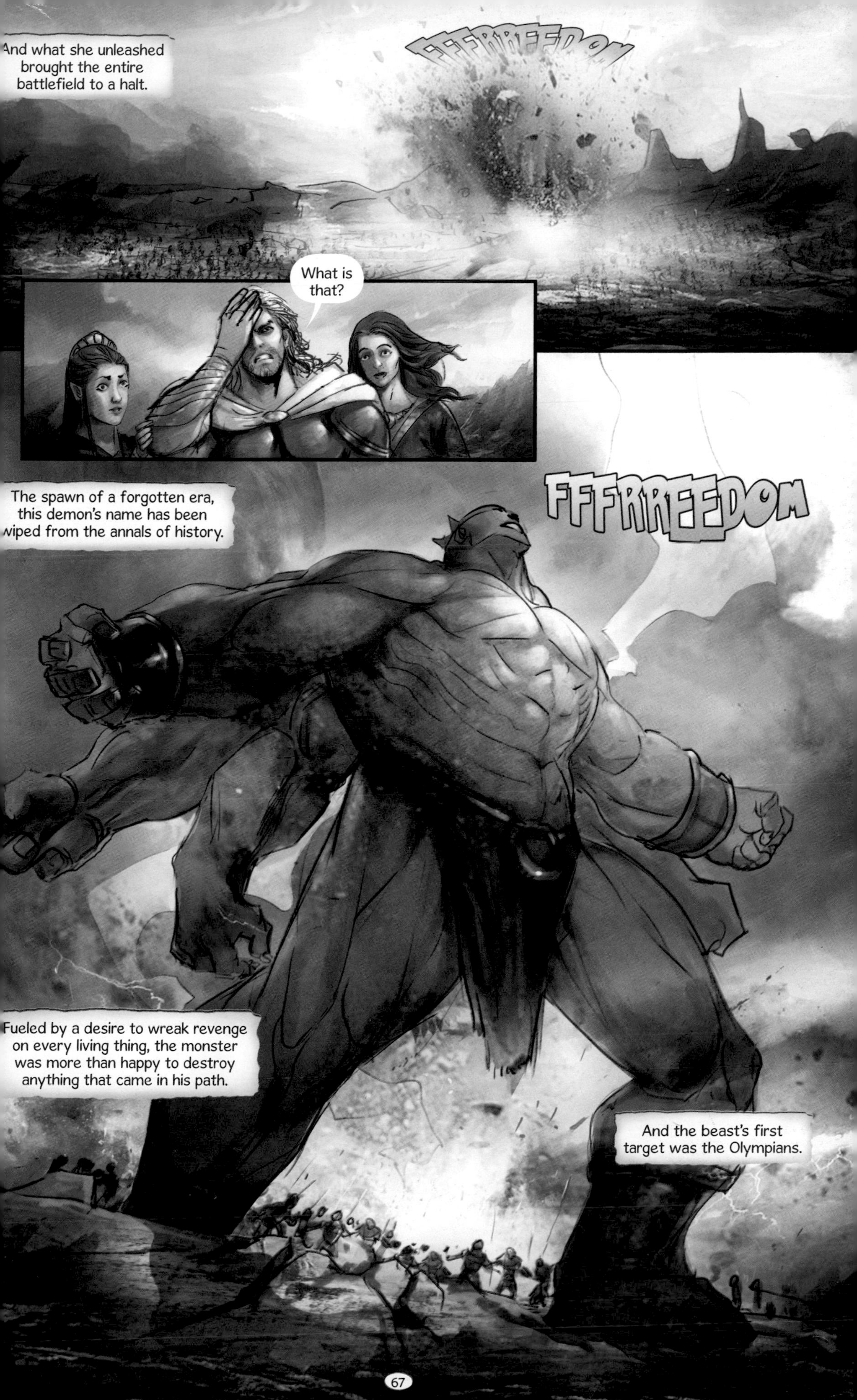
And what she unleashed brought the entire battlefield to a halt.
FFFRREEDOM
What is that?
The spawn of a forgotten era, this demon's name has been wiped from the annals of history.
FFFRREEDOM
Fueled by a desire to wreak revenge on every living thing, the monster was more than happy to destroy anything that came in his path.
And the beast's first target was the Olympians.

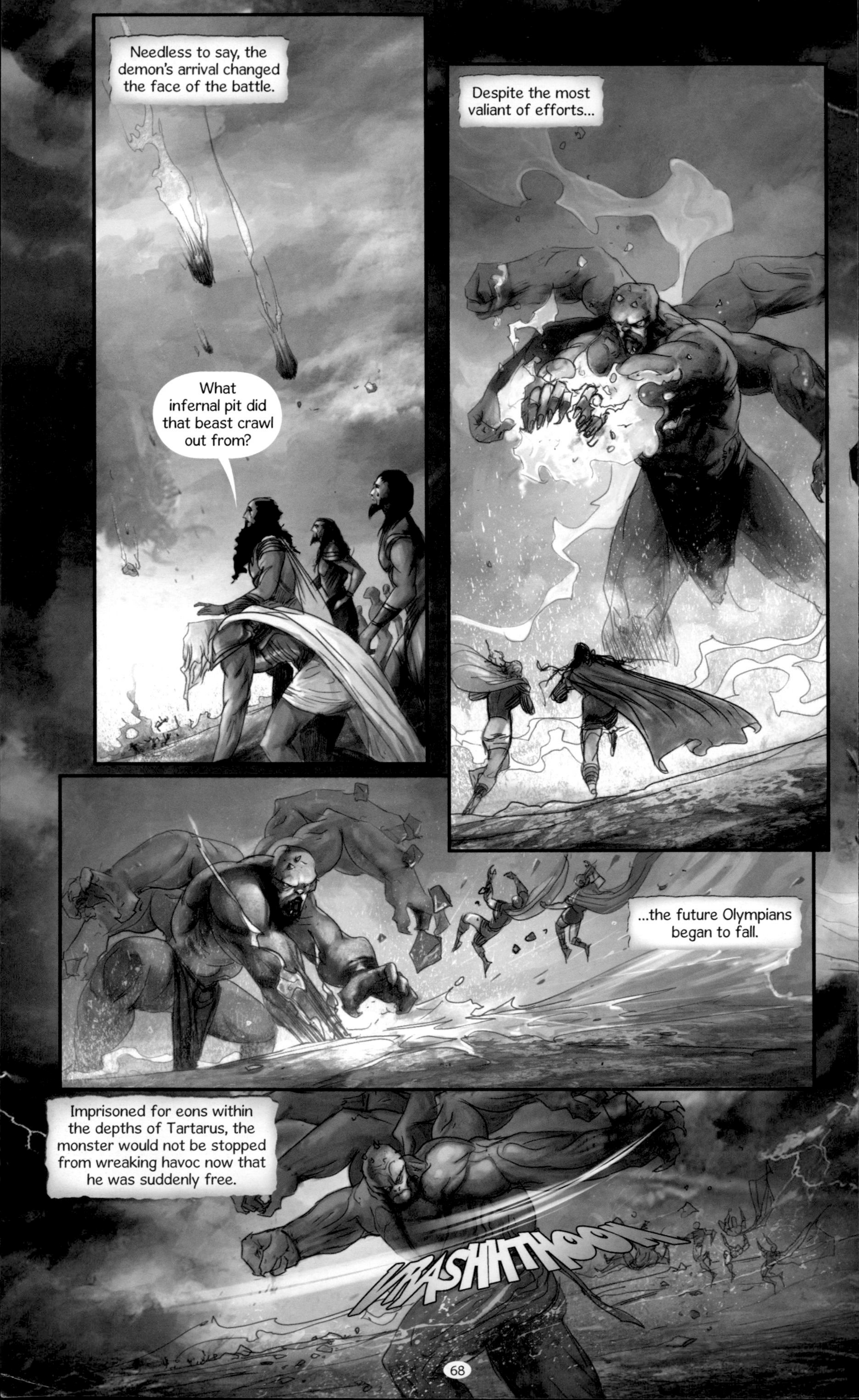
Needless to say, the demon's arrival changed the face of the battle.
What infernal pit did that beast crawl out from?
Despite the most valiant of efforts...
...the future Olympians began to fall.
Imprisoned for eons within the depths of Tartarus, the monster would not be stopped from wreaking havoc now that he was suddenly free.
VRASHHTHOOM

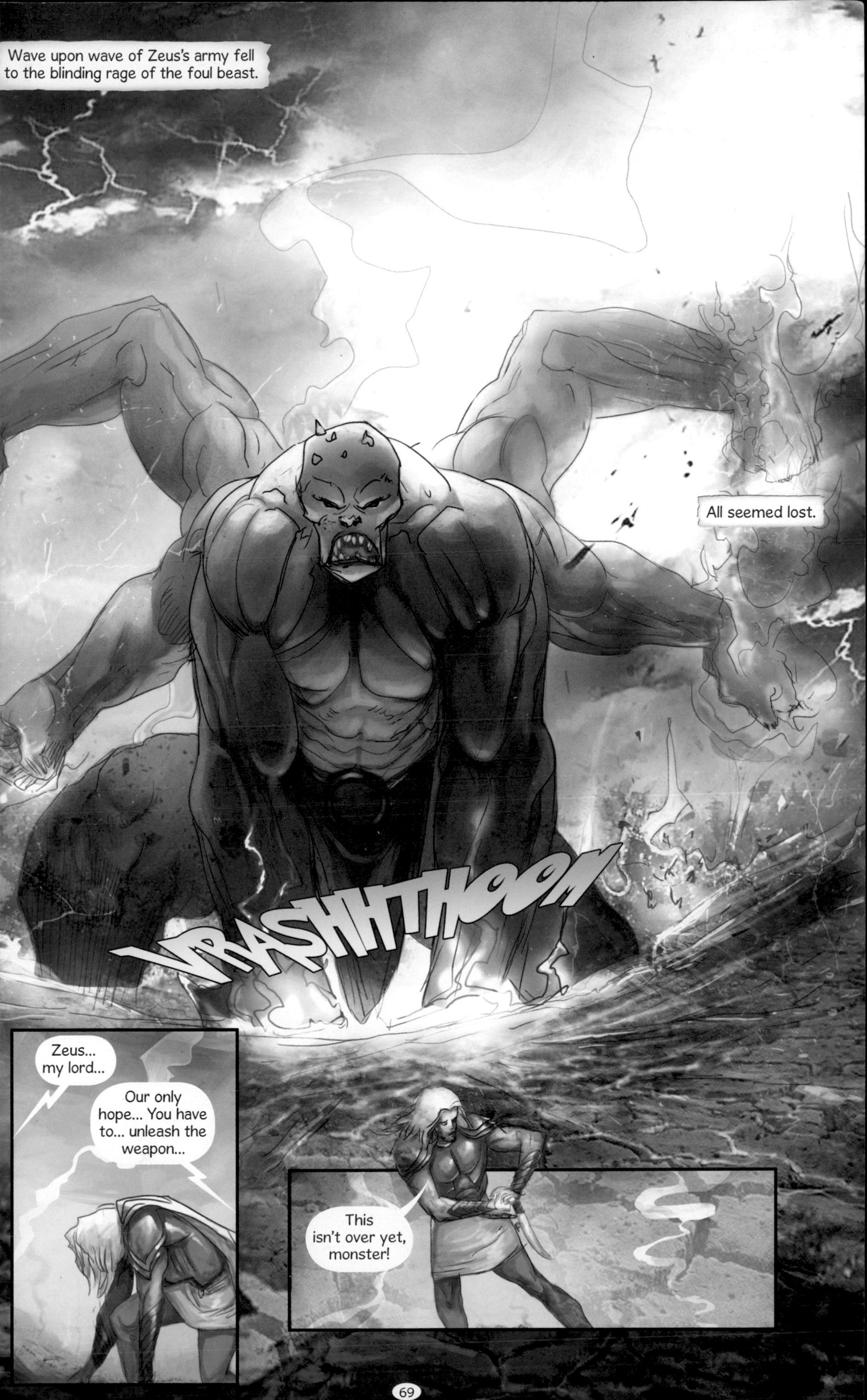
Wave upon wave of Zeus's army fell to the blinding rage of the foul beast.
All seemed lost.
VRASHHTHOOM
Zeus... my lord...
Our only hope... You have to... unleash the weapon...
This isn't over yet, monster!

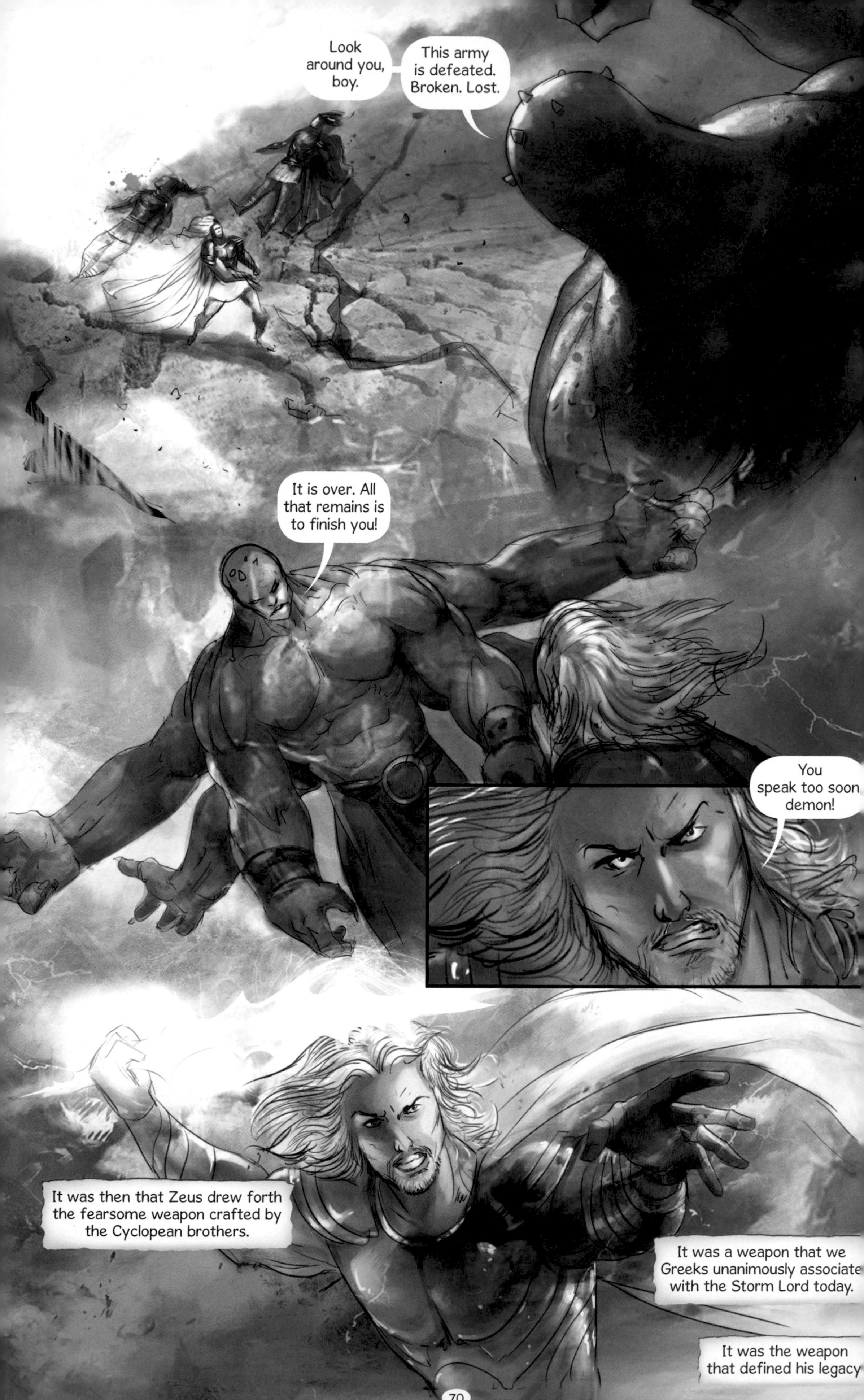
Look around you, boy.
This army is defeated. Broken. Lost.
It is over. All that remains is to finish you!
You speak too soon demon!
It was then that Zeus drew forth the fearsome weapon crafted by the Cyclopean brothers.
It was a weapon that we Greeks unanimously associate with the Storm Lord today.
It was the weapon that defined his legacy

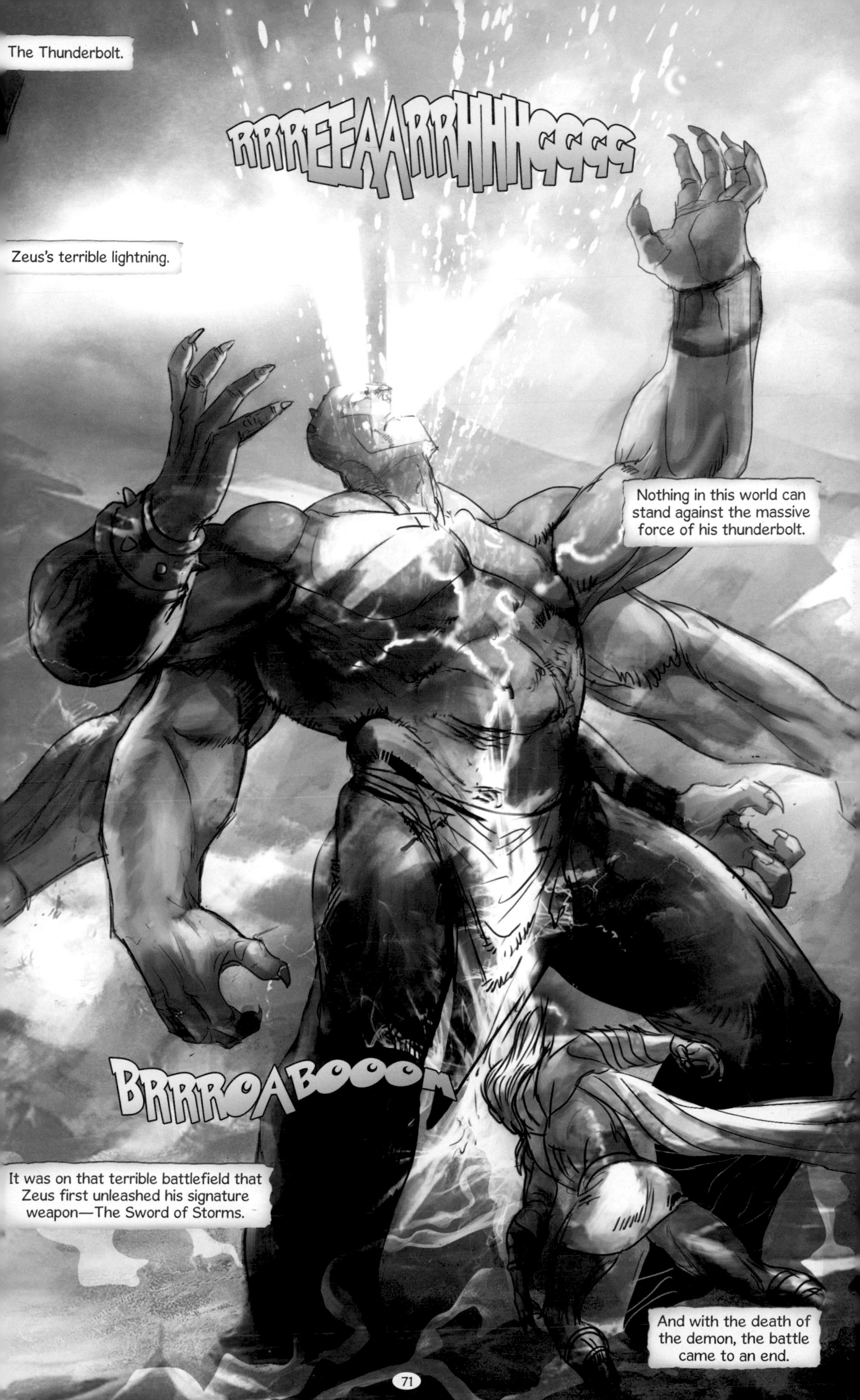
The Thunderbolt.
RRRREEAARRHHHGGGG
Zeus's terrible lightning.
Nothing in this world can stand against the massive force of his thunderbolt.
BRRRROABOOOM
It was on that terrible battlefield that Zeus first unleashed his signature weapon—The Sword of Storms.
And with the death of the demon, the battle came to an end.

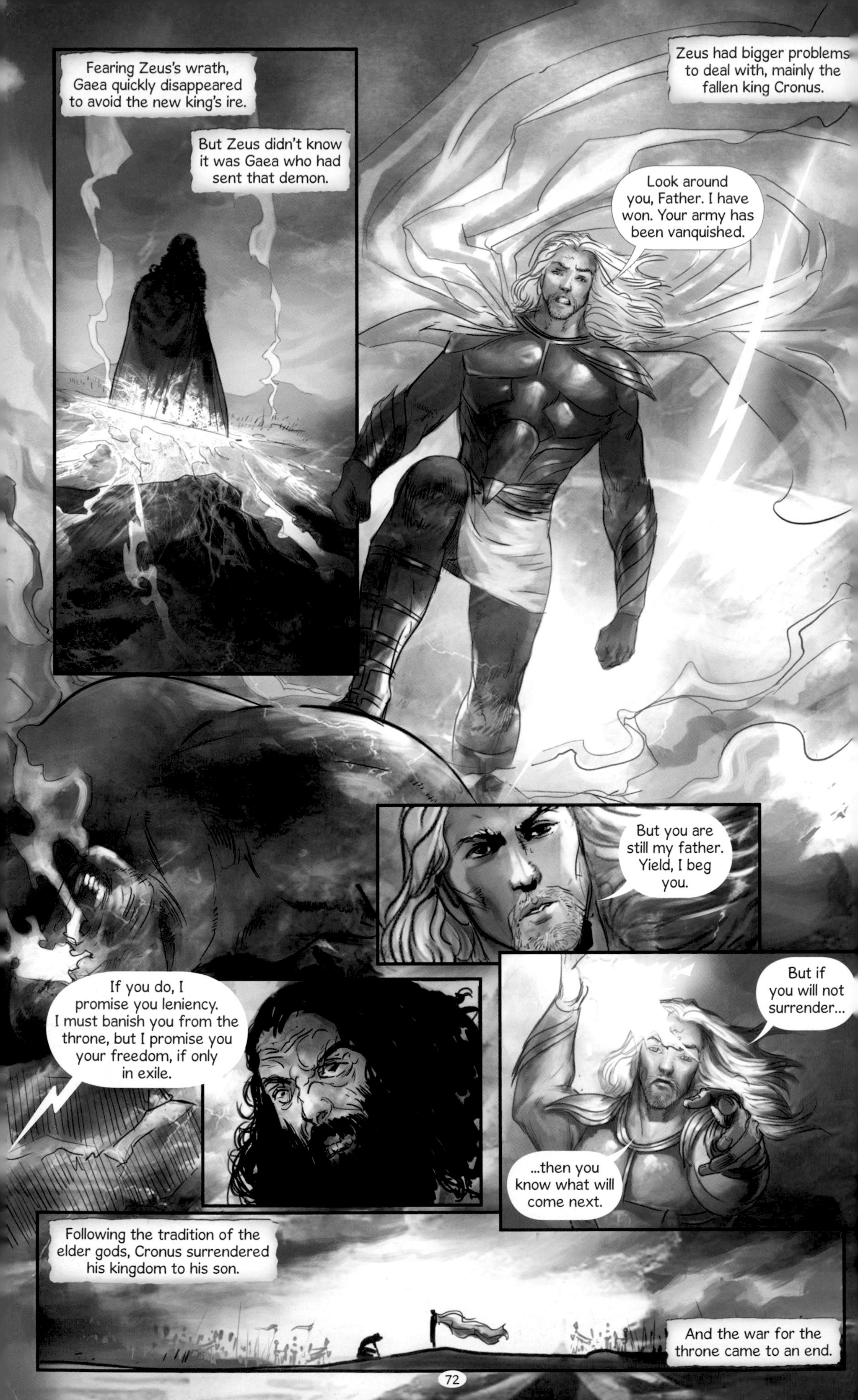

Fearing Zeus's wrath, Gaea quickly disappeared to avoid the new king's ire.
But Zeus didn't know it was Gaea who had sent that demon.
Zeus had bigger problems to deal with, mainly the fallen king Cronus.
Look around you, Father. I have won. Your army has been vanquished.
But you are still my father. Yield, I beg you.
If you do, I promise you leniency. I must banish you from the throne, but I promise you your freedom, if only in exile.
But if you will not surrender...
...then you know what will come next.
Following the tradition of the elder gods, Cronus surrendered his kingdom to his son.
And the war for the throne came to an end.

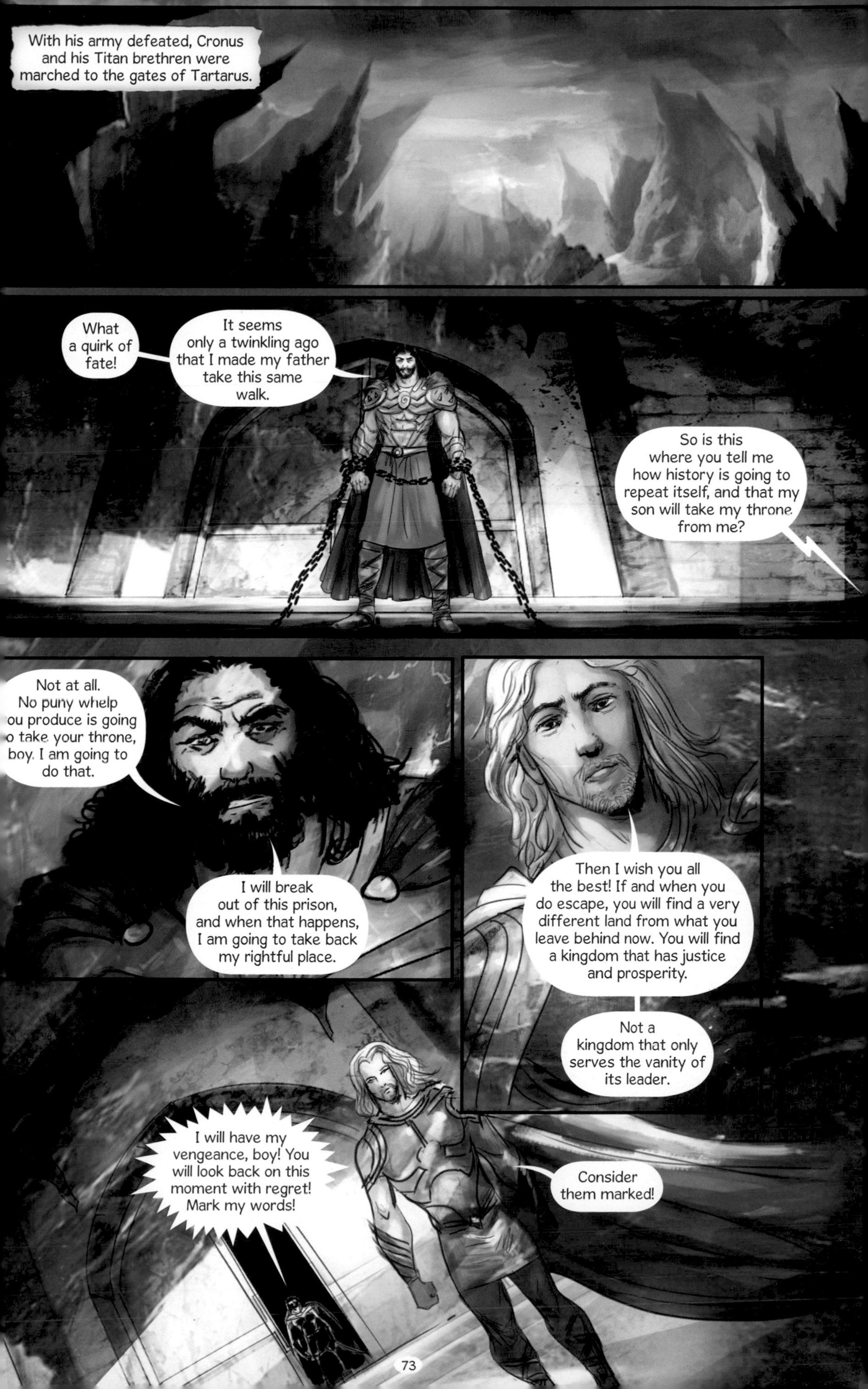

With his army defeated, Cronus and his Titan brethren were marched to the gates of Tartarus.
What a quirk of fate!
It seems only a twinkling ago that I made my father take this same walk.
So is this where you tell me how history is going to repeat itself, and that my son will take my throne from me?
Not at all. No puny whelp ou produce is going o take your throne, boy. I am going to do that.
I will break out of this prison, and when that happens, I am going to take back my rightful place.
Then I wish you all the best! If and when you do escape, you will find a very different land from what you leave behind now. You will find a kingdom that has justice and prosperity.
Not a kingdom that only serves the vanity of its leader.
I will have my vengeance, boy! You will look back on this moment with regret! Mark my words!
Consider them marked!

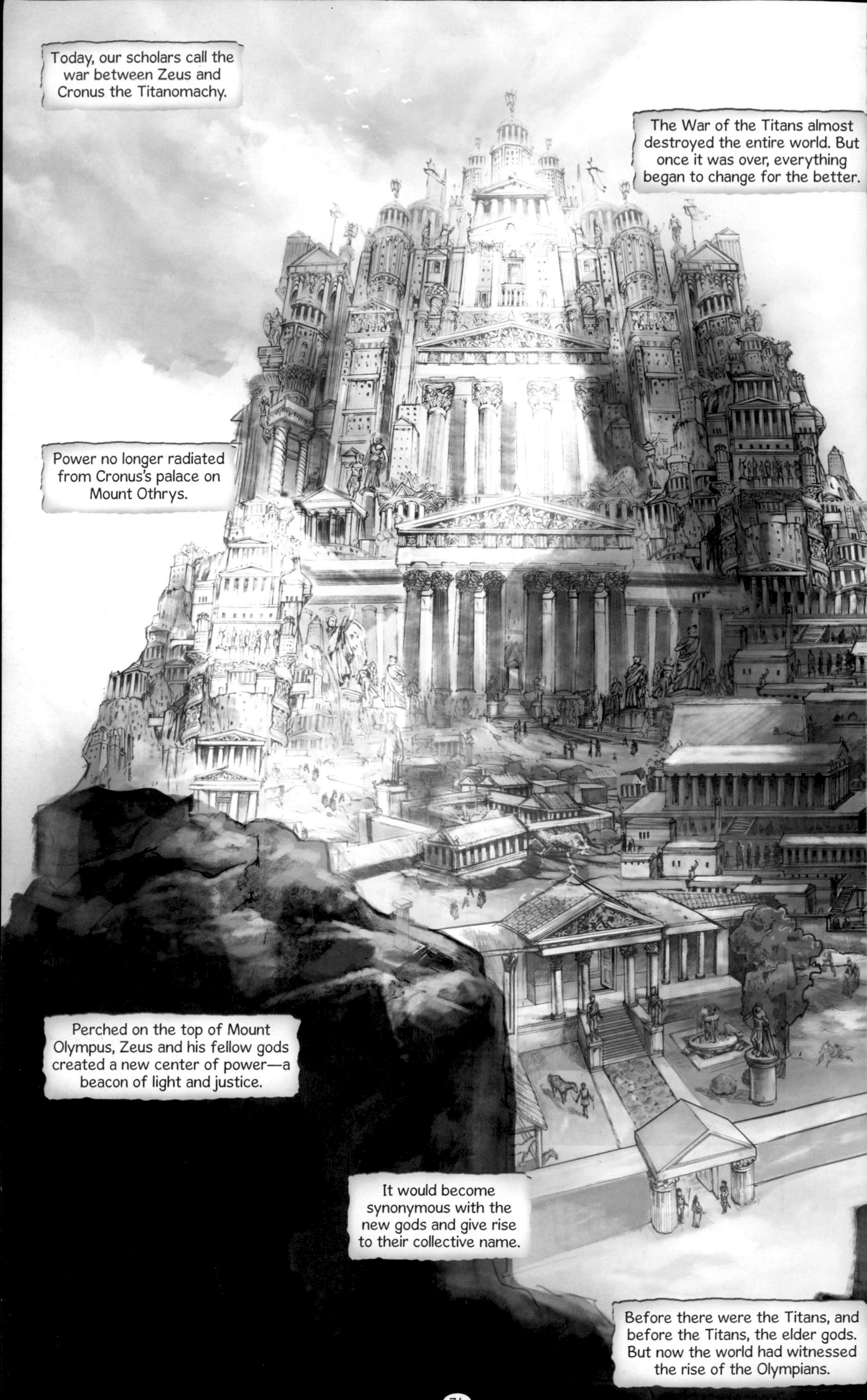
Today, our scholars call the war between Zeus and Cronus the Titanomachy.
The War of the Titans almost destroyed the entire world. But once it was over, everything began to change for the better.
Power no longer radiated from Cronus's palace on Mount Othrys.
Perched on the top of Mount Olympus, Zeus and his fellow gods created a new center of power—a beacon of light and justice.
It would become synonymous with the new gods and give rise to their collective name.
Before there were the Titans, and before the Titans, the elder gods. But now the world had witnessed the rise of the Olympians.

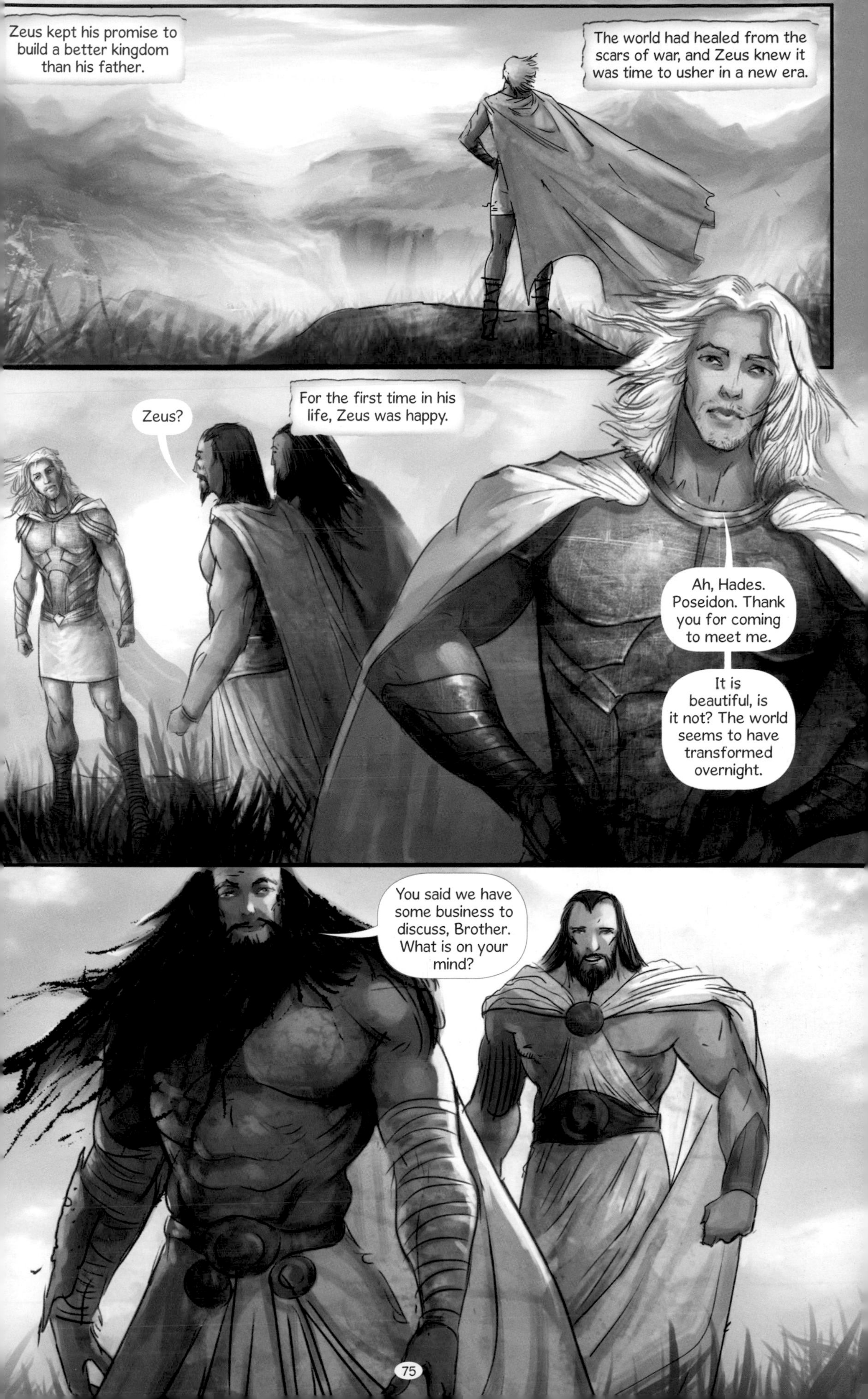
Zeus kept his promise to build a better kingdom than his father.
The world had healed from the scars of war, and Zeus knew it was time to usher in a new era.
Zeus?
For the first time in his life, Zeus was happy.
Ah, Hades. Poseidon. Thank you for coming to meet me.
It is beautiful, is it not? The world seems to have transformed overnight.
You said we have some business to discuss, Brother. What is on your mind?

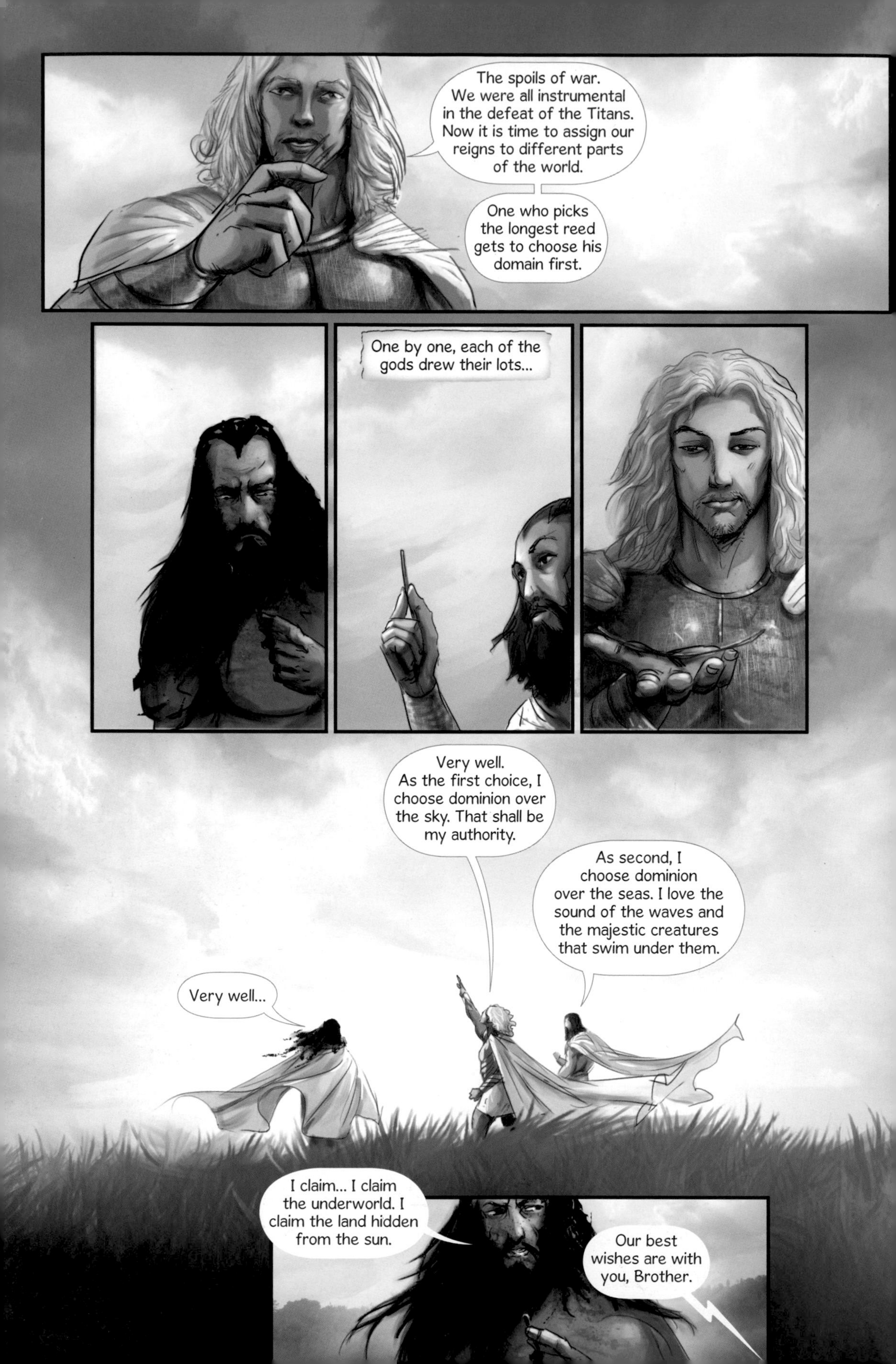
The spoils of war. We were all instrumental in the defeat of the Titans. Now it is time to assign our reigns to different parts of the world.
One who picks the longest reed gets to choose his domain first.
One by one, each of the gods drew their lots...
Very well. As the first choice, I choose dominion over the sky. That shall be my authority.
As second, I choose dominion over the seas. I love the sound of the waves and the majestic creatures that swim under them.
Very well...
I claim... I claim the underworld. I claim the land hidden from the sun.
Our best wishes are with you, Brother.

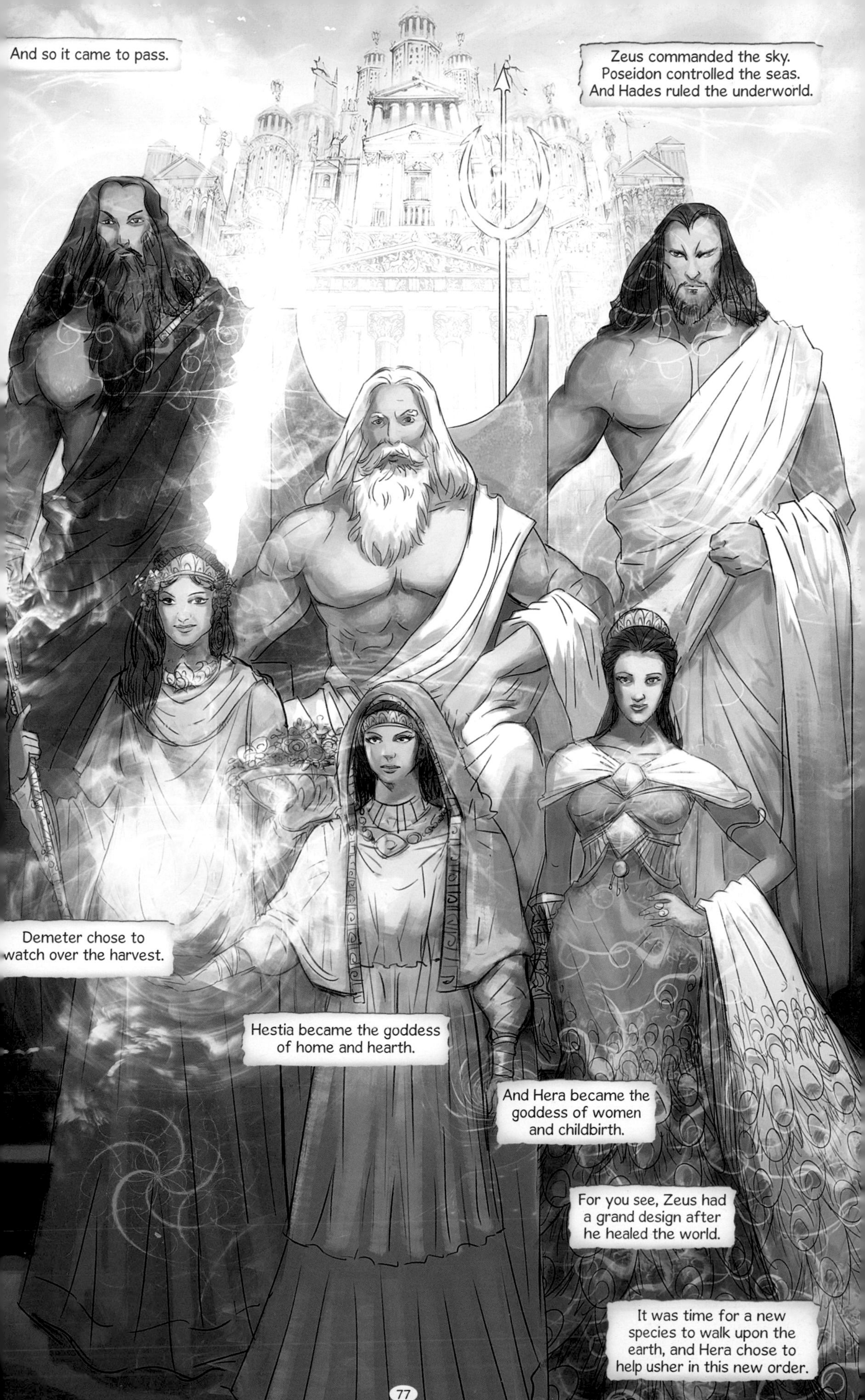
And so it came to pass.
Zeus commanded the sky. Poseidon controlled the seas. And Hades ruled the underworld.
Demeter chose to watch over the harvest.
Hestia became the goddess of home and hearth.
And Hera became the goddess of women and childbirth.
For you see, Zeus had a grand design after he healed the world.
It was time for a new species to walk upon the earth, and Hera chose to help usher in this new order.

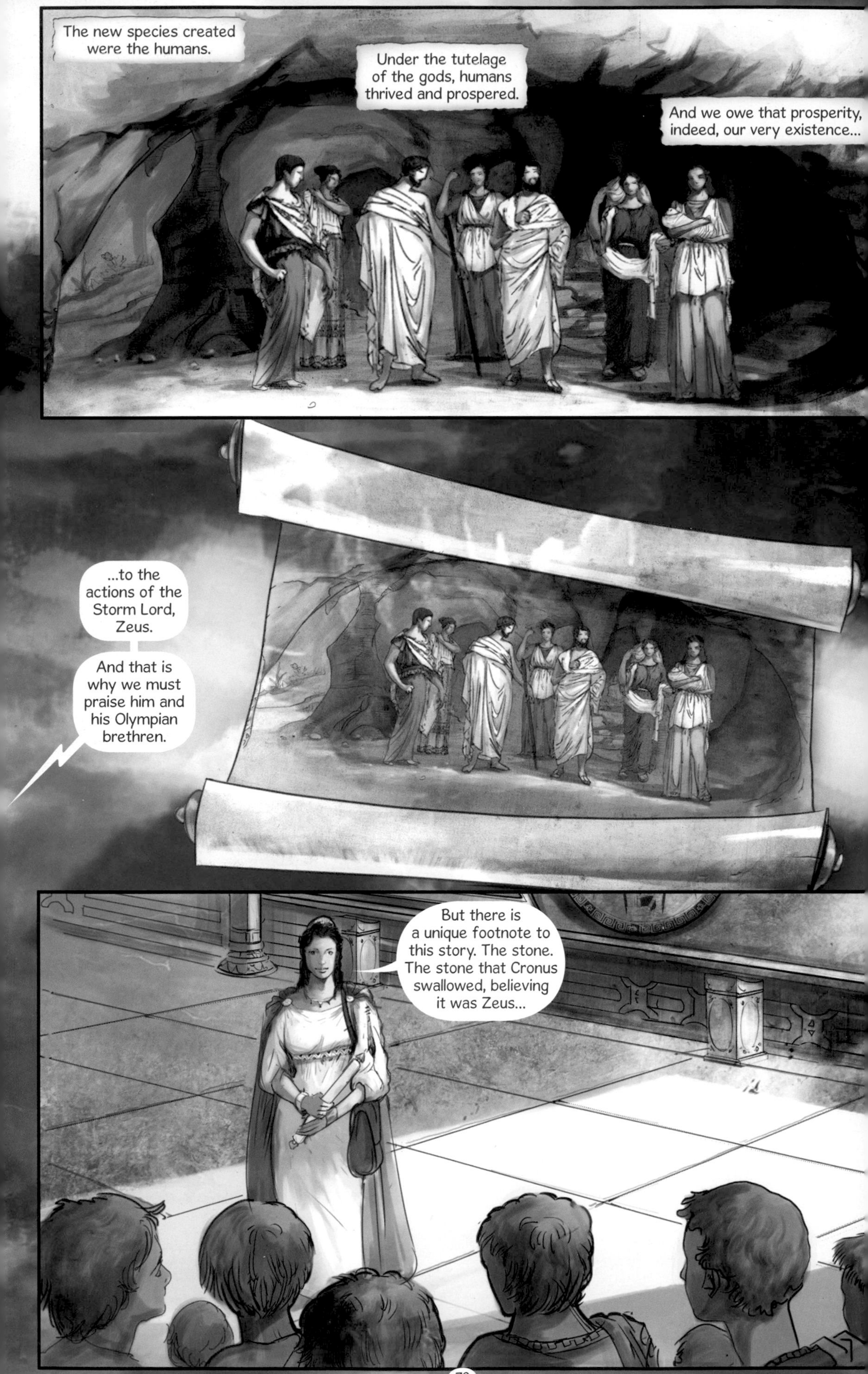
The new species created were the humans.
Under the tutelage of the gods, humans thrived and prospered.
And we owe that prosperity, indeed, our very existence...
...to the actions of the Storm Lord, Zeus.
And that is why we must praise him and his Olympian brethren.
But there is a unique footnote to this story. The stone. The stone that Cronus swallowed, believing it was Zeus...

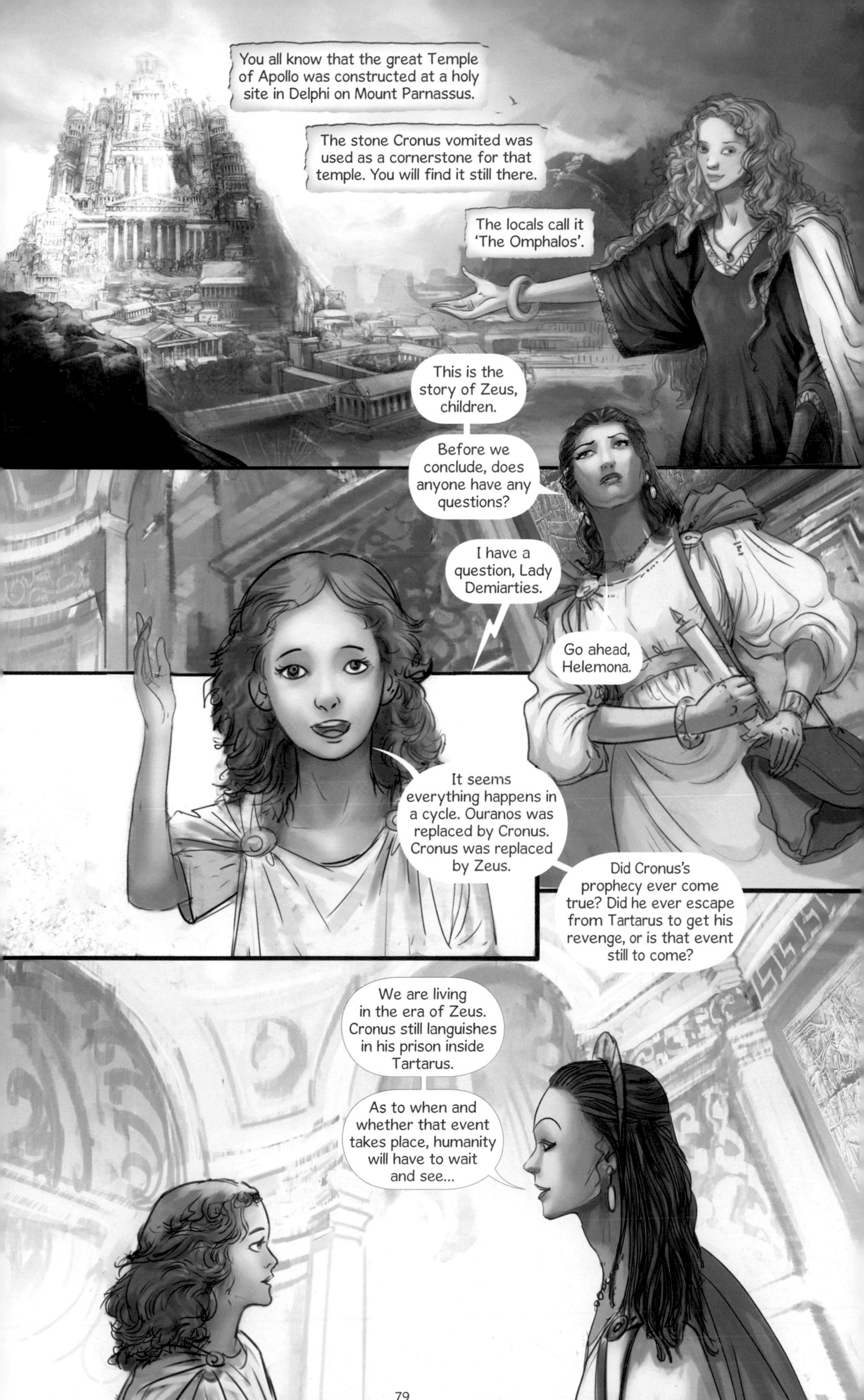

You all know that the great Temple of Apollo was constructed at a holy site in Delphi on Mount Parnassus.
The stone Cronus vomited was used as a cornerstone for that temple. You will find it still there.
The locals call it 'The Omphalos'.
This is the story of Zeus, children.
Before we conclude, does anyone have any questions?
I have a question, Lady Demiarties.
Go ahead, Helemona.
It seems everything happens in a cycle. Ouranos was replaced by Cronus. Cronus was replaced by Zeus.
Did Cronus's prophecy ever come true? Did he ever escape from Tartarus to get his revenge, or is that event still to come?
We are living in the era of Zeus. Cronus still languishes in his prison inside Tartarus.
As to when and whether that event takes place, humanity will have to wait and see...

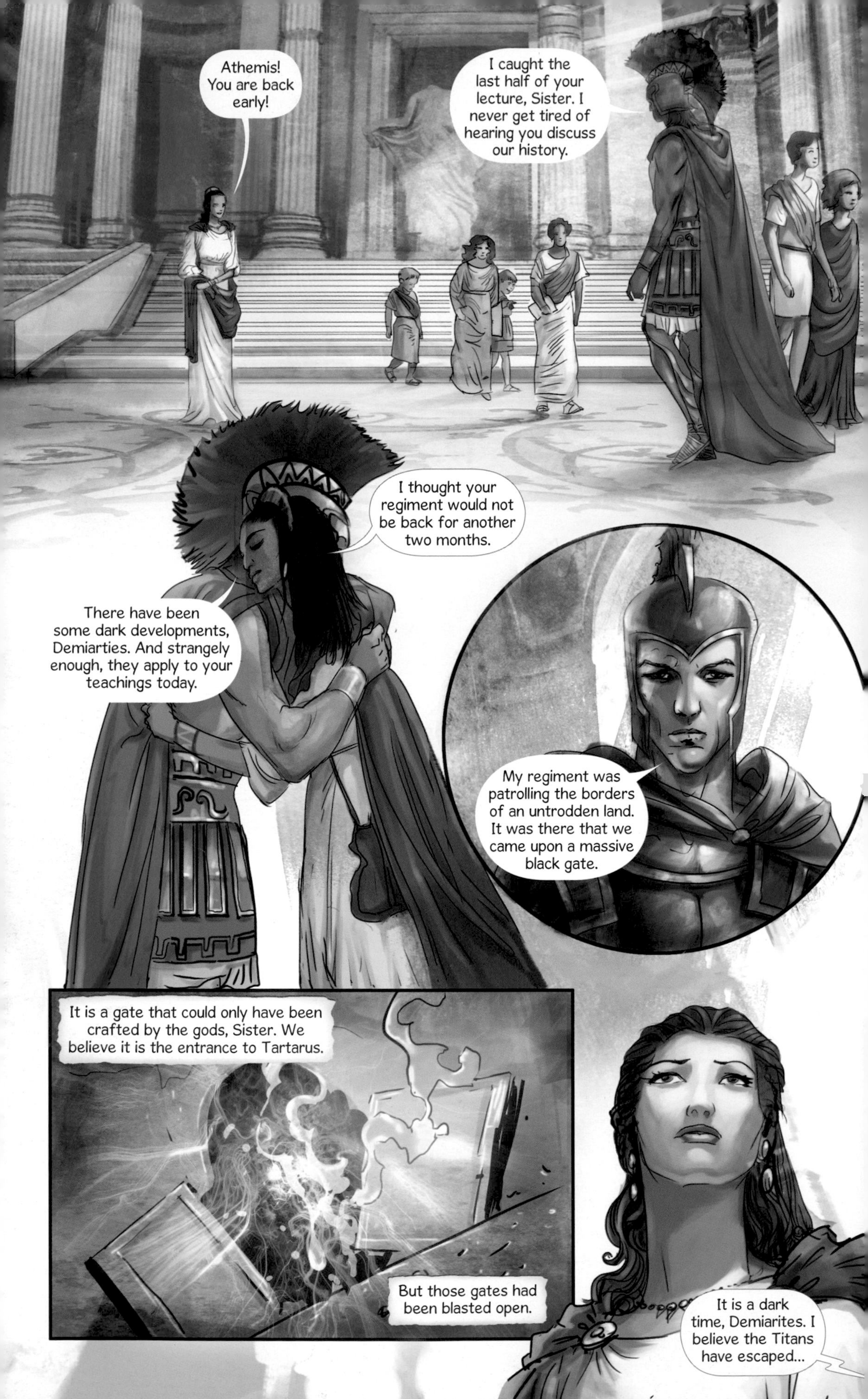
Athemis! You are back early!
I caught the last half of your lecture, Sister. I never get tired of hearing you discuss our history.
I thought your regiment would not be back for another two months.
There have been some dark developments, Demiarties. And strangely enough, they apply to your teachings today.
My regiment was patrolling the borders of an untrodden land. It was there that we came upon a massive black gate.
It is a gate that could only have been crafted by the gods, Sister. We believe it is the entrance to Tartarus.
But those gates had been blasted open.
It is a dark time, Demiarites. I believe the Titans have escaped...

RYAN FOLEY'S
LEGEND
THE LABORS OF HERACLES

Well fought, my friend. Well fought.

Let's humble a king, shall we?

Written by Ryan Foley
Illustrated by Sankha Banerjee

Their first mistake was to assume he would give up...

Heracles has it all: a beautiful home, a loving family, and a reputation as a great soldier who would stop at nothing to defend his homeland. Then his origin brings him into the center of a vicious plot, where he is hypnotized into committing the worst crime of all. Devastated by his actions, he wanders aimlessly, immersed in depression. He finally finds some solace in the fact that he can atone for his sins by completing ten impossible tasks.

Where other men would give up and consider themselves defeated, Heracles uses his courage, strength and intellect to take up the tasks one by one. Will he succeed? Or has destiny other plans for him. Find out...

www.campfire.co.in

WHERE THE OLYMPIANS DWELL!

If the names of the Olympians remind you of nothing more than the story you just read, and video games you have played, read on! Sports, architecture, and language are a few areas where you can find the deep influence of myths! There sure are more, but that's for you to find out!

Faster, Higher, Stronger!

The Olympic Games that happens every four years originated in Ancient Greece in honor of Zeus. In 776 B.C., the first games were held in Olympia, and they were played every four years until Theosodius I banned them in 393 A.D. as part of his campaign to make Christianity the state religion. To oversee the games, a statue of Zeus was erected by Phidias, the Greek sculptor, around 432 B.C. One of the Seven Ancient Wonders of the World, this statue was unfortunately destroyed in the fifth century A.D., but discovered and resurrected during 1954-58.

Much like the present day Olympic Games, they welcomed participants from many corners of the world. An Olympic Truce was made between various countries during the Games. Under this agreement, armies were banned from entering Elis, a district where the games were organized, so that the players could reach the venue without being harmed.

The sports good brand Nike took its name from the Greek Goddess of Victory, Nike! She also features on the Olympic medal with a winner's crown in her left hand, and a palm frond in the right.

The winners of the ancient Olympic Games were awarded with laurel wreaths, but this custom is not followed now. However, the 2004 Summer Olympic Games held in Athens crowned the champions with olive leaves following the ancient tradition.

Like the famous Olympians of today, the ancient Games had their renowned athletes as well. Among them were Koroibos of Elis (the first ever Olympic champion); Nero, the Roman Emperor; and Varastades, Prince of Armenia and many more.

Initially, women, except those from Sparta, were forbidden from viewing or participating in the Games. In the sixth century B.C., the Heraean Games were started, in honor of Goddess Hera. It was held especially for women players and included only foot racing. Cynisca of Sparta was the first woman champion of the ancient Games.

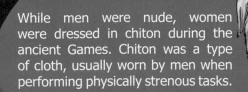

While men were nude, women were dressed in chiton during the ancient Games. Chiton was a type of cloth, usually worn by men when performing physically strenuous tasks.

The Olympian Structures

Great architectural wonders were built in honor of the Olympian gods. Many such temples survive in Greece to this day. Prime examples are the Parthenon, Temple of Hephaestus, Erecthion, and Temple of Aphaia in Athens. At least two of the Seven Wonders of the Ancient World are associated with them: the Temple of Artemis at Ephemus (now in Turkey), and the Statue of Zeus in Olympia, Greece.

None remains as well preserved as the Pantheon in Rome, Italy, erected as a temple to all the gods by the Roman statesman, Marcus Agrippa. Often touted as one of the most influential architectural structures, its mark can be seen on many Western buildings, starting from the Renaissance period to the modern day. Well-known examples include the United States Capitol and National Gallery of Art in Washington, D.C., the Pantheon in Paris, and St. Peter's Basilica in Vatican City.

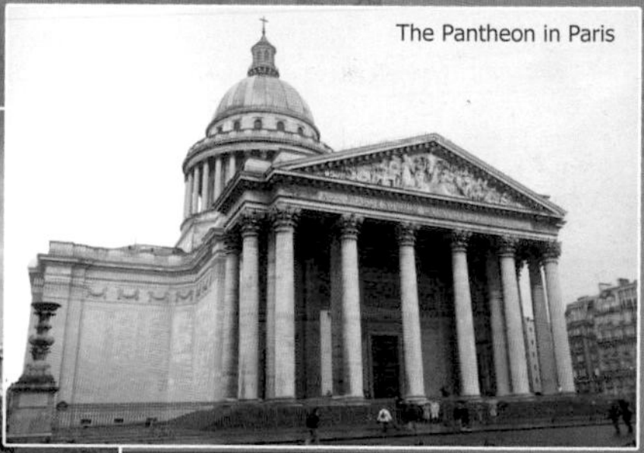
The Pantheon in Paris

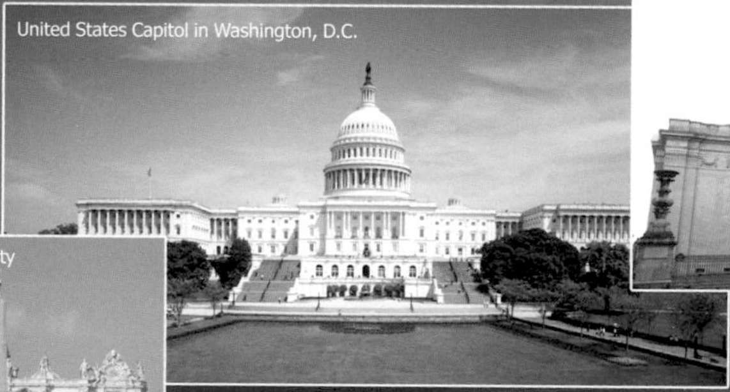
United States Capitol in Washington, D.C.

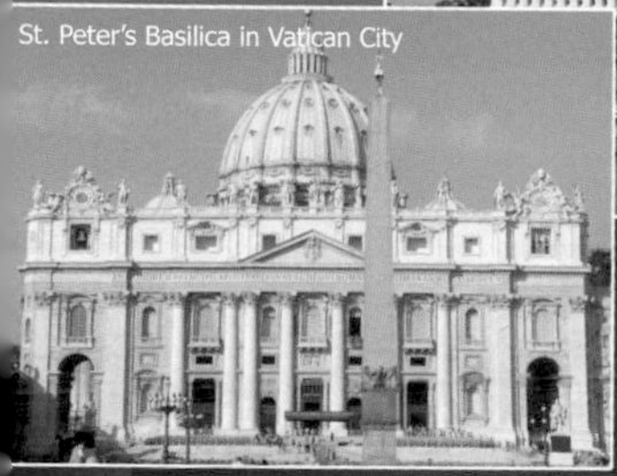
St. Peter's Basilica in Vatican City

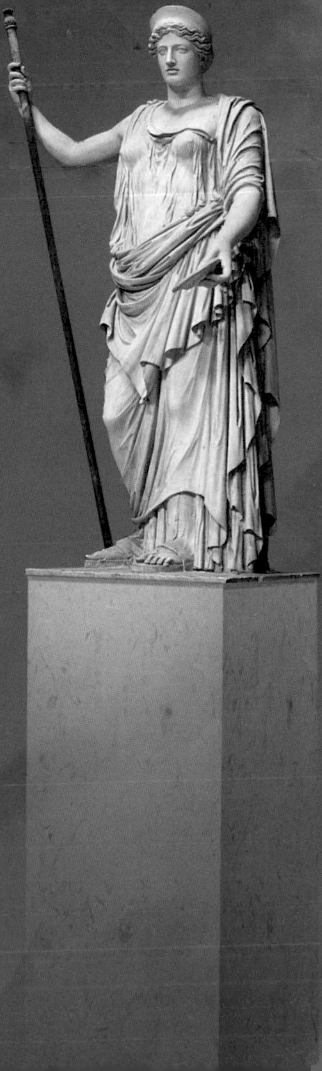

'Olympics' came from the Olympians, but what other words did the Greek gods give us?

- Ceres is the Roman counterpart of Demeter, the Greek goddess of harvest. The word 'cereal' comes from Ceres, referring to her association with food grains.
- The Titans themselves gave names to the metal titanium and the word 'titanic', which means gigantic.
- 'Music' is derived from the nine Muses, who were daughters of Zeus and Mnemosyne, the goddess of memory. Interestingly, the nine Muses were goddesses who inspired creativity in arts and literature. Today, a muse is something or someone who provides inspiration to an artist or poet.
- The word 'Atlas' is derived from the Titan Atlas who was cursed by Zeus to carry the heavens on his shoulders. Interestingly, early map collections had his image on their cover.

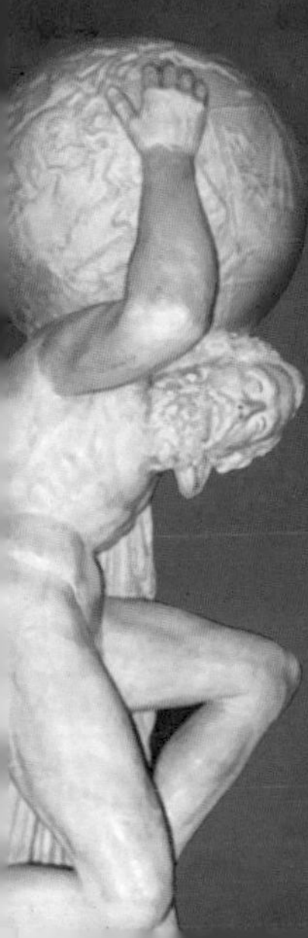

You may also like to read other titles from our

MYTHOLOGY SERIES

PERSEUS
DESTINY'S CALL
WRITTEN BY RYAN FOLEY
ILLUSTRATED BY NARESH KUMAR

PERSEUS DESTINY'S CALL

The life of Perseus, a fisherman, changed the day he was tricked into making an impossible promise to the king of Seriphos. He was sent on a mission to bring the head of the monster, Medusa. To overcome the odds, Perseus must learn to battle intelligently and fearlessly. Read on to find out how Perseus, the Avenger, answers the call of his destiny.

JASON AND THE ARGONAUTS

Jason
and the
Argonauts
Written by Dan Whitehead
Illustrated by Sankha Banerjee

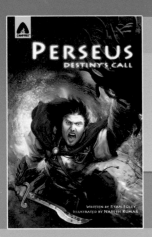

The rightful prince of Iolcus, brought up in exile, Jason has just one goal in mind—to save his people from the tyrannical rule of his uncle, Pelias. In return for the throne, Jason has to retrieve the Golden Fleece from the kingdom of Colchis. An enduring tale of adventure, comradeship, temptation, and betrayal.

ABHIMANYU SINGH SISODIA
RAVANA
ROAR OF THE DEMON KING
ART BY SACHIN NAGAR

RAVANA ROAR OF THE DEMON KING

If any character in mythology has as many apologists as it has denouncers, it is Ravana. This arrogant demon brooks no hindrance to snatching his heart's desire, and his terror seems unstoppable even to the gods. A story that never fails to inspire awe and fear.

Saraswati Nagpal
Sita
Daughter of the Earth
Illustrated by Manikandan

SITA DAUGHTER OF THE EARTH

Sita is the kind-hearted and intelligent princess of Videha. Married to Rama, her journey in life takes her from exhilaration to anguish. Adapted from the ancient Indian epic, the *Ramayana*, Campfire brings you a touching tale of love, honor, and sacrifice that reveals one woman's shining strength in an unforgiving world.